The author's career included 26 years within the fire service seeing him join as a fire fighter, riding the fire appliances and taking orders, up to his role at retirement of being an operational fire officer who gives those orders.

For many years he was intrigued by the human reaction to being given an order which could obviously put the receiver into harm's way. In this modern era of health and safety where giving inappropriate orders can and will lead to certain consequences, it was hard for him to understand the justification of a war of attrition such as the Great War.

Risk should always be weighed against benefit. How this principle could be seen in the actions and strategies of senior commanders in that war is a mystery to the author.

To all those who fell in the Great War,
the war to end all wars.

Let your sacrifice never be forgotten and your
memories never diminish.

AAG Whitehead

PALS WAR –
THE SECOND BATTLE
OF YPRES

AUSTIN MACAULEY
PUBLISHERS LTD.

A CIP catalogue record for this title is available from the British Library.

ISBN 9781786121769 (Paperback)
ISBN 9781786121776 (Hardback)
ISBN 9781786121783 (eBook)

Acknowledgments

To all my family for their support. And in memory of my father, Roy Whitehead, who passed away before the completion of this book.

A Prelude to War

The underlying causes of World War I, which began in the Balkans in late July 1914, were numerous. These causes were: political, territorial and economic conflicts among the great powers of Europe in the four decades leading up to the war. Militaristic causes, involving a complex web of alliances, imperialism and nationalism added to the tensions. However, the immediate origin of the war, was down to the statesmen and generals during July 1914 caused by the assassination of Archduke Franz Ferdinand and his wife Sophie by an ethnic Serb and Yugoslav nationalist, Gavrilo Princip, who was a member of the group, Young Bosnia, which was supported by the Serbian nationalist organization the Black Hand.

In the decade before 1914, tensions in Europe were high. Crisis point was reached after a long and difficult series of diplomatic clashes among the Great Powers (Britain, France, Russia, Germany, Austria-Hungary and Italy). This was due to changes in the balance of power in Europe since the previous century. Austria-Hungary was competing with Serbia and Russia for territory and influence in the Balkans and the rest of the Great Powers were pulled into the conflict through their various alliances and treaties.

During the Bosnian crisis of 1908, Russia had been humiliated because of its inability to support Serbia during the First Balkan War. So, in November 1912, Russia announced a major reconstruction of its military.

German Foreign Secretary, Gottlieb von Jagow told the Reichstag, on 28 November, that "If Austria is forced, for whatever reason, to fight for its position as a Great Power, then we must stand by her". As a result, the British Foreign Secretary and the Lord Chancellor responded with an explicit warning that if Germany were to attack France, Britain would intervene in France's favour.

With the Russian military reconstruction and the British warning, the possibility of war was the main topic at the German Imperial War Council in Berlin on 8 December 1912. This involved some of Germany's top military leadership, including Admiral Alfred von Tirpitz, Admiral Georg Alexander von Müller, Admiral August von Heeringen, General Helmuth von Moltke, General Moriz von Lyncker and Kaiser Wilhelm II. The presence of the leaders of both the German army and navy at this War Council attests to its importance.

Wilhelm II's opinion was that Austria should attack Serbia that December, and if Russia was to support the Serbs, then war would be unavoidable. This would be better now than going to war after Russia completed the massive modernization and expansion of their army that they had just begun. The professional military opinion of Moltke was a war being unavoidable and the sooner it came the better, the military wanted to launch an immediate attack.

Both Wilhelm II and the army leadership were in agreement. However, Tirpitz asked for a postponement for one and a half years because the navy was not ready for a general war that included Britain and its Royal Navy as an opponent. Moltke objected to the postponement but agreed to it reluctantly when Wilhelm II sided with Tirpitz.

With the Russian Great Military Programme of November 1912 the leadership of the German army began demanding even more strongly for a "preventive war" against Russia. Moltke declared that, because the financial structure of the German state, Germany could not win the arms race with Britain, France and Russia, which she herself had begun in 1911. As such, Moltke from late 1912 onwards was the leading advocate for an immediate, general war. This culminated in a near ultimatum demanding for a German "preventive war" against Russia, during May and June 1914 he convinced the Kaiser that in two or three years Russia would have completed her armaments. The military superiority of Germany's enemies would then be so great that they could not overcome them and that, presently, his forces were a match for them and victory was possible. Again, his opinion was that there was no alternative to making this preventive war in order to defeat the enemy while victory was still possible.

Some of the distant origins of World War I can be seen in the results and consequences of the Franco-Prussian War in 1870–71, over four decades before. The Germans won decisively and set up a powerful empire, while France went into chaos and military decline for years. A legacy of animosity grew between France and Germany following the German annexation of Alsace-Lorraine. The annexation caused widespread resentment in France, giving rise to the desire for revenge, known as *revanchism*. French sentiments wanted to avenge military and territorial losses and the displacement of France as the pre-eminent continental military power.

However in 1913, a new French President, Raymond Poincaré, took office and favoured improving relations with Germany. More interested in the idea of French expansion in the Middle East than a war of revenge to regain Alsace-Lorraine, Poincaré became the first French President to dine at the German Embassy in Paris in January 1914. The *Reich* had the opportunity to pursue this possible improvement in relations if they wanted to but in fact preferred a policy of war to destroy France.

Because of France's smaller economy and population, by 1913 French leaders had largely accepted that France by itself could never defeat Germany.

Meanwhile, in May 1914, two factions ran Serbian politics, one headed by the prime minister, and the other by the radical nationalist chief of Military Intelligence, known by his codename Apis. That month, due to Apis's (Colonel Dimitrijevic) plotting, King Peter dismissed his government. The Russian Minister in Belgrade intervened to have the government restored; Serbia was near-bankrupt and, having suffered heavy casualties in the Balkan Wars and in the suppression of a December 1913 Albanian revolt in Kosovo, needed peace, certainly not internal power struggles. Russia also favoured peace in the Balkans; from the Russian viewpoint it was desirable to keep this government in power. It was in the midst of this political crisis that politically powerful members of the Serbian military armed and trained three Bosnian students as assassins to send into Austria-Hungary.

In 1867, the Austrian Empire fundamentally changed its governmental structure, becoming the Dual Monarchy of Austria-Hungary. Historically, the empire had been run in an essentially feudal manner with a German-speaking aristocracy at its head. However, with the threat represented by an emergence of nationalism within the empire's many component ethnicities, some elements, including Emperor Franz Joseph, decided that a compromise was required to preserve the power of the German aristocracy, which made the Hungarian elite almost equal partners in the government of Austria-Hungary. This was not taken well amongst many in the traditional German-speaking ruling classes. As a result, it was extremely difficult for Austria-Hungary to form a coherent foreign policy that suited the interests of both the German and Hungarian elite. Some reasoned that

4

dealing with political deadlock required that more Slavs be brought into Austria-Hungary to dilute the power of the Hungarian elite. Therefore, there was widespread advocacy of a war with Serbia in leading circles both in Vienna and in Budapest.

Russia wanted to strengthen its role as the protector of Eastern Christians in the Balkans (Serbians being a prime example). Russia was being threatened by an expanding Turkish military that was trained by German experts using the latest technology. That was despite enjoying a booming economy, growing population and large armed forces. The situation at this time brought back old objectives: expelling the Turks from Constantinople, extending Russian dominion into eastern Anatolia and Persian Azerbaijan, and annexing Galicia. This would ensure Russian dominance in the Black Sea and consequently access to the Mediterranean.

Military theorists of the time generally held that seizing the offensive was extremely important. This theory encouraged all belligerents to strike first to gain the advantage. This attitude shortened the window for diplomacy. Most planners wanted to begin mobilization as quickly as possible to avoid being caught on the defensive.

The loose web of alliances around Europe existed (many of them requiring participants to agree to collective defence if attacked) included:

Treaty of London, 1839, about the neutrality of Belgium

German-Austrian treaty (1879) or Dual Alliance

Italy joining Germany and Austria in 1882

Franco-Russian Alliance (1894)

The "Entente Cordiale" between Britain and France (1904), and the separate "entente" between Britain and Russia (1907) that formed the Triple Entente

Therefore, if Austria attacks Serbia, Russia will fall upon Austria, Germany upon Russia, and France and England upon Germany

This complex set of treaties binding various players in Europe together before the war sometimes is thought to have been misunderstood by contemporary political leaders. The traditionalist theory of "Entangling Alliances" has been shown to be mistaken. The Triple Entente between Russia, France and the United Kingdom did not in fact force any of those powers to mobilize because it was not a military treaty. Mobilization by a relatively minor player would not have had a cascading effect that could rapidly run out of control, involving every country. The crisis between Austria-Hungary and Serbia could have been a localized issue.

By the 1870s or 1880s all the major powers had been preparing for a large-scale war, although none expected one. Britain focused on building up its Royal Navy, already stronger than the next two navies combined. Germany, France, Austria, Italy and Russia, and some smaller countries, set up conscription systems whereby young men would serve from one to three years in the army, then spend the next 20 years or so in the reserves with annual summer training. Men from higher social statuses became officers. Recent wars (since 1865) had typically been short — a matter of months. All the war plans called for a decisive opening and assumed victory would come after a short war; no one planned for or was ready for the food and munitions needs of a long stalemate as actually happened in 1914–18. The new British Secretary of State for War, Lord

Kitchener, was the only leading official on either side to both expect a long war ("three years" or longer, he told an amazed colleague) and act accordingly, immediately building an army of millions of soldiers who would fight for years.

Supported by Wilhelm II's enthusiasm for an expanded German navy, Grand Admiral Alfred von Tirpitz championed four Fleet Acts from 1898 to 1912, and, from 1902 to 1910, the Royal Navy embarked on its own massive expansion to keep ahead of the Germans. This competition came to focus on the revolutionary new ships based on the *Dreadnought*, which was launched in 1906, and which gave Britain a battleship that far outclassed any other in Europe. The British response was overwhelming, proving to Germany that its efforts were never going to equal the Royal Navy. The Germans had abandoned the naval race, before war broke out, it was one of a major factor in Britain joining the Triple Entente and therefore important in the formation of the alliance system as a whole.

Following the night of 10/11 June 1903, Serbian officers assassinated their unpopular King Alexander I of Serbia. Parliament then elected Peter Karađorđević as their new king. The consequence of this dynastic change had Serbia relying on Russia and France rather than on Austria-Hungary, as had been the case during rule of the previous dynasty. Serbian desire to relieve itself of Austrian influence provoked the Pig War, an economic conflict, from which Serbia eventually came out as the victor.

Austria-Hungary had solidified its position in Bosnia-Herzegovina, by annexing the provinces on 6 October 1908. The Bosnian crisis (as it was known) continued until April 1909, when the annexation received grudging international approval through amendment of the Treaty of Berlin. During this period, relations between Austria-

Hungary, on the one hand, and Russia and Serbia, on the other, were permanently damaged.

In 1912–1913, the Balkan Wars increased international tension between the Russian Empire and Austria-Hungary. With a strengthening Serbia and a weakening Ottoman Empire and Bulgaria (who otherwise might have kept Serbia in check) the balance of power in Eastern Europe shifted in favour of Russia. The conflicts demonstrated that a localized war in the Balkans could alter the balance of power without provoking general war.

All this political and military posturing caused heightened tension with a underlying misjudgement by some of the main players on the European scene that existing allegiances would not be honoured if the cost was a general war, this left "tinder box" Europe just waiting for the spark.

Countdown to Bloody Slaughter

June 28, 1914: A Serbian student assassinates Archduke Franz Ferdinand of the Austro-Hungarian Empire.

June 28–29: Anti-Serb riots takes place in Sarajevo.

July 23: Following their own secret enquiry, Austria-Hungary sends an ultimatum to Serbia containing several very severe demands. In particular, they gave only forty-eight hours to comply. Whilst both Great Britain and Russia sympathised with many of the demands, both agree that the timescales are far too short. Both nevertheless advised Serbia to comply.

July 24: Germany officially declares support for Austria's position.

July 24: Sir Edward Grey, speaking for the British government, asks that Germany, France, Italy and Great Britain, who have no direct interests in Serbia, should act together for the sake of peace.

July 25: The Serbian government replies to Austria, and agrees to most of the demands. However, certain demands brought into question her survival as an independent nation. On these points they asked that the Hague Tribunal arbitrate.

July 25: Russia enters a period of preparation for war and mobilization begins on all frontiers. Their government decides on a partial mobilization in principle to begin on July 29.

July 25: Serbia mobilizes its army, responding to the Austro-Hungarian demands with less than full acceptance. As a result, Austria-Hungary breaks off diplomatic relations with Serbia.

July 26: Some Serbian reservists accidentally violate the Austro-Hungarian border at Temes-Kubin.

July 26: Russia having agreed to stand aside whilst others conferred, a meeting is organised to take place between the ambassadors from Great Britain, Germany, Italy and France to discuss the crisis. However, Germany declines the invitation.

July 27: Sir Edward Grey meets the German Ambassador independently. A telegram to Berlin after the meeting states, "Other issues might be raised that would supersede the dispute between Austria and Serbia ... as long as Germany would work to keep peace I would keep closely in touch"; this hints at Germany wanting war and any reason will do.

July 28: Austria-Hungary, having failed to accept Serbia's response of the 25th, declares war on Serbia. Mobilization against Serbia begins.

July 29: Confusion sees a Russian general mobilization being ordered, and then changed to a partial mobilization.

July 29: Sir Edward Grey appeals to Germany to intervene to maintain peace.

July 29: The British Ambassador in Berlin, Sir Edward Goschen, is informed by the German Chancellor that Germany is contemplating war with France, and furthermore, wishes to send its army through Belgium. He tries to secure Britain's neutrality in such an action.

July 30: A Russian general mobilization is reordered at 5.00 p.m.

July 31: An Austrian general mobilization is ordered.

July 31: Now Germany enters a period of preparation for war.

July 31: Germany sends an ultimatum to Russia, demanding that they halt military preparations within twelve hours.

July 31: Both France and Germany are asked by Britain to declare their support for the ongoing neutrality of Belgium. France agrees to this. However, Germany does not respond.

July 31: Germany asks France, whether it would stay neutral in case of a war between Germany and Russia.

August 1 (3.00 a.m.): King George V of Great Britain personally telegraphs Tsar Nicholas II of Russia.

August 1: A French general mobilization is ordered, Deployment Plan XVII is chosen.

August 1: A German general mobilization is ordered, deployment plan 'Aufmarsch II West' is chosen.

August 1: Germany declares war against Russia.

August 1: The Tsar responds to the king's telegram, stating, "I would gladly have accepted your proposals had not the German ambassador this afternoon presented a note to my Government declaring war."

August 2: Germany and the Ottoman Empire sign a secret treaty entrenching the Ottoman–German Alliance.

August 3: Germany, after France declines its demand to remain neutral, declares war on France. Germany states to Belgium that she would "treat her as an enemy" if she did not allow free passage of German troops across her lands to access France.

August 3: Britain, expecting German naval attack on the northern French coast, states that Britain would give "... all the protection in its powers to France".

August 4: Germany implements their offensive operations inspired by the Schlieffen Plan.

August 4 (midnight): Having failed to receive notice from Germany assuring the neutrality of Belgium, Britain declares war on Germany. British Foreign Secretary, Sir Edward Grey, is reported as saying, "The lights are going out all over Europe and I doubt we will see them go on again in our lifetime".

August 6: Austria-Hungary declares war on Russia.

August 11: In Britain, "a call to arms" is published. Further detail came out dated 21 August. This outlines how Kitchener's new army was to start its building process.

August 23: Japan, honouring the Anglo-Japanese Alliance, declares war on Germany.

August 25: Japan also declares war on Austria-Hungary.

The Early battles: From mobile, dynamic to static, trench warfare.

August 5–16: Belgium, the Battle of Liege; ran for twelve days, was something of a moral victory for the Allies, in this case the Belgians, and resulted in surprisingly heavy losses upon the German invasion force by the numerically heavily outnumbered Belgium's. On the 17 August, the German Second Army, together with First and Third Armies, began to implement the next stage of the Schlieffen Plan, forcing the Belgian army back to Antwerp. Brussels itself was captured without resistance on 20 August.

August 23: Battle of Mons; the Mons battle signified the first engagement between British and German forces on the Western Front, and began on 23 August 1914. The British found themselves heavily outnumbered by the Germans: 70,000 troops as opposed to 160,000, and 300 guns against 600 German. British riflemen exact heavy losses from the advancing German infantry. British Expeditionary Force (BEF) under its Commander-in-Chief, Sir John French, realising how outnumbered they are start an extended retreat to Marne.

August 26: Battle of Le Cateau; part of the Great Retreat and one of the early major German victories. This takes place between the French Fifth Army and the German Second and Third Armies. Ultimately the French decision to withdraw probably saved the French army from destruction. By retreating, the French were able to hold northern France and remain in the war.

September 5–12: Battle of the Marne; since the beginning of August the war had been a mobile affair. The German advance is brought to a halt, stalemate and trench warfare that typifies World War I ensued.

September 13–28: First Battle of the Aisne; an offensive by the Allied forces against the right wing of the retreating German First and Second armies. It was a rather belated pursuit of the Germans. The British and French were slow, owing to tired troops and over caution by commanders. The Allies realise that the Germans intended to halt their retreat at the Aisne. The two German armies, joined by the new Seventh Army, were able to entrench themselves.

10 –2 October/November: Battle of La Bassée, Race to the Sea; the French Commander-in-Chief Joseph Joffre, moves his forces north-west so as to attack the exposed German right flank at Noyon (the First Battle of Albert). Ultimately, this failed as German defenders firmly dug in behind formidably prepared trench lines.

19–22 October/November: First Battle of Ypres; Sir John French and Marshal Ferdinand Foch both retained the hope of launching a joint offensive following the Race to the Sea had ended at the North Sea coast after each army attempted to outflank the other by moving north and west across Flanders. The new German Army Chief of Staff, General der Infanterie Erich Georg Anton von Falkenhayn has different ideas. Fighting around Ypres would linger on until 22 November when the onset of winter weather forced a break in hostilities. Less than half of the 160,000 men the BEF sent to France came out of the encounter unscathed.

Co. Durham 1914

Life at Home

Daniel looked across the fells of the northern Pennines. He marvelled at its wild, unforgiving natural beauty. Time here stood still and the bleakness of the Teesdale Moors added to its majesty with the backdrop of the Mickle Fell and Cross Fell standing as two monolithic sentinels, north and south of the Castle Estate.

Daniel was assisting his Uncle John who everybody but family called Jack, a localism that Daniel could not explain. Jack was the head keeper of the Castle Estate belonging to the Neville family whose family seat had been at the castle since the Middle Ages. Jack had left the village of his birth when he was 16 years old after working on the neighbouring estate as an apprentice gilly to become a professional soldier serving gallantly with the Durham Fusiliers in the Second Boer War. He had worked himself up through the ranks to the rank of Regimental Sergeant Major with the award of the Military Cross for valour in the Battle of Spion Kop where it was reported that, although injured himself with a bullet wound to his left thigh, he rescued his fallen major whilst carrying out a tactical withdrawal from the ridge. On returning to civvy street some years later, Jack went back to his previous profession with a glowing military record and the thanks of the nation. It was Jack's military grooming of precise planning and strict discipline that saw him rise to head keeper on the Castle Estate. It also helped that the now Lord Neville had been that major he had saved back in that fateful Battle of Spion Kop.

Daniel looked across at his uncle and saw a man at one with his environment. They were both camouflaged and lay in a peat scar checking the distant deer herd to assess the health of the animals and in particular the dominant stag. His uncle had as usual taken all the precautions to get as close as he could without spooking them to get a good look at the herd to see which would be culled during the coming season. This was a life so far removed from his normal working day he savoured every time he got the chance to come here. It didn't happen so often now but, over the years, Uncle John had spent as much time with him as his parents. Jack had no other family. It was hard to believe just a few miles to the east of this magnificent scenery was the industrial heartland of the County Durham coalfields and on its western edge sat West Auckland, the family home and his place of work, West Auckland Colliery.

As they slowly reversed off the ridge and down into Lunedale that familiar feeling of not wanting to leave a place of serenity came over him. This was because leaving this lofty height meant he had started the long ride back to the estate and ultimately back home and his real life of working in the midst of the industrial might that was the driving force of the British Empire. Of course he should not complain too much as there were hundreds, no thousands, worse off than him.

His father Patrick Byrne was the blacksmith at West Auckland Colliery. A good job and one his father was perfectly built for. At well over six feet tall, it was he who gave Daniel his height but his father was broader than Daniel by half and a life of blacksmithing had given him immense strength and power. Some saw his father as a wild man who was hard to control but his work ethic meant he was very highly thought of by the Colliery Manager. His reputation as untamed was further enhanced by his means of earning extra money during the agricultural show season and the annual Appleby Fair where his father was a major attraction as a prize fighter. Even at the age of forty he was still unbeaten and made a healthy income of side bets with his brother's help. Over the last two years, Daniel had been allowed to go along with the two of them but his father was adamant that he would never allow Daniel to get involved in the betting or the fighting. However, he had gone to great lengths to teach Daniel the art of unregulated pugilism. "A man needs to be able to defend himself and his own" was the mantra his father would use time and time again. This was especially saved for Daniel's mother, Florence, when she would remonstrate with her husband about teaching such base skills to their son. For all the preconceived opinions of his father that people had, they all understood his skills at work and on the football pitch where he had played for the village team in the Northern League and had made himself a bit of a celebrity in his day. The club was most famous for being the winners of the Sir Thomas Lipton Trophy, an international football competition, twice, in 1909 and 1911. This was something else that Daniel had inherited from his father and indeed he played for that same village team mirroring his father's somewhat overly competitive nature and a never wavering will to win. This all added up to giving his father this reputation of a somewhat aggressive, uncompromising individual. However, when faced by his mother, his childhood sweetheart, he was nothing but placid and totally loving.

Daniel's mother, Florence, was the local school teacher and with every spare breath had given Daniel the benefit of personal tuition during his formative years. He had good written and mathematical skills with a true interest in science. He also had a good grasp of the French language which was totally unheard of in West Auckland. If his father was the uncompromising individual that people saw, his mother was the polar opposite and it had made such a perfect match. It was his father's love for his mother that had made him stop at home when Uncle John had left to join the army separating the brothers for the only time in their lives. His mother's education had paid off when Daniel had been taken on as an apprentice working on the steam engines that drove the winding gear and the pit carts up the Leazes Incline. This had kept Daniel away from the pit face until he had started showing a thorough understanding and aptitude for blasting. This science and its power for destruction were almost as alluring as the beauty of the north Pennines.

With his family in a good financial state and he with very good prospects, Daniel should have been settled and looking forward to a life that would see him marry and have a family that reflected the good upbringing that he had received. But there was something missing, something nagging at him. It was a desire to see more, to become more. The urge to travel and have greater experiences than his village could offer was burning within him. This was one thing he hadn't inherited from his father but from his Uncle John.

As Daniel and his uncle moved down the reverse side of the ridge out of site of the deer herd there was a great thundering of hooves across heather moorland. At first it was more of a distant swish of continuous noise, however as the noise grew greater and obviously closer you could make out the separate placing of heavy hooves and the alarm calls of adult stags. Suddenly over the ridge came a stampede of the deer herd that not so long ago was several hundred yards away on the opposite side of the valley. Daniel and his uncle just got to their horses before they were driven off by the bolting deer and as soon as the deer saw them they changed direction to avoid these human trespasses in their natural world.

"What in Christ's name caused that? They were totally at ease a few minutes ago!" said Daniel's uncle leading his horse back up toward the ridgeline.

Daniel followed realising his uncle wasn't expecting an answer.

On reaching the ridge they looked over towards the area where, until a few minutes ago, the herd had been happily feeding. Shooting up from the blind side of the ridge on the other valley was a series of huge tongues of flame appearing in the fading light like bolts of lightning but instead of coming from the sky to earth these seemingly came from earth up into the sky.

"I know I am repeating myself", said Daniel's uncle, "but, what in Christ's name is that?"

This time Daniel answered, "Never seen anything like that, but we better go over there and take a look, don't you think?"

Having tied the horses up amongst a small copse they started to make their way down to the valley floor where they followed How Beck up towards its source at How Beck Head from there they could easily drop down to a small plantation at Long Rigg which backed on to the army gunnery ranges at Battle Hill. Approaching from this direction they would be in the incoming area of the light artillery range, but knowing the area like they did and also knowing the red flags were not flying and that would indicate no live firing that day, they continued to approach the area where they had seen the flames from the western flank. The flames had died down and Daniel had not seen any further demonstration of these bolts of flame since they had crested the source of the stream. It was now quiet dark and with dusk descending creating a whole different feel to the exploration of the flame source. Daniel's uncle put his finger to his mouth signalling they needed to be silent on the further traverse of the moor side. Suddenly there was a spark about two hundred yards to their front. It was just a spark and no further flame, following this there was a stream of cursing and, in the dark, Daniel saw a group of men in army uniforms in a small crowd. Daniel looked at his uncle who was now stalking his prey with all the skill that he had shown Daniel over the years, he used the scars in the peat to manoeuvre the pair of them within twenty yards of the group.

"I can't get the bastard thing to fire up!" cursed one of the group, "here you have a go" passing a wide barrel-like device to another of the group. It was connected to a back pack on the original man.

The man unknowingly pointed the barrel at Daniel and his uncle; there was a hissing sound but nothing more.

"Damn flamethrower, if those fools at the War Office think they can rely on this as a weapon they should be out here right now, let's pack up and we can try again tomorrow".

At that, the group turned round and left passing within a few feet of Daniel and his uncle. They stayed motionless for ten minutes after the group had left, although it seemed considerably longer to Daniel. His uncle finally moved up to the point at which the group had been struggling with the device and touched the ground with his hand and bringing it back to his nose. He took a sniff at his hand and then offered it up to Daniel's nose, there was a petroleum/oil smell on his uncle's hand.

"I think it's time we were not here! Let's get back to the horses".

Daniel set off up the valley side but was stopped by his uncle.

"Going that way will silhouette us against the skyline, come on lad you need to keep your wits about you, those who stop thinking are the ones who get left behind"

They got back to the horses in good time although it was now completely dark. It did not pose a problem to Daniel and especially his uncle and as they descended the moor back to the castle the two of them discussed what they had seen. Daniel also realised the excitement and the euphoria that was coursing through his veins was the kind of drug that left him wanting more. He had talked to his uncle many times about different battles he had been involved in when he had served in South Africa and, until that night, Daniel had always thought his uncle must have had a death wish or was just plain crazy to have gone through that and gone back for more, but now he understood.

A few weeks later whilst visiting his friend Henry, Lord Neville's only son, he met up with Uncle John again and his uncle could not wait to pass on the "intelligence", as he called it, he had gained about the events of that evening. He had learnt from Lord Neville who was a member of the House of Lords that there were major concerns about the political crisis across Europe and into Asia. It appeared that different countries were allying themselves together and right across the continent these allies were looking at other confederations and flexing their military muscles. Lord Neville had used the phrase that Europe was like a "tinder box" and, unfortunately, the assassination of an Austrian duke had been the spark for "all hell to break loose". Everybody knew the country was at war and things were not going to plan. Lord Neville also had let slip that the army ranges that had been purchased from the family estate several years earlier were to be used for some clandestine experimental trials of new weaponry. This was the explanation to the mystery of the flamethrower. Daniel's uncle had told Lord Neville about unexplained burnt areas of moorland close to Battle Hill Ranges and had been told that it was probably what the army was calling a flamethrower. It consisted of flaming fuel being pushed out of a barrel by compressed gas. The burning fuel could reach many yards and burn anything in its path. The problem was, it was proving to be very unreliable and had in fact killed a group of soldiers who had been trialling it just a few weeks ago when, without explanation, it had exploded. The slightest leak from the fuel tank if ignited would cause a fireball that, as was the case in question, could have engulfed all around. This was one new-fangled invention that would not be being used anytime soon!

So that was the mystery explained, but Daniel's rather pleased uncle had pointed out how, by following his training, they had entered the army's secret base, observed some trials and got back to safety without anybody realising they had been observed. Put that way, Daniel felt the rush course through his veins once again.

Daniel met up with Henry Neville and immediately started talking about the disturbing but somehow exciting news from across Europe. Henry and Daniel had been friends since childhood. Daniel's mother had been used to give extra tuition to the heir to the Neville estate when it had been recognised that his ability in dealing with numbers was, for some reason, below average. With the help of Florence Byrne and her patient gentle teaching technique the young lord had managed to improve manifold to a point where he might not excel but he could hold his own without the fear of embarrassment. Daniel always went up to the castle during these sessions and met up with his uncle for his tutoring in field craft. The two young lads grew up as the best of friends despite the chasm between their class statuses. Lord Neville not only appreciated the excellent progress his son had made under Florence's tutorage but the confidentiality that all the Byrne family had shown in not making the young lad's deficiencies common knowledge across the area. What with the extra teaching, visiting his uncle and visiting his friend Henry,

Daniel had spent as much of his formative years in the castle as he had at his own home. As the two lads grew older Henry had gone off to boarding school and then to university whilst Daniel had started work at West Auckland Colliery. Fortunately, with his education and the sponsorship of the lord he was fortunate to work with the colliery engineers. This difference in path did not stop them meeting up when the young lord came home and, when he did, their relationship was just as strong, if not stronger, than if they had not been apart. By the time Henry Neville came home from university, Daniel was an experienced member of the engineering team. He was considered one of the most trustworthy at blasting on the larger faces, this involved the coalface being undercut, holes being drilled for blasting and the charges being placed and detonated. Daniel had earned this reputation by demonstrating an almost sixth sense for impending danger and an ability to react with such decisive speed that others with far greater experience in the mines would always heed his warnings and follow his lead.

On the 30 September 1912 at the age of seventeen Daniel had been working at the Brockwell Face and at 56 fathoms the undercut was almost complete. Daniel was waiting to start the drilling to lay the chargers when there was a "blower", a sudden discharge of gas from a fissure within the coal face. Further down the face, colliers were working their hacks into the bottom of the face which in places was up to 6ft 6ins high. During this work the hacks regularly sparked due to catching bedrock and not coal. To his left, Daniel picked up on the unmistakable foulness of the flammable air as a blower released and, to his right, his mates were swinging their hacks. With an astonishing turn of speed Daniel shouted whilst at the same time hurling himself at the hewers who were cutting the coal, thus stopping that next contact between hack point and rock face. Within seconds, all the men on the face smelled the tell-tale stench of the blower and the realisation and relief of what Daniel had done. This was the first time they realised that this young lad had a unique gift.

This sixth sense went beyond work; it manifested itself on the football field also. With a quick glance he could judge where the ball was going to land when his full backs had driven a clearance kick hard up field. His timing was such that he regularly got the better of defenders and his uncanny awareness of where his team mates were would allow him to feed the ball to them, sometimes without needing to look. This ability to pass the ball very quickly was the main reason his partner "up front" and boyhood friend, Henry Neville, recently returned from Durham University had become the team and the Northern League top scorer with Daniel himself in second place in both areas. This sixth sense was something Daniel was very aware of; even when several things were happening at once he had always seen these events in ultra-slow motion. Within this twilight time zone Daniel seemed to dissect the independent constituents of the situation, analyse, prioritise and react at a speed others could not fathom, although Daniel found it quite normal. It was about this time that Henry had been mysteriously going missing for a few weeks at a time and would not, or could not, discuss why, but it did have a serious impact on the team's performance. When approached over the matter by Daniel, all the young lord would say was, "it's family business that I cannot walk away from!"

On 28 June 1914 a Serbian student was reported to have assassinated Archduke Franz Ferdinand of Austria. For reasons unknown to Daniel and most of the working class this meant Europe was at war. The spark that Lord Neville had spoken about had set fire to the tinder box!

Daniel's birthday was 12 August; he was 19 years old, the "Glorious Twelfth", the start of the grouse shooting season. This would be when all the hard work that his uncle had done over the previous twelve months hopefully paid off. Although the nobility had still come to the shooting days, there was much to divert their thoughts and conversations. It was common knowledge that when the Germans, already having been given the nickname of "Fritz", had invaded Belgium and France the British Expeditionary Force had set sail and entered the war to aid its allies. They were having a hard time of things but fortunately they had brought a halt to Fritz's advance across a broad front from the Belgian coast in the north to the Swiss border in the south. Daniel understood that the British seemed to be in an area of Belgium called Flanders.

The day before, a recruiting officer who his uncle knew had visited the village trying to get young men to volunteer for the new army, *Your King and Country need you: a call to arms* had been published and brandished by the officer. Further details came out later in August 1914. Army Order 324 specified that six new divisions would be created from units formed of volunteers, collectively called Kitchener's Army or K1. Great emphasis was given to joining up as a group; "pals together" and "you better be quick" because everyone was saying the war would be over by Christmas. So, across the land, young men of all walks of life volunteered in droves. That was no different in the area around West Auckland, Co. Durham.

Wednesday evening was training night for West Auckland Town FC. Lord Neville and the colliery manager, George Burrows did not see eye to eye on many things, actually on very little. However, sport and, in particular, football was an area which they both supported with great passion. Both had sons of a similar age to Daniel and, although not the best player, just a poacher earning a living off Daniel's skills, nor even a natural leader, Henry Neville, son and heir to the Neville estate, did bring financial support as well as a reasonable degree of skill. Charles Burrows known as Charlie was a dependable full-back and his place in the team guaranteed all team members who worked at the colliery had an early finish on training night. With all these ingredients, West Auckland Town FC was in good shape after recent problems and saw a reasonable amount of success, however not as much as it had in the past, something that his father never failed to mention to Daniel when they talked football!

The training session had started and finished with the topic of conversation being of one thing and one thing only, the words of the recruiting officer from the Durham Fusiliers: 'Your King and Country need you" and be quick about it because the war will be over by Christmas! The national swelling of patriotism was just as strong in West Auckland and the surrounding areas as anywhere else in the country. It united not only the working class but all classes including the nobility in a desire to do their duty for king and country. The additional excitement of doing this together with your mates seemed to make it the most natural thing to do; forming a "Pals Battalion" from the areas of West Auckland, Bishop Auckland and St Helens Auckland, calling themselves the "Auckland Pals". All the team members went to talk to their friends and even Bishop Auckland FC their rivals to drum up support and arrange to meet at the recruiting office in Bishop Auckland the following Saturday.

Daniel felt that surge of excitement that had come over him during his Battle Hill adventure. He knew this was his calling, he had to answer it, if not he would be forever left wondering what he had missed. He did not want that, he had seen all too often that look in his father's eyes when his Uncle John talked of not just his war experiences but life experiences, the fact that he had seen so much more of the world than his brother. There always was just that hint of regret on his father's face regardless of the deep love he had for his wife, Daniel's mother.

He discussed it with his father firstly and, to his surprise, he learnt that his parents had already discussed this possibility. His mother was totally against him going off to fight a war that was, "no more than a fall out between royal families and governments who were driven by nothing but greed for the right to conquer other countries to strengthen their own empires", was his mother's take on the situation. But his father had argued that they could not really stop him as he was a man and, as such, needed to make his own mind up. Daniel knew why his father had supported that view and felt a tinge of sadness that his father still lived with that regret of what might have been. Daniel would make sure he would have the experiences for both of them and return to retell the stories for his father. When he entered the scullery where his mother was preparing this year's batch of apple and blackberry jam, the sweet smell and the warmth was such an overwhelming atmosphere of homely security he faltered in the doorway. His mother turned towards him, she had been crying. She looked up at him and the tears began to roll down her cheekbones that were still high and of a complexion that a girl half her age would be proud of. But on this occasion it was not his beautiful mother he saw before him but a frightened little woman who, as she looked past him at her husband in the doorway realised what was about to be said. Before he could say anything she threw herself at him, weeping and, in between the sobs, made him promise to come home safe and stay in touch so she would always know where he was and that he was safe. As usual she had made a difficult situation easy for him by understanding him and taking her pain and hiding it as best she could. It wasn't a surprise to Daniel. Finally, he went to see his uncle, who had already guessed what Daniel would be saying seeing as he had made a special trip to see him so late at night. He had heard from his lordship that his son and the boys from all across town intended signing up. He sat Daniel down and there followed two hours of compressed conversation where his uncle went over all his experiences that he had in actual fact told him many times before. That said, Daniel was not so arrogant to think it was not worth listening to again, besides Uncle John was a proven war hero, something he only aspired to be. Finally, his uncle brought out a small canvas pouch that was designed to fit on the rear of a belt and a Mauser auto-loading pistol with ten-round box magazines which he had brought back from the Transvaal. Firstly, he explained that he was only to use them when just about to go into battle, as the army would "haul him over the coals" for not using standard issue. But the Mauser with its ten-shot magazine would give him a good advantage in close-up fighting, although his uncle had some spare rounds, he explained it was a German pistol so he would have to "re-supply directly from Fritz". The canvas pouch which carried his uncle's prism compass, with its mother of pearl face to catch any light available could be used at night to keep the user from straying off track. Uncle John explained that firepower always won the day and all armies only gave their troops the bare minimum, so to carry more and be able to carry on firing would always give him the advantage. The compass that Daniel had been taught to use by his uncle was something that Daniel had always quietly coveted and was thrilled to receive. It was at this moment, following this sudden deadly advice, that it dawned on Daniel that this was for real and that if he was ever to use the equipment his uncle had just given him it would be because he was face to face with an enemy who was trying to kill him. Suddenly there was that rush of excitement again. How like his uncle, to give sound advice and practical help, not hugs and farewell kisses, just a firm handshake and a "look after yourself and the others". Then they parted.

Recruitment and Training

On the Saturday, young men from both football teams, West Auckland, St Helens, Bildershaw, Auckland Park, Bishop's Park, Black Boy and Eldons' Harry, Henry and John Henry Collieries, formed a massive queue outside the recruitment centre that had been established at the town hall. The recruiting officer Sergeant Bob Howel was a veteran of the second Boer War and a long-standing friend of Daniel's Uncle John, "if you turn out to be half the soldier that your uncle is then God help Fritz" said Sergeant Howel as Daniel signed his papers. He swelled with pride at the thought of now being in the Durham Fusiliers. They were the 2nd Service Battalion of the Durham Fusiliers which, along with the West Riding Regiment, Northumberland Fusiliers and the Green Howards, formed the 32nd brigade (11th Northern Division) of the K1 army group. They were to be marched to Brancepeth Training Camp just outside Durham city where they would be issued with their uniform and equipment and start their basic training. This was the group's first introduction to the one thing they would all get to know very well, a forced march. In this case it was a relatively short distance from the town hall to the Bishop Auckland railway station to entrain into cattle trucks and detrain at Brandon and a two mile march to the camp. This was just as well as some of the lads had not got the sort of footwear that would allow easy marching. They only wore their pit clogs and these

29

certainly were not made to walk distances, less still to march.

"We'll see what you're made off now Byrne" said a voice from across the other side of the mess hall, "now you are away from all your family you'll have nobody's reputation to fall back on, you'll have to make a name for yourself!"

It was Ray Murray, "Big" Ray Murray as he was known, and for some reason he and Daniel had never really got on. It wasn't as though he had not tried but, ever since they had been kids, Ray had made it clear that he resented Daniel, so Daniel in turn had never had anything to do with him.

Ray Murray was slightly shorter than Daniel but very thick set. He had never been involved in the football team unlike almost everybody amongst the "Auckland Pals" who had or still played at some level or other. He just didn't understand the team ethic and working together to achieve a common goal, it was always about himself and if that was to the detriment of others, so be it! It was a bit of a surprise that he should have joined up with the rest of them, it would be the first time he had ever been part of a team.

It was a shocked group of young men who arrived at Brancepeth Camp half way through that afternoon. Daniel had no idea how many there was but it must have numbered in the hundreds, and a big percentage of those who had entered the camp were limping badly following the unexpected march, if you could have called it a march! When they had detrained they had been taken by an instructor, Sergeant Wainwright and he had left them all in no uncertain doubts that they were in the army now and they now belonged to him. Gone were the pleasantries of Sergeant Howel from the recruiting office. Daniel knew from discussions with his uncle, this was more akin to how it was to be. He thought back to Uncle John's advice about surviving basic training; "Keep your head down, your mouth shut, never answer back. You must remember at all times basic training is just that, it will be thirteen weeks of hell when you will be driven hard to see if you will break. Just think of it as a thirteen-week compartment in your life and all you need is to get through it!"

As they had signed up in their most intimate groups, they were set up in the barracks in those same groups which the instructors had called platoons and further sub-divided into sections of twelve men.

Having been allocated to a hut, they were told to put their belongings on one of the two-tier bunks. They were bunk beds and Daniel was able to get an upper bunk! Unbelievably, Ray Murray had been allocated to the same hut and had ended up on the bunk below Daniel. They then had to fall in outside and were given a knife, fork and spoon each, marched to a long dining room full of very noisy solders all clad in denims, which were the working uniform of the time. They queued up and received a meal of re-constituted potato, boiled tasteless haricot beans and a piece of tough stringy meat, which was so tasteless and burnt it was hard to distinguish which type of poor animal had given up its life in order to feed this hungry rabble. Even so, the men around shouted for them not to throw anything away, but to scrape it on to their plates. These soldiers did not understand where some of these lads came from; this was good grub to a lot of the Auckland Pals! Outside the hut was a large tank full of hot water to plunge their eating irons in to wash them. They were then marched back to the hut for a first night on a hard camp bed with a pillow filled with straw and three army blankets. Again, for some of the lads this was quite good, being in the army to date did not seem all too bad, however:

Reveille was at 6.00 a.m. followed by a difficult shave in a room full of jesting squaddies, some of whom used cut-throat razors! Later, they were taken down to Brancepeth Castle to the stores where they were issued with two battle dress uniforms, an overcoat, rifle, bayonet, denims, two pairs of boots and all accoutrements required for soldiering; then to the barbers', where their heads were shaved to a stubble.

Within the next few hours, their civvies had been changed for denims and smart khaki uniform with good heavy boots. At least to most people this was considerably smarter than their normal attire, but by far the most coveted and pride-swelling part of the uniform was the cap bearing the crest of the Durham Fusiliers. That shining star with its blue shield holding the golden cross, crossed rifles and four rampant lions brandishing swords was a fascination to Daniel. There was a cloth badge to be sewn on to the arm of the jacket but the cap badge was metal and shiny. It seemed whatever angle you looked at it from it managed to pick up the sun and gleam almost as though it was the beating heart of the regiment. Daniel did look at it from every angle. The more he looked, the greater the smile on his face it just felt … well … right, almost as this was what he was meant to be and everything in his life prior to this was a build-up to this moment and now life started for real. Every day followed the same pattern. They were rushed from pillar to post, never having a minute until lights out at 10.00 p.m. Continual rifle drill, physical training, bombing (Mills Grenades) training and marching at a pace varying from fast to even faster (or so it appeared). The first Saturday morning they were all inoculated against various diseases. Each man stood in a queue with a bared arm into which was plunged a large blunt needle and, the more men who received this injection, the blunter the needle became! Some men fainted. Their arms were very sore and tender for the weekend, but when Monday came along it was more marching, rifle drill etc.

Within Daniel's section was:

Charlie Burrows – Charlie – left-back

Gordon Lascelles – Lazzer – right-back

Ronald Metcalfe – Ronnie – centre-half

Arthur Moore – Art, due to him being a very good natural artist – goalkeeper

John Anderson – Anders – midfielder

Kenneth Thomas – Kenny – left-winger

Raymond Thompson – Tommo – right-winger

George Horner – Jack – midfielder

Harry Fowler – Fouller – midfielder

Henry Davison – Davy – centre forward

Ray Murray – Big Ray

With the exception of Ray Murray, all belonged to West Auckland Town FC; but one person was missing from the group, this was Daniel's closest friend and fellow forward Henry Neville (who was always called Henry due to being the son of Lord Neville). At the recruiting office, he had been earmarked immediately for officer training and there the two friends had been separated, promising to stay in touch; however neither knew where the other had gone!

Half-way through the fifth week of the basic training, Sergeant Wainwright suddenly announced that following a discussion between Lord Neville and General Smythe, who was in charge of the training camp, a football match was to be arranged between a team from the camp and the local team, Crook FC. When Daniel's section heard this they knew who would be the team to represent the camp. If it had been the brainchild of Lord Neville it would effectively be West Auckland Town FC with a few guests from Bishop Auckland FC. Sure enough, almost to a man as they predicted, it was West to play Crook which over the years had been a regular season fixture but this was to be their farewell match because after this they would be travelling south to Hillsborough Barracks, Sheffield, for further training.

The day of the match was something to behold. Hundreds of troops on manoeuvres, but not to war but a few miles down the road to see the match. It would only be a war on the pitch for the Durham Fusiliers. Over the years, the animosity between Crook and West had grown from being healthy, competitive rivalry to open disregard for each other which usually ended in some major fracas which saw the game disintegrate into something resembling a brawl! The young fusiliers team did not march to the game; instead they rode in style, at the expense of the team's benefactor, Lord Neville, in a motor bus hired for the day from the Eden Bus company of West Auckland; the same bus company that had supplied the transport that brought family members of the team from West to watch their sons' grand farewell. On the same day that Sergeant Wainwright had broken the news of the match he had delivered the West Auckland FC kit of black and gold and all the lads' boots, so it was like a regular season match. As the bus pulled up to the ground, the lads could not believe their eyes, hundreds of khaki-clad supporters,

"Hey Charlie, this is what it must be like when you arrive at St James' Park?"

"Yeah, well make the most on it Ronnie. Cos this is as close as you'll get!" replied Charlie Burrows.

"Danny", shouted Kenny Thomas from the other side of the bus, "here's your dad and uncle"

"We'll be aright if it kicks off then", added Art Moore.

One by one, each saw their relatives awaiting the arrival of their sons, the gladiators!!

And gladiators they had to be when the match kicked off. To everybody but Crook FC they were heroes about to bravely march off to fight the Hun. However, to the players of Crook FC it seemed they had only one mission and that was to ensure as many of the Durham Fusiliers were not fit for duty at the end of the game. After the first few minutes of the game where most of the tackles seemed to be knee high or higher the game began to spread out and settle down to a pace that the Durham Fusiliers found well within their capacity. It very soon became clear that the last few weeks of intensive physical training had given the West lads a pace which normal civvies just could not keep up with. With a half time score of 2 – 0 to the fusiliers, the game ended in a rather one-sided score of 5 – 0. After the match players, families and dignitaries were treated to another luxury thanks to Lord Neville. At the side of the changing rooms and club there had been erected a marquee/beer tent. The rest of the khaki supporters had either moved off into town if they had a pass or had trudged back to camp before furlough.

As the conquering heroes entered the marquee there was great applause much to the embarrassment of the whole team, but with such a score line, the general was well pleased his team had shown their physical superiority and an overwhelming team ethic which was exactly how the empire was to defeat the Hun. Lord Neville was beaming with pride and it wasn't just because his team had performed so admirably. Stood beside him was his son, Henry. He was dressed in the uniform of a lieutenant of the Durham Fusiliers. Daniel could not contain his joy at seeing his good friend and hugged him forgetting all the military protocols that had been drilled into him over the previous weeks. When the general saw the beaming smile on Lord Neville's face grow even wider, he decided that it was probably not a good time or place to reprimand this private, but just coughed somewhat uncomfortably. This brought everybody back to the here and now so both lads slightly parted. Henry commented in his usual tongue in cheek style, "you were getting a little slow during the second half, maybe it's your age catching up with you".

Daniel retorted equally as tongue in cheek, "If you had bothered to get your boots on, then I would not have had to put up with those Bishop lads up front with me!"

Then Daniel saw his father and Uncle John standing in the background. Henry saw his friend's attention drift as he saw them and, as a good friend would, said, "go over and see them, we've got all night to catch up, I think the bus will be leaving soon so you've no time to lose".

Uncle John draped a big arm over Daniel's shoulder as he neared drawing him into the family and from nowhere a pint of Cameron's Best was presented to him.

"To your health and a safe journey" toasted Daniel's uncle and they all drank.

"Where's Mum?" asked Daniel, half knowing the answer before he received the answer.

"She couldn't come and go through saying goodbye again, son," replied Daniel's father in an unusually quiet voice. It was apparent he was finding it hard to retain his composure in this short and very public opportunity to say what father and son had to say. There was a strange sense that Daniel picked up on, a sense that his father was out of his comfort zone. He could see his father was upset at this farewell and that this massive bear of a man was crying inside and was fighting not to show it on the outside.

Daniel quickly said, "Tell Mum I will be fine and I promise to write. When I return I will have you all proud of me with the medals I am going to win and the stories I will be able to tell will even rival Uncle John's. Now drink up and make sure you catch that bus it's too long a walk at this time of an evening".

With that he pulled his father and Uncle John together in a great hug, released them and walked away into the crowd to find his friends. He really didn't want to foreshorten the goodbye but he couldn't bear to watch his father so upset.

Patrick and John drained their glasses in one and started to walk towards the door, Patrick turning to his brother, said in almost despair, "I have so much I wanted to tell him, but couldn't".

His brother threw his arm around his shoulder and led him outside leaning his head towards Patrick and whispering, "He knows and that's why he left us so quickly, for the first time I have ever seen, he was protecting you. Our boy has grown up to be a fine man, you should be proud", John said with all the reassurance he could.

Patrick nodded his head in agreement but couldn't trust himself to say anything and, with that, the two brothers walked off into the darkness of the evening.

Henry hadn't missed his friend's situation so was quick to his side, "Come on Danny, let's go and see the lads", and with that they immersed themselves in the crowd where there seemed to be such an expectant buzz as to what the future held for the Auckland Pals.

After a couple more pints and several conversations with a host of people, Daniel came face to face with Betty Hibbert, a young lady he had shared plenty of time with over the last couple of years. Betty was from Crook and Daniel only saw her at the dances that were held at Bishop Auckland Hippodrome. They had always seemed to be at ease in each other's company and there had been some sessions of heavy petting and groping but it had never amounted to what you could call a relationship. But tonight there seemed to be a much greater intensity to everything they were saying and their body language suggested much more was on offer than ever before. Very shortly they were outside the marquee walking hand in hand down towards the Old Meadows Farm where they stopped in the hay barn.

Without a word, Betty put her arms up and around his neck and pulled him down towards her waiting lips. She pushed her hips forward so as to grind her pelvis into his. There was a latent passion in the air so potent that it could be tasted. After several minutes of kissing and exploring each other's body, Betty pulled him towards the loose hay at the base of the stack where she dropped on to the hay pulling him on top of her. Daniel resisted and pulled away hoarsely whispering, "Betty, we can't do this, I'm going away and there is a possibility I won't come back."

"I know and that's why we have to. I don't want you to promise me anything but to keep yourself safe over there. Now come here".

With that she pulled him down on top of her and this time Daniel didn't pull away! It was nearly half past eleven when Daniel had walked Betty to her home and kissed her goodbye. He had been walking for about ten minutes back towards the football ground hoping he would find some of his mates still there and that there was some sort of arrangement to get them back to camp, although he had a pass until morning. He was feeling very good with himself and every sense seemed to be at attention and he was buzzing with the joys of life. As he passed the rear of one of the town centre pubs, a back door opened and there stood Ray Murray.

"Now look at what we have here, if it isn't everybody's hero, Daniel bleeding Byrne [he managed to spit the two Bs of bleeding Byrne] I've been waiting for this moment for a long time" slurred Ray and staggered towards him.

Daniel backed off not wanting to spoil what had been, until then, a pretty good evening, but at the side of the pub just next to the Front Street, Ray threw a huge hay maker punch which if it had landed would have knocked down Jack Johnson let alone Daniel Byrne. However, Ray was so drunk that it was easily avoided and Daniel tried to calm Ray down. This only annoyed Ray more and he came at

Daniel with both arms mowing the air like a demented windmill, without realising, Daniel had backed himself into a tight spot so had to duck and spin to the left to try and avoid this second onslaught. As he did he slipped slightly and did not get the speed and direction to his move he required and a poorly timed punch caught Daniel just above the right eye. Unfortunately for Ray, this brought an immediate and uncompromising reaction. As the partially unsuccessful evasive action was completed, Daniel immediately turned and was ready for Ray to turn. To be quite honest, as a result of his size and his state, Ray presented Daniel with an easy target which he took with full advantage. He hit Ray with a straight left and then a right so quickly that they almost landed simultaneously. Ray was almost as quickly on his backside on the floor leaning against the side of the pub, he was not getting up after that. However, the punch that had caught Daniel had left him slightly dazed so Daniel cupped his head in his hands and tried to steady himself. At that point there was the piercing sound of a whistle and two policemen came running up. It's surprising how the sound of a policeman's whistle can clear the head! And it certainly cleared Daniel's, as the police sergeant asked for an explanation, Daniel realised that they had not seen what had actually happened. Very quickly Daniel pointed down around the rear of the pub in the direction he had walked and shouted, "Quick they went that way". The younger of the two policemen set off in the direction Daniel had indicated. Meanwhile, the sergeant listened to how Daniel had been set upon by two locals and, if it had not been for the timely intervention of his friend, he would have been in a worse state than he now was. Unfortunately, the two ruffians had managed to punch his friend and that was why he was in the state that he saw before him. Although Ray was fairly dazed he was not so far out of it that he did not pick up on the story that Daniel was spinning. On questioning, he confirmed all that Daniel had concocted, the real time dazed state of Ray added to the believability of the story. When the younger policeman returned he recognised Daniel because he had been watching the match that afternoon.

"Hardly surprising you are not welcome round these parts after the drubbing you gave them this afternoon".

This seemed to tilt the scales so the sergeant believed their story and set about helping the lads back to the ground where they could hopefully get help back to camp.

When the two fusiliers arrived at the ground, the company who had supplied the marquee and fittings was packing up the fittings by the lights of their motor lorry.

"If the lighter things aren't removed tonight then we will not have them by morning!" explained the foreman.

Daniel and Ray's luck held when they were offered a lift back to camp if they lent a hand finishing off.

"We are based at Willington so can drop you off there and that will leave you a walk of about a mile or two to your camp added the foreman".

Within the hour the two were travelling in the back of the lorry back to the camp where Daniel would have no problem having a pass until morning; however Ray should have been back before 8.00 p.m. prior to the normal 10.00 p.m. lights out.

Ray had been very subdued in the lorry and when they struck out for the camp from Willington, he rather sheepishly asked, "Why didn't you drop me in the shit? You know I would have dropped you in it!"

"Ray, we are about to go to war where Fritz is going to be doing his best to blow our heads off. We West lads have got to look out for each other because if we don't, nobody else will. We will be stronger and safer together, we need to watch each other's back and not fight amongst ourselves," stressed Daniel in a way that almost erred on pleading for Ray to see sense, "anyway why have you always hated me? What did I do to you that was so wrong for you to try the stunt you tried tonight?"

With that Ray stopped dead in his tracks and sat down on the floor, his shoulders hunched and head bowed in an almost submissive posture, "You have always been good at everything you did and everybody seems to like you, even the toffs from the castle" sobbed Ray, "All I had was a father who beat me and died leaving me to go and earn whatever I could to help my mum. To me you have had everything I wanted and you are what I wanted to be!" burst Ray in the way a pressure relief valve would vent.

"Ray, did you ever think of asking for help from any of the lads? Any one of them would and still will help, including me. If there is only one thing we all have in common, it's we are from West and we look after each other," encouraged Daniel.

"Well, thanks but it's too late now. I am late for furlough, so that's me in the trouble and you lot are off to Hillsborough tomorrow."

"I wouldn't be so sure of that, I have my pass 'til morning, so I will get in and start talking to the guards, when I have them talking, you should be able to sneak in"

"Here," said Ray producing a small bottle of rum, "if you use this you should be able to attract their attention for a while"

"Sounds like a plan Ray" announced Daniel, "come on it will be better if we get back before the guards change so they are ready to get their heads down. The last thing we want is to try this with alert guards who are as fresh as daisies".

With that the two strode off with the appearance of two pals out on a jolly.

The plan worked a treat especially as the two guards had been at the game and recognised Daniel. It was they who insisted he told the story of the two goals and this was washed down with the rum. In fact, it was the new guards coming on duty that broke up the party and by that time Ray was safely in his bunk. When Daniel climbed up on to his bunk, Ray grabbed his leg and said, "Thanks mate!"

Even after a somewhat extraordinary day for the camp and its occupants the following day saw the same pattern return. The army likes its routine. Up at 6:00 a.m. and, after squaring away their kit, they had physical exercises prior to breakfast. But then it was full inspection prior to a march to the train station for the trip to the big steel city of Sheffield. The trip was fairly uneventful apart from the pals could not get over the change in Big Ray, especially when they teased Daniel about what he had got up to during the previous night, "Jealous! That's what you lot are, none of you could have had the kind of game Danny had. Had a good drink and got a woman!"

The train rolled into Pond Street Station and, from there, they picked up a familiar type of train that took them to the front of the barracks. It was a goods train with some wagons that they were herded into, but also there was the so familiar smell of coal, obviously bound for one of the steel mills in the area. So in the early hours they set foot in what was to be their home for the next few weeks.

Hillsborough Barracks was a walled variety of buildings between Langsett Road and Penistone Road in the Hillsborough District of Sheffield. This foreboding range of military buildings covered a vast area of 22 acres and dated from the 1800s; unfortunately, it appeared they had not been maintained since their original construction.

The barracks was divided into three terraces. The first (top) terrace faced on to Langsett Road. This contained the mess establishment, quarters for around forty officers and a similar number of servants, and a chapel. This building had a length of about 400 feet and a width and height of about 40 feet; it was three storeys high and had a mixture of gothic and castellated styles. The other buildings of the barracks consisted of a large five bedroom house serving as the Garrison Commander's quarters outside the walls, a 58-patient two storey hospital for treating the soldiers and a clock-towered building. The cavalry soldiers' quarters were on the first floor and had stabling for 260 horses on the ground floor (total accommodation for over 900 NCOs and other ranks). Also a gun shed housing six field guns, the barracks store with living quarters for the barracks sergeant, a guard room, incorporating a police room, detention cells, and an exercise yard plus a vehicle shed which could house twenty-six motor cars seemed to have been a later alteration, as well as a veterinary infirmary large enough to house eighteen horses, a granary, four cookhouses and various workshops. This was on an altogether grander scale to what the lads had experienced at Brancepeth. They started to get the idea of the immense scale of the empire's war machine. To them it was a small town in itself and the mighty city of Sheffield was a true metropolis, but the barracks were a dark and depressing place to be and it required the lads to pull together to brighten up the picture.

Training for ordinary Tommies began with basic training; physical fitness, drilling, marching and also essential field craft. This was something that Daniel could teach them with the experience he had been afforded by his uncle. However, he remembered his uncle's advice; keep your head down and your mouth shut. All the lads could testify to this, with the exception of the football match that was all they did at Brancepeth. However, here at Hillsborough each soldier was to specialise; in the infantry, it would be, as a rifleman, machine gunner, rifle grenadier, signaller or bomber. They would receive courses of instruction relevant to their role. The lads had been assessed at Brancepeth and on arrival allocated their specialist roles:

Danny – rifleman

Charlie – rifleman

Lazzer – rifleman

Ronnie – bomber

Art – bomber

Anders – bomber

Kenny – rifle grenadier

Tommo – rifle grenadier

Jack – rifle grenadier

Fouller – signaller

Davy – machine gunner

Big Ray – machine gunner

The training was relentless and very soon Daniel was seen to be an excellent marksman and the instructors had seen for themselves his field craft skills. It was soon known via his friends to all the instructors where Daniel had got these skills from and he was quizzed about these skills and how far they extended. They were then tested and pushed further with field trials and tests of survival and endurance on the Pennines of the Peak District. Daniel was not just a rifleman, something which he was very proud of, he was a sharp shooter, which he was even more proud of. His progress was relayed back to his family by regular letters just as he had promised his mother.

A gruelling seven weeks passed with all the lads gradually becoming efficient killing machines using their adopted specialism. Yes, they could use their weapons. But could they use them on another human being was the big question. This was a regular topic of conversation within "A" Section of 14 Platoon. Their instructors constantly vilified the Hun as demons that had to be exterminated to save mankind. Even so, each member of the section held that doubt and, to a certain extent, fear, that they would only know the answer to this when they faced Fritz for the first time and it was becoming more evident that the time was drawing ever nearer. Just as had happened at Brancepeth, during the eighth week, the instructor announced that there was to be a night's furlough on the Saturday night. Every member of the platoon expected to be ready for a full inspection at 8.00 a.m. on the Sunday prior to being transported down to Dover by train to embark for Calais, France.

"Ruddy 'ell! It's actually going to happen then," was the stunned reaction from Tommo, who was rarely heard to swear at all.

"We'd better make the most of Sheffield on Saturday then, it maybe sometime before we get a night out anywhere, if at all!" replied Charlie, with a somewhat dry mouth.

"Relax lads," said Ray, "we are only going for more training but this time it's in France, so we can have a crack at the Sheffield lasses on Saturday, then some French lasses a few days later," this light-hearted front seemed to calm the nerves and lift the edge of the strained atmosphere.

As if the army knew the lads' intentions before they had even had time to think them up, they had received an educational lecture on the perils of VD and the dire consequences to your health as well as your paybook, if you were unfit for duty. They also learnt of their destination in France. It was another training camp, just as Ray had predicted. It was called Etaples.

With sore heads and some forgotten promises to Sheffield ladies, the lads boarded the train and settled down to see the last of England and compare notes about the night before. The banter was light-hearted and really showed what a close knit team they had become, none more than Ray and, as usual, Daniel seemed to be the focal point of the group. They soon passed through the Midlands and neared London, pulling up at Kensington where they changed engines. This, in the half light of the dawn was the first glimpse the lads had had of their capital city, London, and they ran right through to Folkestone with only one stop at Maidstone. Pulling into the harbour station about 9:15 a.m. and after a wait of some thirty minutes boarded the boat which was due to leave about 11:45 a.m.

Further Training in France

Every man was given a lifebelt as a precaution against submarine attacks and, thus attired they crossed the Channel, most of them for the first time. The journey took one and a half hours and if any of the lads were not sea sick by the motion of the ship pitching, then they were sick from the mixed smell of the sea of vomit on the decks and the fumes from the funnels. However, prompt to time the ship entered the bay in which Boulogne stands and the escort of two destroyers, who had convoyed them across, took their leave.

The platoon made their way down the quay and across the bridge and formed up in the main road. While waiting for stragglers, two of which had fallen overboard whilst disembarking and had had to be fished out on to the quayside via loading derricks. They had their first encounter with French street vendors and with great difficulty they successfully negotiated the exchange of their English money into French, this was aided by one or two men who had been out before. For an English shilling they received value to the extent of f1.20 although the proper rate of exchange was f1.40 but the French people always gave this amount thus always standing to gain the difference of 20 cents. It all meant very little to the lads who were all mesmerised by their new surroundings with the new language and smells of a foreign port.

At last they moved off and marched into the town, turning up a side street which proved to be the beginning of a very long hill on top of which stood the camp. With the aid of two halts, which were badly needed for the weather was unseasonably hot for February and they were carrying heavy packs, bearing in mind they had to carry all their worldly possessions. They succeeded in reaching the camp which was composed of a large number of tents divided into sections, so many tents to each section. The camp also had some very large tents, the dining halls etc. being large, marquees with one or two wooden buildings dotted about. There were also one or two large hospitals adjacent to the camp and these were composed of several wards, each ward consisting of three marquees.

Here, they were supposed to be billeted into ten per tent. However due to the number of new arrivals not meeting the number expected the lads got the benefit of only having five in each tent. After dinner of bully beef stew they stowed their kit, had the regulations of the camp read out to them, drew blankets and were then dismissed for the day. Having made themselves at home in their new surroundings, they set out to make a tour of inspection of the camp, visiting the YMCA Church Army Hut and Tipperary Club. This latter, together with Lady Angela Forbes' rest hut, were the two best places in the camp, for such delicacies as tea, bread and butter, eggs, custard and fruit and such like could be obtained very cheaply.

The next day was Sunday and they were up early and had roll call exactly at 7:00 a.m. at the same time being warned that they were bound for the training ground at 2:00 p.m.

"Not bad here, hey Danny," beamed Ray, "I never thought I would be holidaying by the French coast, I could quite get to like this war, if this is what it's all about," Ray paused then added, "but I somehow doubt it!"

Since their arrival the noise of the distant artillery fire had been a constant, sometimes just sporadic and sometimes continuous, but constant.

"Yeah Ray, somehow I think that very shortly we will be much closer to those guns than is good for our health," answered Daniel.

After lunch they fell in and marched to the ground which was known as the "Bull Ring". Passing through the various hospitals, they got their first sight of the grim reality of war. There were men with the most horrendous injuries in full view of the lads and, as they marched, their demeanour became much more sombre, so this is what war is like? On they marched up to the main road to the training area which was some two miles away. On all sides could be seen sand: on the left it stretched away to the sea, while on the right it rose sharply into a large ridge which extended all along the route and was a continuation of the hill on which the camp stood. Arriving after about 30 minutes marching, hot and perspiring, because it was midday and very hot, they turned off the road and made their way to the position set out for the 2nd Service Battalion of the Durham Fusiliers. About half way up the ridge they waited for the arrival of the sergeants, their instructors. They soon appeared, three of them accompanied by an officer, all wearing a wide yellow band on their sleeves to denote that they were instructors. During the afternoon, under the supervision of the sergeants and closely watched by the officer, the lads went through rapid loading, extended order drill, and bayonet fighting and were much relieved when they finally made their way back to the road. The instructors took their leave and they made their way back the way they had come, towards the camp.

The next day found the lads once again on the Bull Ring but this time in the morning from 8:15 a.m. to 1:00 p.m. with a break of half an hour. They were bayonet fighting, bombing and marching in extended order, all that morning and beyond, finally arriving back in camp somewhere about 2:00 p.m.

In a similar manner, the whole of the next ten days with four exceptions were passed. On two days, the monotony of training was relieved by a route march. At 8:15 a.m. about 1000 to 1500 men from the various depots fell in at the appointed place and leaving the camp by the bridge across the railway at Etaples set out on the march. The other two days were spent learning how to operate and construct trenches. If there was one thing a group of pit lads could do and do well it was dig. To the Auckland Pals this was a breeze and represented a bit of an easy day, however that could not be said about all the troops. The second week of their training consisted of a series of attacks carried out on a set of trenches, the exact representation of those they were to be facing when they went into the line at a place that HQ kept secret from all but the officers. For this the lads had to march about 5 miles, prior to the attacks each day and that day the weather turned from bright and sunny to torrential rain, it continued relentlessly for the next few days.

It was just before this second phase of the training started that the platoon was to be introduced to its new lieutenant who had just arrived from Officer Training School in Blighty. The platoon was assembled for its daily inspection and up strolled Lieutenant Henry Neville. Henry had difficulty hiding his grin as he marched front and centre of his new platoon. He was accompanied by his immediate superior, Captain Charles Johnson, who, being aware of the surprise he was about to unleash on to his men let go the hoots and cheers the lads gave when recognition struck home. It appeared that, yet again, the long arm of the Neville family and its connections had managed to find the future heir a position that suited him. But it also suited the rest of the section who now had almost the whole of West Auckland FC in the same section. The big difference would be instead of fighting side by side on a football pitch it would be side by side facing the Hun across no-man's land and sometimes an awful lot closer!

"How did you wangle that?" was the first thing Daniel enquired through his beaming smile following the platoon's fall out and getting his first opportunity to speak to his commanding officer.

"Rather easily, actually."

"Well go on then, let me in on it."

"It seems Father is very good friends with General Haig, they fought together against the Boers. Apparently he also has a very high regard for your uncle too. Anyway, after unsuccessfully trying to convince me that I should take a post with the general staff at HQ, he had a word with good old Dougie and sorted out my first choice posting."

"This was your first choice?" questioned Daniel, unable to hide the disbelief in his voice.

"Of course it was Danny! If I am to face old Fritz down the barrel of my revolver, I want my mates watching my back. I've looked at the section names and we've got the whole bloody team with us, apart from that idiot Murray, how did you get landed with him?"

"It's a long story but take it from me he's a changed character, there's nobody else you would want alongside you when you face old Fritz".

"Well if you say so, I'll give him the benefit of the doubt. However I have to disagree with there being nobody else to have by my side, you have that posting and to that end myself and Captain Johnson have been looking at the training reports and it appears you have been making quite a name for yourself with the instructors." Suddenly Henry's face became very serious and he added, "We have been taking one hell of a beating on the frontline and the regiment, like most others, are losing NCOs faster than they can be trained. With your skills in the field and some of the specialist training I have received, our platoon, especially our section, is to be used for certain special operations when we get up there. I would like you to be platoon Corporal!"

It wasn't very often that Daniel was speechless, but just at that moment he was.

Henry took his silence for doubt and added, "You're a natural leader, all of the platoon will follow you even more than they would me, they always have done; it's an obvious choice, Danny. When we get closer up to the front I will be able to tell you more, but at the moment just accept the rank. We cannot afford anybody around camp knowing our business; Fritz seems to have too much knowledge about troop movements as it is. It's going to be our job to turn the tables a little!"

Daniel still looked a little stunned, when Henry said, "Well that's sorted, then, get these stitched on the arm of your jacket!" and handed over a pair of stripes.

For the final week of training the platoon were separated from the rest of the battalion and started night training, operating in their small groups, independent to the rest. Working on perfecting stealth and hand to hand combat where the emphasis was to get around trenches and open ground without discovery, learning how to overcome a foe without the commotion caused by shooting him. Daniel was in his element just as Henry had expected, with years of staking deer, which were naturally wary prey animals, actually stalking men was relatively simple to him.

It was a fine Friday morning at the end of March 1915. Kit inspection had just finished and just before they fell out Lieutenant-Colonel Pickering, the Battalion Commanding Officer (CO) had made a rather uncommon appearance. There was an immediate buzz of expectation in the air.

"Gentlemen, at 8:00am on Monday morning we will parade here in full field dress, prepared to move out for the front, the exact deployment will not be disclosed until we are underway and nearer our objective. Until then gentlemen you have furlough until midnight on Sunday." With that he was gone.

Major Manners, the Battalion Second-in-Command added, "You have all had a pretty intensive few weeks of training here at Etaples. Go out and enjoy the next couple of days rest, but do not get yourself in to any trouble and undo the good name you have earned for the battalion." Again the officer turned without further word and was gone.

It was down to the company and platoon officers to put the warnings into the sort of language that the lads would understand.

Captain Johnson spelt it out for them, "Lads, you've got money in your pockets and have been cooped up for a long time without letting off any steam. Go out and enjoy yourselves, keep you noses clean even if you can't keep other bits of you clean," titters rose throughout the lads, "if you can't be good, be careful and I expect all of you to be here by midnight on Sunday, dismiss!"

Furlough Prior to Deployment
Le Touquet

As the platoon made their way to the mess tent for breakfast, Henry got his section together and arranged to get them transport into Boulogne. He had arranged lodgings for the whole section, apart from himself and Daniel. Even in such a short amount of time, Ray had shown Henry that Daniel's assessment of him to be true. So, leaving Ray in charge of the group and with the arrangements being to catch up with them for a meal on Sunday evening prior to their return to Etaples, Henry and Daniel set of for Le Touquet, a coastal resort just over the Calais Road where Henry was to meet up with his fiancée, Lady Catherine Bowles. It seemed a little strange to Daniel that he should be asked to accompany his friend and, to be quite honest, he felt a bit uneasy being a gooseberry.

Henry as usual could read Daniel's feelings, so put his mind at rest by explaining, "Danny, relax, Catherine went to finishing school over here and has a very dear friend who she met and stayed in touch with. Marie is from a fine French family who has had some dreadful ill fortune over this war. Both her brothers and father have been killed fighting Fritz, which has driven her mother into such decline that she has taken to her bed. She is the only member of this generation, her mother being her only other living relative left of the de Créquys, a family that can trace their lineage back to the 16th Century. She is in need of cheering up so Catherine has come over to support her and it was only logical that we should meet up and you can make up a foursome. Besides, tonight after our meal we have a lot to discuss. I need you to be aware of our true role and what exactly is going on."

With that, Henry dropped the subject and started to talk about football, in particular the situation at St James' Park, home to Newcastle United, the lads' favourite team.

"Stan Dixon and Tom Curry have joined the Engineers Corps; Curtis Booth and Alex Higgins the DLI; Tommy Goodwill, Northumberland Fusiliers; Bill Bradley, the York and Lancs, and George Wilson, Royal Navy. That was just the few I have heard about. Newcastle United will all but officially close down soon, the club is effectively being mothballed until the end of the war. Wouldn't it be great to go in shoulder to shoulder with the likes of them?" enthused Henry.

It was only a short walk to the Hotel Westminster in Le Touquet where, following placing their belongings in their rooms and after introductions, the four sat down to afternoon tea overlooking the English Channel. Although they were miles from the front and absolutely safe, the occasional percussion of distant artillery bombardment interrupted the peace. Looking out across the Channel it seemed that the whole of the Royal Navy was patrolling the waters. Daniel was trying not to stare but found it very difficult to take his eyes off the fine noble beauty that was Marie de Créquy. Her features were small and dainty which made her eyes all the more stunning. They looked like two blue pools of the clearest water; her complexion was like porcelain without blemish. He did not think he had ever seen a more perfect example of the female form; even his own mother could not have looked that beautiful at the same age?

"Danny! Snap out of it," laughed Henry, realising his friend's attention was elsewhere, "I was just saying to Marie that it was your mother who first taught both you and me to speak French and what a wonderful woman she is. When the girls come up to the castle to visit they must meet her, don't you think?"

Daniel was trying to stay composed, it must have been so obvious that he had been staring at Marie he was a little flustered but managed a weak reply, "Er yes, that they must. However, your grasp of the language must be far greater than mine now; I have only ever had my mother to practise it on".

"*Aimeriez-vous aller faire une promenade dans les jardins et laisser ces deux à rattraper*, Daniel," Marie enquired as she stood up keeping her request slow and clear to allow Daniel to clearly understand, if in fact he did speak French as well as Henry had made out.

"*Bien sûr, pourquoi n'ai-je pas pensé à cela, veuillez nous excuser*," replied Daniel nodding to his friends hoping he had picked up the phrase from Marie correctly.

Both Catherine and Henry acknowledged their friend's desire to walk in the gardens to allow them time to catch-up.

"Bravo Daniel," Marie complimented him and gave a little playful clap of her hands before offering an outstretched hand to guide him away from the others to let them have some time alone.

They spent the next hour or so strolling around the grounds of the Westminster Hotel with Marie leading the conversation questioning Daniel about his home town and the beauty of the Durham Dales. She had obviously heard this from Henry and he had managed to leave out the industrial side of the area, the way Marie painted the picture of the area, Daniel didn't quite recognise it! Both seemed very much at ease in each other's company and, far too quickly, Catherine and Henry appeared suggesting it would be a good idea if they all had a stroll along the beach before they returned to the hotel to prepare for their evening meal. Even though there was a bracing wind blowing, the weather was very pleasant for that time of the year with the sun shining. It was Daniel who noticed that Marie was feeling the coolness of the wind so offered her his uniform jacket and Henry followed suit with Catherine. There was a man selling kites on the beach and Henry bought two and soon the two couples were in deep competition to see whose kite could fly the highest. The time, as well as the kites, flew by and it wasn't until both kites collided with each other and tumbled to earth that they realised what time it was. In great spirits and arm in arm the four returned to the hotel laughing and joking with the familiarity of two couples who had known each other for years and not just hours. With a knowing glance at Daniel, Henry suggested that they should meet back in the bar for aperitifs at 8:00 p.m.

When the girls had left for their rooms, he turned to Daniel, "Right we should be ready in half that time, we'll both have to wear our uniforms unless you have a secret stash of clothing I don't know about? We can get the hotel to launder all our stuff overnight so we will be as smart as two carrots come morning. Back down here for 7:00 p.m. and I will put you in the picture about all this cloak and dagger!" he slapped Daniel on the back and laughed, "I knew you two would hit it off. Catherine has just said it is the first time since she got over here that she has seen Marie really let her hair down and lose that look of pain she has been carrying around with her for so long."

Daniel was pleased to see the Westminster was of the top quality that he expected his friend would only ever settle for. It was something that he had never experienced and could not think he would again so vowed to make the most of it. His room had a large soft double bed in it with en-suite facilities and all the grooming equipment he required. It even had a bath with hot running water! He couldn't help himself, although he was working to a tight deadline. He would have a bath and, whilst in there, he would have his shave. What a day, surely this was as close to heaven as you could get! How ironic thought Daniel, with hell just awaiting a few miles to the north.

Again he was snapped out of his daydream by a knock on the door. Still with his towel around his waist, he opened the door slightly to see his friend standing there with a bottle of red wine and two glasses in his hand.

"I should have known an ugly mug like that would take some time to get presentable," as he pushed past Daniel, "actually this is probably a better place for us to talk rather than down in the bar".

"That is the umpteenth time you have made a comment about security and cloak and dagger. What's it all about?"

Henry poured the wine into the two glasses and handed one to Daniel whilst sitting down on the chaise-longue by the window and started to explain the situation that had brought the Auckland Pals together in war.

Following Henry finishing university, he had looked to a career in the military until he was needed back on the estate. With war looming and with his father's connections, he had been drawn into the Intelligence Corps, part of the Intelligence Department at the War Office. His training had started prior to the outbreak of war and that is why he had been going missing and letting the team down so many times. When they had split up at the recruiting office in Bishop Auckland, he had gone to the Intelligence Corp base for further intensive training.

From the outset of the war, the Germans had known all the movements, strengths and weaknesses of the allies and exploited this knowledge to make the rapid progress they had in the early stages. Hopefully, other members of the

Corp had dealt with those leaks but from escaped allied prisoners it was clear that the Germans had been aggressively taking prisoners from the allied trenches and vigorously questioning them to gain all the information they could. Henry had been selected as part of a cadre of officers who should put together teams who could infiltrate the German frontline and repay the compliment, with interest. When Henry realised that the lads were all joining up together it was obvious to him that there could not be a better team to have around him. He had meant what he had said back in Etaples, *if he was to face old Fritz down the barrel of his revolver he wanted his mates watching his back.*

So the plan was, when they went into the frontline, their mission would be to patrol no-man's land and see if they could kidnap a few of the Hun guards and pick up any other useful intelligence. This needed to be done prior to the next stunt that was to be at a place where the two enemies had faced each other for some time. Ypres. To the allies it was known as the Ypres Salient due to the fact the frontline just north of the town jutted out into German-held territory so the troops had the enemy on three sides. This was obviously not an ideal position to defend so the Commander-in-Chief of the British Army, Field Marshal Sir John French had sought to straighten the line and push the Hun back.

"So we are to operate on our own in front of our own frontlines?" confirmed Daniel.

"Yes, that's about the size of it Danny?" It was Henry's turn to be a little hesitant, not knowing how his friend would take to him placing all the Auckland Pals in this situation without giving them any say in the matter.

"Sounds brilliant, should be good fun, certainly better than standing around knee deep in water-filled trenches waiting for Fritz to drop a shell on you. That's what it sounds like happens most of the time if the word at Etaples is true. If I can get up within a few yards of a herd of deer then I should be able to get close enough to the old Hun to pick his damned pockets!"

Suddenly the last trace of doubt that Henry had had dispersed with his friend's reaction.

"You're right there old pal," raising his glass towards Daniel he toasted, "The Auckland Pals!"

"To us," countered Daniel, with one swig from the glass, the two drained the wine and Henry recharged them, "I could get quite fond of the old vin rouge," laughed Daniel.

"If I was you I would concentrate on putting your clothes on or Marie will get a little more than she bargained for when she sits down to her main course!"

"Do you think so? I was considering a more relaxed approach to my attire this evening," the banter between the friends was as free and easy as it ever had been, surely with a team built on such friendships nothing could stop them?

In the short period of time that the hotel staff had been given they had made their uniforms presentable for the evening but they assured both lads that they would be in first class order come morning. They cut a rather dashing picture as they entered the bar to await the arrival of the girls. Everything was a lot less formal over in France, it was something that Henry did like about the country; Daniel didn't know any better but took his friend's word on the matter. Obviously the girls had not travelled as light as the lads so, when they entered, they turned the heads of the few customers that were in, including Henry and Daniel.

Getting up and raising his glass in toasting the ladies he brought his glass in front of his mouth and whispered to Daniel, "Do try to pick your bottom jaw up off the ground," and was moving across the room to take the arm of Catherine, with Daniel following suit towards Marie.

He again was amazed by her beauty but in the black sequinned evening dress with the shoulder-less, low cut top he was also staggered by her incredible figure.

"*Marie, tu es absolument magnifique ce soir,*" Daniel whispered to Marie as he extended his arm and bowed his head.

"*Vous êtes monsieur plus galant,*" Marie ever so slightly blushed at Daniel's compliment and, taking his arm, they followed Henry and Catherine into the dining room.

The meal seemed to be over in a flash; at least it did to Daniel. Just when he thought it was getting close to the end of the evening Henry saved the day by suggesting they all took a stroll in the garden to get some fresh air. It might have been Daniel's imagination or just wishful thinking on his part but it did appear that Marie was very keen to keep the evening going and was very quick to agree to Henry's suggestion. So arm in arm the couples took to the garden with again the ladies using the gentlemen's uniform jackets to fend off the evening chill. Daniel and Marie led the way and, after a few minutes, Daniel realised that Henry and Catherine had taken a different route, so they were alone.

"I have really had a fabulous day Daniel, thank you. It seems such a long time since I have had reason to be happy, not since before ..." her voice trailed off slightly and she did not finish her sentence, but just pulled Daniel closer and they continued to walk in silence with her head slightly tilted resting on his upper arm. "You know Daniel the only men that I have known and cared for have gone from my life. Catherine does not know what you and Henry are to be doing when you go into the line but knows it is something special and therefore probably dangerous. I have only just met you but feel as if I have known you a lifetime, please be careful out there. Look after Henry, as I know Catherine is asking him to look after you."

By now they had stopped walking and were stood looking into each other's eyes holding both hands. Daniel could see that her eyes were slightly moist and the first signs of tears were forming.

"We always have done and we always will do. Besides there's another dozen of us to look after each other's backs, you'll have to meet the rest of the team sometime. Once you see the full team you will realise that we are in good hands," smiled Daniel, trying to lighten the mood.

It seemed to work as the smile that had been on Marie's face all evening had returned. She moved towards him lifted on to her tiptoes and kissed him lightly on his cheek, "Thank you".

At that moment there was a cough from over Marie's shoulder and Henry and Catherine came into view.

"Well I am completely beat and we have a full day tomorrow, a spot of horse riding on the beach if the weather holds and a visit into the town for lunch followed by the matinee show at the Excelsior! What do you think Danny? Are you up for that?"

"Sounds like everything is planned to a tee and I will need all the rest I can get to keep up with the ladies."

With that, he offered Marie his arm once again and the couples returned to the hotel where the gentlemen saw the ladies to the suite that they were sharing then they retired themselves.

Although Daniel's head was spinning he was asleep as his head hit the pillow. He awoke at 6.00 a.m. feeling refreshed and still in a spin from the events of the previous night. As he recounted those events in his head, he still could not quite take on board just how well he and Marie had hit it off and the fact that she had kissed him on his cheek!

Breakfast had been planned until 8.00 a.m. so, after his morning ablutions, Daniel had a short walk into the town.

The Westminster had been good to their word his uniform was cleaned and pressed, so Daniel was careful not to get himself too dishevelled prior to breakfast where he prayed the events of the night before would be further built upon. However, he did half expect that Marie would have realised that in her moment of sadness over the thoughts of her father and brothers that she had been overly forward with the kiss and she would therefore be a little stand offish this morning. Nevertheless, that would not hold him back from trying to win her heart. Daniel strolled towards the main entrance of the Westminster when Henry came out towards him beaming from ear to ear,

"Danny, I've been looking for you for ages, where have you been? Never mind, just come with me, have I got something to tell you!"

"Henry, steady down you are talking faster than I can listen! What's all the excitement about?"

"Well it appears that the girls did not go straight off to sleep when we left them last night. Far from it, in fact they did quite a bit of talking and the main topic of conversation from Marie was you! There's really no accounting for taste is there? You have a lady of the highest French social standing who, in a matter of hours, has fallen for a County Durham lad!"

This was music to Daniel's ears, but there was that one thing that had been mentioned by Henry and it was the only negative thought he had had during his walk around the town. The social divide!

Daniel's face took a serious turn as he looked at his friend with a questioning expression, "Henry ... I think you've hit the nail on the head, how on earth is a lad from West Auckland actually going to be allowed to escort such a stunning member of the French upper class?"

Daniel's question was delivered in a near state of desperation to his good friend.

Momentarily there was a look of non-comprehension on Henry's face, almost as though he had not thought of it. Slowly he smiled and taking his friend by the arm he guided him into the front garden of the hotel by the water fountain.

"My god you had me worried there for a minute! With that expression I actually thought that you did not reciprocate her feelings."

"Reciprocate! I would walk over red hot embers from my dad's furnace if I thought it would win her over!"

"Well then that's all right then and as for the matter that seems to be of such an issue to you. Remember, the only people who could object to the two of you being an item are the other senior members of her household and following the disastrous events of Mons and Aisne for the French Army, Marie is the head of her family and she can make all her own decisions. Besides this is France, they are a lot more laid back about this sort of thing than they are in England!"

There was a moment's silence whilst Henry allowed Daniel time to digest his explanation, then threw his arm around Daniel's shoulder turning him around at the same time and marched him off for breakfast adding, "Now that that is settled can we join the girls for breakfast? I'm starving, oh by the way try and look composed and ignorant of this conversation, be natural and keep your bottom jaw off the floor," coached Henry.

The two friends sat down opposite the ladies for breakfast and it seemed, although nothing was said, that everybody was aware that there had been a major change to the relationships around the table. Catherine and Henry had manufactured this beautifully and both Marie and Daniel were very willing participants in the plan. After breakfast, the four had another walk into the gardens and the ease and spontaneity with which Marie took Daniel's arm put him totally at ease. Not twenty-four hours since meeting each other there seemed to be an air of ease between the two that should in most cases only come after months, even years, of being in each other's company. As the four walked there was the start of constant rat-a-tat-tat from the Bull Ring training area at Etaples just across the main Calais road. It was not going to allow the four to have a pleasant day with this constant reminder of what the two lads would be facing in a couple of days.

"Would you be able to arrange transport to Abbeville, so we can rid ourselves of that din, Henry?" enquired Marie, "it would be far more peaceful if we spent the remainder of the weekend at Château de Noyelles and it would be nice for the old house to hear some laughing and joy once more."

"What an excellent idea Marie," agreed Catherine, "can you get that sorted at short notice darling?" she added looking at Henry, with a knowing smile that Henry recognised as the look that Catherine usually had on her face when trying to look innocent but not being able to hide the smugness of outflanking her fiancée.

"Not a problem, the Westminster will be able to arrange a road taxi and we will keep our rooms for Sunday night when we meet up with the lads. Would you like to come with me whist I make the arrangements Daniel?"

The Château de Noyelles looked on to Somme Bay with its landscapes reflecting the ebb and flow of the tides with large breakers like hills and cliffs on the side of the valley and the rolling swell of the valley bottom that seemed to be a patchwork quilt of arable fields. As the taxi rounded the bend at the top of a steep hill which had the vehicle slowing down to a snail's pace, Daniel saw before him a countryside not dissimilar to his native County Durham, well at least the rural side of it! The D940 road which ran from Calais down the coast of the Cote D'Opale to Mers-les-Baines gave an astonishing view of the Chateau that Marie knew has home. Daniel saw the pride in which she looked at her home, but also a certain sadness lay behind her pride. She realised he was looking at her and she steeled herself against her sadness and gave him a smile,

"*Bienvenue a mon domicile*, Daniel," she whispered and reached out for his hand.

"*Vous avez une belle maison*, Marie," replied Daniel gently taking her hand and giving it a gentle squeeze.

Unsurprisingly, Henry had come up trumps with the road taxi. The Renault XB had been given two rows of seats behind the driver so both couples had been allowed a little privacy and that made it all the more intimate for Daniel. It was only 50km from Le Touquet to Abbeville according to the driver; however with the roads in poor repair due to most of the maintenance being saved for the roads leading from the coast to the frontlines, little work had taken place on this road for some time. For this reason and a top speed of 40mph, at best the journey had taken a couple of hours, not that Daniel had minded being sat next to Marie for that time. They had talked about something and nothing, about the beauty of the French coast and compared it to the wild features of the upper Pennines and it was agreed that when the war was over Marie would see for herself what he described to her.

The chateau was a grand house. Not in the same league as Teesdale Castle, the seat of the Neville family, but way beyond anything Daniel envisaged he would ever live in. Marie explained that the estate covered 300 hectares of mixed agriculture and vineyards and had several tenant farms on land to the north of the chateau, the land boundary being the Foret Domaniale de Crecy.

She squeezed his hand and with that little tremble of sadness in her voice, she said, "I have to try to run the family affairs now, even the farms on the land have lost their menfolk to this war".

"The chateau was built at the beginning of the 17th century as a hunting lodge. Louis XV and his court met here in the 1720s on hunting trips," explained Marie, "my family were granted it by the king for services rendered. My brother would have been the seventh generation to take the seat and now it's down to me."

"Is your mother going to be a little put out by our unannounced arrival?" it was a question Daniel had been wrestling with since they had set off.

"Mama is not at home, she resides in a sanatorium in Abbeville where she can have staff who can give her the care she needs, and since our bereavements she has been very disturbed. Until recently, I was looking after her and running the estate. It was very trying and I'm afraid I was not doing a good job of either, however since she went there I have visited most days and try to give her a little comfort."

"You have such a huge cross to bear but carry it so well, who would think behind all that beauty there is the most capable of ladies. You are a most extraordinary woman, Marie de Créquy," complimented Daniel bowing his head in salute.

With that heartfelt compliment, Marie's smile returned just as the taxi pulled up outside the chateau. The driver helped with the luggage and took his orders from Henry, "Return here at 2.00 p.m. tomorrow, we need to be back at the Westminster for 6.00 p.m., no later".

The main buildings were incongruously ornamented by the elaborate towers, spires and steeply-pitched roofs typical of 16th/17th century châteaux, the late Gothic and Italian Renaissance influenced architecture was clear to see.

The main rear garden was flanked on both sides by outbuildings with small doors allowing access but had their larger access through double doors facing out on to the grounds. The outbuildings formed an enclosed garden; this section of the property was given over to the *chambres de verdure*, a series of gardens that were divided by boxwood hedges. At the bottom of this area a teak bench stood next to climbing roses over trestles; gravel paths wound around the many apple and pear trees set out symmetrically like a battalion on parade.

Daniel should have been taken aback at the grandeur, but having spent such a large part of his formative years playing with his lifelong friend up at the castle he was impressed but did not feel unduly out of place. Soon, an elderly lady in formal but not a uniform style dress appeared. She beamed at Marie holding outstretched her two arms and walked towards her. The two embraced to show this was not the standard maid/mistress relationship.

"This is Madame Albert, Margot to all in this house, she is like a second mother to me and she and her family live in La Baie Ferme which is the farm that sat on the hill, we passed it when we entered the chateau entrance gates, Margot, *vous savez*, Catherine."

Catherine gave Margot a hug of someone who obviously knew her well, "*C'est* Henry, *fiance de* Catherine *et* Daniel, *un ami tres special.*"

Daniel had noticed that Henry had remained rather formal and had just bowed his head in recognition of the introduction; he copied but added, "*Mon plaisir,* Madame Albert,"

"*Non, non,*" corrected Madame Albert, "Margot *s'il vous plait,*" with that she looked directly at Daniel with the cheekiest of smiles and repeated Marie's introduction with exaggerated emphasis on special, "*un ami special,*" with that she turned and left the entrance hall ordering all to go into the salon and she would bring wine and would have their bags taken to their rooms. Not that Daniel and Henry had much in the way of baggage.

As they entered the salon, Daniel couldn't help but think of the way he had been introduced, a special friend! Once again he was taken aback by the speed in which their relationship had moved, and it all seemed perfectly natural!

Margot entered carrying a decanter with four wine glasses, charged them and offered them around. On leaving the room, she invited the two couples to join her family for the evening meal at the farm, she explained that due to not expecting Marie back so soon she had not started preparing anything but her daughter would have started their meal and it would only be a simple case of adding a few places at the table. Marie thanked her and kissed her on the cheek accepting the invitation on behalf of all.

They finished their wine and Daniel noticed Margot in the entrance hall starting to lift their bags, realising that there was nobody else to do the heavy lifting he went out and insisted on doing the carrying. Henry was close behind and the two carried the bags upstairs under the direction of Margot. They placed the girls' bags in their respective rooms and were shown their rooms by Margot, who also showed them wardrobes that were full of male civilian clothes which Daniel presumed belonged to Marie's brothers. Apparently it had been Marie's idea to suggest to the lads they might want to leave their uniforms to one side for a little time.

By mid-afternoon they were all changed and had returned to the original plan for the day which was to have a ride. Unfortunately, there were only the field horses available due to the army having taken all but what had to remain on the grounds so it could continue to function as a viable farm. Even that was due to the army needing food to feed its hordes, the very lifeblood of France as well as the other countries involved in the war was being sucked dry by the conflict. It didn't seem that anything or anybody had not been touched by loss and tragedy, even Margot who had an invalid husband following a farming accident some years previous was mourning the loss of her son-in-law. Annette who was two years older than Marie had lost her husband just months after their marriage in the same battle as Marie's older brother. The Battle of Aisne was one of the early battles of World War I and Germany just swept any resistance to one side. Annette's husband had been shoulder to shoulder with Marie's brother fighting a rear guard action protecting the flank of the retreating French Army when both were hit by shrapnel from the same shell. They lay where they fell but witnesses had confirmed both had taken the full brunt of the exploding shell. So at the tender age of twenty-one Annette was a widow, although you would not guess this, she was young and vibrant and, like Marie, didn't wear mourning black for her loss. It was Annette who explained that when you have a farm to run you have no time to mourn.

The four rode into Noyelles-sur-Mer and had bowls of onion soup with freshly baked bread in a little brasserie before heading back to the chateau to prepare for their visit to La Baie Ferme. Although he looked forward to anytime he could spend with Marie, he was not quite so sure about a meal with a French family who would probably talk too fluently and with the same Normandy accent that made Margot slightly difficult to follow. During the ride he talked freely of his horse riding experiences, explaining to Marie he was much more used to riding heavy horses up on the Dales where he would ride and guide the pack horses during stalking trips. When he explained his anxieties about the coming meal, Marie put his mind at rest complimenting his French and reassuring him that Annette spoke very good English and that she would be close at hand if he got into difficulties with Margot or her husband.

Daniel had nothing to worry about. Following their return to the chateau, they got ready for the evening with yet again Henry being ready first and appearing in Daniel's room with two glasses and a bottle of vin rouge in hand.

"By, you take some getting ready, anybody would think you are out to impress! Mind, with your limited good looks you need all the help you can get!" teased Henry.

"I really hope you don't think you are funny, because have I got news for you. You aren't!!" replied Daniel draining his glass and offering up his empty glass to Henry as though he was the hired help, "I say boy, just fill that glass, there's a good chap".

"Cheeky bastard!" was the immediate, although not the most imaginative, riposte.

Henry then got serious and, out of the blue, asked Daniel what he would need to create some sort of camouflage so they would blend into the environment and would not stand out so much when they started doing the type of stunts they had talked about.

"Nothing much more than we wear when stalking and it's easy enough to make gillie suits out of old sacking. We will need one large flour sack and two or three sandbag sacks per person," replied Daniel after a bit of thought. "I have been giving these stunts into no-man's land some thought and I do have a couple of suggestions if you are interested."

"I was hoping you would have, you always were the sneaky type, that's why I needed you with me in the section! What are you thinking about?" asked Henry.

"Well, if we are to go out on a limb we will be isolated and I will always remember what Uncle John said to me about the weight of firepower keeping their heads down when he handed me his Mauser. If we take a route into our objectives and leave our machine guns at a point where if we could get into trouble they can give support, we might keep sufficient heads down long enough for our withdrawal. Especially if those machine guns were the new Lewis guns that Ray and Davy got a go at last week. They actually could operate them on their own. I know they are only just being used by the army but think of the support we would have, Ray said they kicked out 500-600 rounds per minute and the pan magazine carries 97 rounds. He can carry several magazines himself and we could all carry extra with us and leave them with the two guns as we go forward," enthused Daniel.

"Well you have been thinking about this haven't you?"

"Oh, there's more to come."

"We can talk about this further tomorrow evening when we get back to camp. We don't want to keep the ladies waiting do we?"

When everybody was ready they walked the short distance to La Baie Ferme. They all wore heavy, warm and comfy clothing that also left Daniel feeling very much more at ease. Not long after arriving and having had another couple of glasses of rather good local vin rouge, Tomas, Margot's husband who seemed to be setting the pace of the drinking became very serious with an official toast welcoming his guests.

"*Pour les héros de l'Angleterre, qui se battent pour notre liberte,*" he boomed out, raising his glass high.

Marie must have realised that with the accent and the red wine there might be little or no understanding of Tomas's felicitations so she translated, "To the heroes from England, who fight for our liberty."

For the rest of the evening, the food and wine flowed freely with the Calvados being offered by Tomas, and the cigars by Henry at the end.

As they were about to leave for the stroll back to the chateau, Tomas managed to single Daniel out to talk to him on his own. For all they had drunk, he was very clear and slow to enable Daniel to understand what he was saying, "*Vous avez apporté le bonheur retour à la petite* Marie, *regardez vous-même et aftre retour en toute sécurité,"* he fully understood the sentiment, "You have brought happiness back to little Marie, look after yourself and return safe," with a lump in his throat he promised that this was just au revoir and indeed he would return.

It was a pleasant walk back to the chateau, although the breeze was cool. Both couples, realising that come morning they would be soon facing their enforced parting with a very uncertain future, took care to allow each other space so as not to compromise this limited time for intimacy. As they came to the chateau, Marie steered Daniel along the west side into the rear garden and they walked down towards the orchard where the teak bench waited. They sat in silence for some time then, almost simultaneously, they turned their heads to look into each other's eyes.

"I don't want this moment ever to end," Marie whispered.

Daniel put his arm around her shoulder and drew her gently into him, she lifted her head up towards him and he moved his down towards her and very slowly and deliberately they kissed. They kissed as though the world was about to end if they stopped. Daniel didn't want it to end and would have been happy to just stop there for the rest of the evening, however after a few minutes, Marie gave a little shiver and Daniel realised it was time to go inside as the cold had started to bite. In silence, he stood and led her round the front of the house to the main entrance. They entered and immediately realised that Henry and Catherine had disappeared, so locking the front door, they too went upstairs. Daniel walked Marie to her bedroom where he kissed her goodnight and turned to walk away, Marie held on to his hand and pulled him back round to face her, she was a picture of beauty and with her back to the door she reached behind her with her free hand and opened it leading Daniel inside.

Breakfast was a late affair, a very late affair. Daniel had woke early full of the joys of spring and had intended to go for a walk into the gardens to try to comprehend what had happened. But Marie had other ideas and the walk was soon forgotten for a more pleasurable exertion. There were two slightly embarrassed couples who sat down in the parlour to sort themselves out with breakfast. It was clear that Henry had not bothered with his bedroom the previous evening also and, as Marie poured coffee out into everybody's cups, she looked at Catherine. Catherine looked back and smiled and then started to laugh, and then all four were laughing. After all what had they to be feeling guilty about? Four people, two couples, best of friends and in love.

Margot came up to the house around lunchtime with some cold meats and cheese as well as more freshly made bread. She kissed both the lads and wished them a safe journey and made them promise to look out for each other. This was something that, if she had known them better, she would have realised was not necessary. Even so, Daniel and Henry promised and thanked her for a wonderful evening and she took her leave. There was now that sort of awkward period of waiting for something unpleasant to happen and you know it is going to happen, so really it would be better if it happened sooner rather than later. Unfortunately, the taxi driver had been given clear instructions and to his credit was good to his promise. This allowed a final walk hand in hand for both couples where they tried to make light conversation not wanting to spoil the magic of the weekend by facing up to the inevitable parting. They talked about the future and what they could do when the war was over and surely it could not go on for too much longer, could it? Not knowing what the future held for either of them made it easy to suggest plans without the problem of thinking too deeply about the practicalities. One thing was for sure they would write to each other as often as possible and whenever Daniel got any time away from the frontline, Marie would be nearby so they could see each other and not just correspond.

Just before 2.00 p.m. the taxi arrived and tearful farewells made. Both couples openly showing their affections in front of each other, for the umpteenth time the girls made the lads promise to look after each other and bring each other back safely. With promises made and quiet vows of love given, the taxi headed back to the Westminster in Le Touquet. Tomas, Margot and Annette waved from the farm as the taxi drove past. So ended Daniel's whirlwind introduction to the woman he had fallen head over heels in love with in just a weekend.

The lads were sat outside of the Westminster when Henry and Daniel arrived.

Specialist Training

"Ray, we haven't lost anybody have we?" questioned Daniel.

"Why no," replied Ray in mock surprise that he should think such a thing could happen, "Although Charlie seems to have attracted a few little bits of wildlife from his romance in Boulogne."

The rest of the lads started to laugh and as Henry and Daniel looked at him, Charlie just shrugged his shoulders and said, "I was in love,"

"Aye, every bloody night, with a different tart each time!" Art could not contain his shame on Charlie's behalf.

Again the group burst into raptures of laughter and followed Henry up the street to the nearest bar where he bought the beers. Due to the excesses of the weekend and the fact they all knew they had a hard march ahead of them the following day nobody really wanted to have a session on the drink. It was Ray who said on behalf of the lads that they intended getting back to Etaples for about 10.00 p.m. so they got a decent night's sleep and could rise early to have plenty of time to square their kit away ready for inspection at 8.00 p.m. and be ready in good time for the "off" soon after. Henry gave an acknowledging nod to Daniel as if to give final approval and agreement to Daniel's assessment of Ray.

"We have one thing extra to do before we leave Etaples lads," announced Henry, "before we leave I have arranged for the section to have a photograph taken outside the old Tipperary Club, I will get it sent back to the castle and make sure that everybody's families get a copy as well as one for the wall of the 'Wests' clubhouse wall. When we get back tonight I suggest you write home to your families to let them know how things are going. I don't suppose any of you have done for some time?" he looked around the group with an accusing look. "Just as I thought, like me you have been too wrapped up enjoying yourselves, but tomorrow it gets very serious, so best you put pen to paper tonight."

As he looked around the room he saw some sombre heads nodding in agreement.

On the walk back to Etaples, Ray came alongside Daniel, "You've got a twinkle in your eye since you got back, anything you want to share, Danny?"

"You wouldn't believe what happened," admitted Daniel and gave Ray a very brief outline of how he had fallen hopelessly head over heels in love.

When he had finished, Ray joked, "Slightly higher league than Betty Hibbert. Anyway, good for you, I think having something other than king and country to fight for is going to be a bonus in the months to come."

Daniel immediately looked at him, put his arm over his shoulder, "We all have far more than that, we have each other mate! And don't forget it!"

On their arrival at Etaples, Daniel took Henry's counsel and wrote to his parents telling them about the weekend, obviously leaving out the more intimate details, but leaving them in no uncertainty that this lady was very special to him. He then spent far longer composing a letter to Marie telling her that it would be a few months until he got any time off but if she was in agreement that they should meet up and share that time together. He was full of excitement and at the same time dread, that when the letter finally got to her, her feelings may have changed for some reason. But how could they? Everything had been so spontaneous and natural. However, he still had that little nagging doubt in the back of his head about the class difference, regardless of what his friend had said.

Morning of 1 April 1914 saw them at the rear of the battalion with their platoon, their section on the rear of that. Inspection had gone without a hitch; they had breakfasted and had the promised photograph. Many people had commented on it being all fool's day and that possibly the war was actually over and they were marching back to Boulogne to ship out to Blighty. Unfortunately, the distant rumble of heavy artillery spoilt that theory. The first day marching saw them cover 25 miles due to the roads being in reasonably good condition but the next two days saw these distances get less and less as the amount of military traffic increased whilst the road conditions deteriorated. On the fourth day, without warning, the battalion carried on marching to the east of the small town of Poperinge while the section headed to the west and set up in a billet at an old farm on the outskirts of town. One large barn was just about intact and this acted as living/sleeping quarters and the one remaining barn was the admin block. The farmhouse itself had been destroyed during the first battle of Ypres and was therefore totally unusable. Here the section found their supplies had been dropped off by the quartermaster who stood guard to officially hand over the consignment; a pile of sacking in various sizes, two brand new Lewis machine guns with boxes of magazines and enough food, tea and rum to last a small army a month, let alone a week of training. Davy and Ray thought it was Christmas but nobody quite understood what the sacking was for and why they had left the rest of the battalion. Henry explained that once they had got their food sorted and everybody was billeted he would put them all in the picture and that they would be staying here for the next few days getting some final training and preparation.

There was a silence in the barn as the role the pals had been given was explained. It was apparent to all that when they went into battle they would be very much on their own. Once again, it was Ray who broke the silence and the tension.

"Well, at least when we go on a stunt the whole bloody German Army aren't going to be waiting, having been warned by our artillery bombardment! So it's down to us to keep as quiet as possible and, with Danny being a sneaky bugger, we have a good teacher," there was laughter from the lads and also a realisation that what Ray said was actually true. It was a dangerous game they would be playing, but success and failure did very much come down to them, that and, like everybody on the battlefield, a lot of luck.

Over the next few days, Daniel and Henry worked the team constantly, everybody had made a camouflage suit out of the bigger sacks by cutting a head hole out of the centre bottom and cutting and unpicking the sides to create a smock to which they attached twigs and covered it in mud and charcoal from their cooking fires. The smaller sandbag sacks were used to the same effect to cover their helmets, with strips of the hessian bound around the rifles and over other equipment to break up the shape of the normal Tommy.

"Anything that might chink or clunk needs to be bound," explained Daniel, "Fritz is no fool so let's not give him any help in locating us."

Hand signals were practiced so the lads could communicate without a sound. All this was a straight copy of field craft used on the castle estate, so both Henry and Daniel were well versed in the practices. Following an evening of discussion, they also came up with training sessions of moving forward in stealth, leaving behind the machine gunners to cover their withdrawal back through a pre-set route, with the final emergency plan of "everyman for himself!" After each practice run if any of the lads had heard anybody's kit they told them so extra hessian was used to muffle the offending object. Within five days of solid practice there was to be a nocturnal practice assault on their Battalion HQ. The objective was to breach the external security and place a small milk churn with the word bomb painted in bold letters on it in front of the door of the farmhouse being used as HQ.

The evenings were drawing out so dusk was around 7.00 p.m. with total darkness not being until 10.00 p.m. It was a perfect night for the assault with a constant rain storm overhead which would dampen the alertness of the sentries. The plan was briefed; the group would approach the barbed wire perimeter fence across an open field. These were the rules of engagement set out by the "powers that be", some of which seemed to be in the shadows of the barn listening to the briefing. At the edge of the field, immediately before the road in front of the target, was a small ditch and the two machine gunners would set up there some fifty yards apart to give a wide arc of fire that would protect the flanks of the team. They were all to mark the centre of the gap between Ray and Davy and this would be their route of retreat. The team line-up was given just like a Saturday match day:

The cover was given by Ray and Davy on the Lewis's with extra support by Ronnie and Anders two of the bombers and Fouller the group signaller. Fouller's job was to put up the SOS signal for artillery cover if needed. Moving forward to cut the wires were Kenny, Jack and Tommo the rifle grenadiers who would stay at that point to give further cover. Charlie and Lazzer the two riflemen would cover Henry, Daniel and Art when they moved up to their objective. Art was to be used for his artistic talents, to observe the reproduced sketches later. The plan went like clockwork. Having planted the churn and retiring, they got back to the wire to see that, Kenny, Tommo and Jack had taken a rather confused and slightly frightened sentry prisoner. Apparently, the sentry had walked past the hole in the wire but had stopped for a pee. When it became obvious to the three there was a good chance of him seeing the cut wire they had sprung on him knocking him to the ground covering both the sentry and Kenny in pee! When the forward party had returned they found the guard with a hessian gag in his mouth and his heavy trench coat pulled up over his head so he could be led by the collar and not see anything but his footing, light permitting. It was something that neither Henry nor Daniel had thought about; how will you actually lead a prisoner away from enemy lines without giving the game away? Something to think about and discuss during the evening debrief. The team fell back past the machine guns and on to the final rendezvous point in the woods beyond the field. From there they formed up and marched back to their farmhouse with Kenny and Tommo covering off in front and Charlie and Lazzer guarding the rear. There was much merriment when they got back to the farm, not least towards Kenny who was still covered in his prisoner's urine which, with his body heat, had now started to smell!

"Kenny you smell like an old lady's piss pot!" laughed Charlie.

"I would not know what one smelled like, you probably do after the horrors you were with back in Boulogne!" was the best response Kenny could think of under the pressure of being laughed at by all the lads.

They had removed the trench coat from the sentry's head and reassured him everything was alright and they were not German spies as they entered their quarters only to be met by a host of top brass.

Henry stopped in his step and gave the order, "Squad, squad shun!" Every last man came to attention on the spot.

It was Lieutenant-Colonel Pickering, the Battalion Commanding Officer who stepped forward and directed Henry to get rid of their prisoner and line the men up prior to being introduced to the rest of the top brass. Clearly the most important of these was the Army Corps OC, General Haig. Haig had been appointed Aide-de-Camp to King George V in 1914 and there was a widely known poor relationship between him and Sir John French, Commander-in-Chief of the British Expeditionary Force. Some even tipped him, with his royal patronage, to take French's place! After moving down the line and being introduced to all the men he turned to Henry and spoke to him in very familiar terms calling him by his first name, this was picked up by all present. He talked to Henry but in a way that also delivered the same message to all in earshot, including the other top brass present. He spoke of the need to know what the enemy planned and where their strong and weak points were, also when they were amassing for attacks. He explained he wanted to fully exploit ariel reconnaissance, but that could only give partial intelligence and men on the ground were the ultimate source of reliable intelligence. Intelligence, he further explained, would be the single most contributing factor to a successful outcome to the war. That was the role of this group and it was his idea that had brought them to the point where they all found themselves; therefore, he would be keeping a close eye on the exploits of the group over the coming months and years (this was the first time anybody had heard anybody talk of the war going on for years!).

General Haig took one last look at the group and said, "Henry you have done a sterling job putting these fine young lads together and for that I am pleased to reward your endeavour by promoting you to captain with immediate effect; however you need yourself a sergeant. I will leave you to sort that out, you know your men better than me." He turned to his Aide-de-Camp and Lieutenant-Colonel Pickering stating, "I know that this is not usual protocol to have such a rank structure within a section, but we have never had a specialist section like this before! Working in such isolation and independence there needs to be clears lines on command and communication, so who would you suggest should be your sergeant, Henry?"

Without hesitation Henry turned to his friend and introduced Daniel, "I have the honour of introducing you to Corporal Daniel Byrne, sir. He would be my selection."

"Ha! The young man you have spoken so highly of?" Haig turned to take Daniel's hand and added, "Knew your uncle I believe, I will never forget the sight of him carrying young Henry's father over his shoulder whilst still firing that ugly German pistol at the damn Boers. If you are half the soldier he was, God help Fritz! So Henry you will now need a corporal, let's get all this sorted before I leave".

Henry looked at Daniel and then back to Haig, "My sergeant is best placed to make that decision if it's alright with you sir?

"Only right too," approved Haig and then both turned to Daniel.

Again without hesitation, Daniel turned to Ray and introduced him as his selection. Haig noticed that Henry's head was nodding with approval and at that Haig brought the audience to a close by wishing them the best of luck and confirming his high expectations from the entire section.

"Lieutenant-Colonel Pickering, make sure these promotions are implemented immediately."

With that, they were gone.

The group stood still at attention in silence for a few seconds until Ray let out a huge sigh followed by, "Bloody hell Henry, you could have warned us of that, at least we would have cleaned Kenny up, he still stinks of piss!"

With that, the whole group fell about laughing with congratulations being heaped on each other for a fully successful mission and their new captain, sergeant and corporal. Prior to hitting their billets, there was a celebratory rum issue and the lads toasted a successful night's work.

Having slept well and not even been disturbed by the ongoing "tit for tat" barrage that seemed to follow a nightly pattern they breakfasted on bread, bacon and tea then were straight back to working out how best to bring a prisoner under their control in the quietest way. If they knocked them unconscious there was the problem of transporting the now deadweight and the possibility of knocking them senseless so as to make them useless for intelligence. No, that must be the last option. They needed to overpower their victim in a way that gave them no chance to make a noise but left them capable of moving under their own steam. It was agreed that once under their control and back in no-man's land their charges would be more willing to co-operate because, if they made any noise, the German sentries and machine gunners would open up indiscriminately. So the basic technique they agreed upon was to hopefully bring the victim down from the back with one hand over their mouth and the other arm crooked around their neck. At this point, a second member of the team confronted the victim with the threat of the bayonet. By binding their hands and leaving plenty of rope they could lead the unfortunate individual like a dog. This was practised plenty of times by all and an acceptance that they would have to adapt their style to the situation and no one technique would be correct was highlighted when Art who was fairly small tried to practise on "Big Ray". He could not reach up and around Ray's neck let alone have the power to drag him down!

When they stopped for lunch break, Art went off and started one of his sketches. Daniel went over to see what he was working on. He knew how good he was from their childhood schooling but even so was amazed how quickly he could sketch the ruins of the farm in the foreground with some of the reserve light artillery in the mid ground, whilst also capturing the detailed contours and features in the distance. This gave Daniel an idea and he discussed it with Henry and Art. If Art could sketch the land out in front of no-man's land with the sort of detail he had just demonstrated, all the team could familiarise themselves with the terrain prior to setting foot out there and without risking their lives. They would therefore at least have a fair idea of landmarks and routes to and from their objectives. Admittedly, this would be a different prospect in darkness but at least they would have some knowledge and be able to find a good site for the Lewis's. Henry agreed and sent Fouller the signaller off to HQ with a request for a trench periscope so Art could see his landscape without putting his head above the parapet.

By evening the whole group were well and truly tired out. They had eaten and had double rations of rum. The new captain, sergeant and corporal insignia had duly arrived so Daniel and Ray were busy sewing. That was the moment Henry announced that,

"Tomorrow night we will be moving up into the front line with a view to making our first mission in towards the enemy lines that following night. We will do some more light training in the morning and then rest up whilst we wait for nightfall and our guide to take us up to where the rest of the battalion have been for the last ten days. The following day we will be given our orders, have time to get our bearings and to plan what we are tasked with. I would suggest that you all take the opportunity to write to your loved ones again, but remember no mention of what we are about or exactly where we are."

Davy turned to Ray and whispered, "Wish I flaming knew, haven't had a clue since we left Brancepeth, but that seems a lifetime ago!"

Again, Daniel wrote to both his parents and to Marie. He assured his parents of his well-being and explained about his rapid promotion and asked them to tell Uncle John about the kind words from General Haig. To Marie he wrote thanking her for the letter that had been delivered just that day, where she put his mind at rest about her feelings for him. He wrote about their future plans and how he was still in a spin since meeting her, that he a simple lad from West Auckland could be so blessed to be in love and to be loved by such a wonderful lady. He tried rewriting it several times due to it always sounding a little formal and not reflecting his passion for her, but he was not a skilled enough wordsmith to do his feelings justice.

The next day dragged while they all waited for the guide to arrive just before dusk. They all had too much time to think of what was to come; to a man, they just wanted to get on with it. The waiting was giving them too much time to reflect. Sergeant Daniel Byrne was about to go into the frontline and very shortly after that into battle for the first time and he already had received two promotions! Was he up to the task? How would he cope when under fire? Would he be able to lead the lads without letting them down? So many questions, only one way to find the answer. The opportunity finally arrived when the guide arrived nearly one hour late apologising and explaining he had got lost just after leaving the battalion in the frontline. Apparently, the front line was very disjointed at the point they were to be stationed and that he and another guide who had been sent to fetch a group of replacements for the Northumberland Fusiliers had been exposed to direct machine gun fire from Fritz's line until they had got to the first of the communication trenches nearly fifty yards to the rear. It was the hope of the guide that under the cover of darkness they would get back without the same amount of grief.

The Front Line, Ypres Salient
Hooge

They moved off with the guide at the front with Henry close behind and Daniel behind him, Ray brought up the rear with all the others between. The going at first was easy and quick with the artillery explosions getting nearer by the minute. It was a cacophony of percussion with a light display of different colours that, although very sobering, was so dramatic to be fascinating, Daniel knew enough about explosives to realise that the different colours depended on the charges in the different shells, each one suggesting different ways they would kill and maim. Daniel started to get that feeling of excitement that took him back to that day on the estate with his uncle when they spied on the soldiers experimenting with the flamethrower. Oh, the irony of it, just a few months later and here he was doing it for real in the name of king and country! He was almost laughing when he was suddenly stopped by running into the now stationary Henry.

"I say Danny old boy, I didn't know you cared," was his friend's reaction, trying to sound light-hearted in front of all the lads.

As the group gathered together Henry explained that the guide had said that from here until they got into the front line there was to be absolute silence so as not to alert Fritz. It was quite busy in the communication trenches and the sound of the artillery exploding was as loud as they had experienced and it got louder and louder with every step. As they got to the end of the communication trench and into the second line, or support trench, they saw it was in actual fact what had been the front line until recently. The new front line they realised was no more than a series of deepened shell holes that did not interconnect nor did they reach back to the point at which they found themselves. It was quite dark now and the message was passed down the line from their guide that when they started moving to keep low, quiet and not to lose contact with the man in front. The guide waited, judging the best time to move off. As he did, the whole group followed, they had no sooner got above ground than all hell broke loose. There was a sudden and unbelievable increase in the artillery barrage which was directed in their general area. It was so heavy that there did not seem to be any one explosion just a continual thunder roll and wave after wave of pressure waves hitting them side on. The noise was so great that it nearly drowned out the staccato rattle of the German Maxim machine guns that had simultaneously burst into life trying their best to end the lives of any Tommy who happened to be unfortunate enough to be in their sights. Just behind Daniel there was a sickening thud and the expulsion of air from lungs that, although he had never heard before, he somehow knew exactly what it was. They were only a few yards from the trench and, no matter how much he wanted to throw himself into it, he turned to confirm his worst nightmare. He saw Ray bent over on his knees and for a moment thought he had been hit but then realised that he was bent over Davy. Daniel went to help Ray telling the others to make for the cover of the trench. Ray had now got the two Lewis guns over one shoulder and was trying to drag Davy towards safety. Daniel reached down to get his other arm and braced himself for the load he was about to haul, he nearly lost his balance. Instead of all of Davy's weight, there was just the arm, he almost screamed with shock but composed himself and placed the arm across Davy's chest and grabbed his tunic shoulder around the collar. Together, Ray and Daniel got him into the trench where the others looked on in disbelief. In the slight moonlight they could see that not only was Davy's arm severed but his neck was sliced open on the same side from front to back. He was quite dead and they all knew it instantly. Daniel looked up to the heavens wanting to scream his frustration but as he looked across no-man's land he saw one lone figure walking towards their line. It was the silhouette of the biggest Tommy he had ever seen, he was totally alone and stumbled as if dazed or drunk, Daniel could not make out which. But whichever it was, he slowly made his way towards them oblivious to all the explosions and machine gun fire going on around him. Nothing touched him. In one hand, like any other man carried their rifle, was another Lewis gun. He stopped just above the parapet of the trench, making no effort to enter. Realising that this man was not drunk but very much in a daze caused by shock, Daniel jumped out of the trench into the same tide of death that this man ignored and pushed him forward into the trench, or so he thought. It was just like pushing against a pit prop, it did not move so much as a fraction. Quickly taking a different tact, he used the flat of his boot to kick into the rear of the giant's knee, with a sideways twist he keeled over, landed on top of the parapet and slid down into the trench with Daniel quickly following.

"Wholly Jesus," screamed Ray, above the ongoing barrage, "Danny, Davy's dead, and you nearly were you mad bastard, what did you think you were doing?"

Struggling to get his breath, he replied, "Couldn't let him cop a packet not just after Davy copping it, it was only a matter of time until something hit him."

"Christ knows how they missed him, not like he's a small target, look at the size of him he could have crushed any of us if he had landed on us."

It was true; Daniel took a closer look at the man he had just saved. He had righted himself into a sitting position with his knees drawn up to his chest, he completely blocked the trench.

Ray was big but this man was huge and all he kept repeating was, "They're all gone, where is everybody?"

Henry had been too far in front to do anything about helping get Davy's body into the trench. He had sorted the rest of the shocked section into safety and could only look on as Daniel had gone to the aid of the strange giant.

"Gutsy work Danny, but Ray is right, you could have got yourself killed up there and for what? We don't even know him; this section needs you in one piece!"

At that moment, a captain from the York brigade from their battalion came running over and presented himself to Henry. After introductions, he looked at the men on the floor and pointed at Davy's shattered torso, "One of yours?"

"Yes he didn't even make it into the front line."

"So who is he with?" pointing at the big man.

"I don't know he just staggered in from the front and Danny here saved him from ending up like poor old Davy."

The captain examined the giant's insignia. "That explains what kicked it off then; it must have been the replacements from the Northumberland's. One of the sentries said somebody had just walked between the two trenches heading toward the Hun's lines. Their guide must have got lost and led them straight into slaughter, poor bastards. We were told to expect seventy of them as well as your special unit. Lieutenant-Colonel Pickering would like to see you as soon as possible, he's just down the trench a little way, in what was a Hun concrete bunker about fifty yards away. You get your section straighten up and I will tell him you will be with him shortly, I'll explain what's happened. I shouldn't think he will mind you taking a little time in the circumstances, besides there's nothing much happening and we aren't expecting anything out of the ordinary tonight."

He tapped Henry on the shoulder in a friendly manner and disappeared the way he had come.

"Did you hear that?" asked Henry to Daniel, "he's just said that there's nothing much happening and we aren't expecting anything out of the ordinary tonight. Good God, what is extraordinary then?"

Daniel had managed to pull himself together and recover his composure, quietly saying, "You get yourself off to see Pickering and find out what's going on, I'll sort the boys out."

"Are you sure Danny? He looked into Daniel's eyes and saw steel," he nodded and added, "Okay, give the lads a good ration of rum that should help settle them. If we needed any reminder that we are in it up to our necks, then we've just had it; what a damn awful way to start," he turned and moved up the trench to report to Lieutenant-Colonel Pickering.

Things had settled down considerably and working parties had arrived and started to connect the separate shell holes into one continual trench as well as extending the communications trench from the old front line to the new one.

A sentry had come over to Daniel and reported, "Sergeant," Daniel looked round wondering who he was addressing until realising it was him! "There's a dugout just before you get to the bunker that Fritz used for the crews who manned the bunker. It will be a bit of a crush but your whole section should be able to get in it, Lieutenant-Colonel Pickering said it was to be kept available for you section. The lads are saying you are a special unit, is that true?"

Daniel looked around at his friends who all looked dumbstruck and, almost under his breath and quiet enough not to allow the sentry to hear, "Yes, special alright, so special we have one man killed before we have had the chance to take a shot at the damn Hun," then added as his proper reply to the sentry, "right thanks we'll make our way down there."

"Right boys, let us head off down the trench to the dugout," ordered Daniel, pointing the way so the lads knew where he wanted them to head.

"What about Davy?" asked Ronnie, almost sobbing.

The sentry inadvertently came to Daniel's aid, "Oh just get his pay book and leave his tags, when the working parties finish I will get them to take him down the line and out of the way, at least he's one of the lucky ones who will get a proper burial."

They got up and slowly moved along the trench, heads kept low not only in sorrow but as the sentry reminded them, so as not to give Fritz a target.

Daniel looked at the big man who was still in the same spot, "Ray give me a hand here, we can't just leave him."

Together, they got him into the dugout where Daniel gave all the section a double ration of rum. He came to the big man and offered it to him and he duly drained the quarter-full flagon.

Daniel needed to say something and he knew it, he really needed Henry to help but with him away getting their briefing it was down to him. It was something his father used to say about leading a football team. "Any fool can lead a team that are winning; the true measure of a leader is to get the team up when they have taken a knock." He knew this to be right, but what a knock.

At that point, the giant looked up and around and said in a soft Irish brogue, "I'll be thanking you, I think I have lost my whole section, I saw them fall one by one and nothing hit me, how could they miss me?" he slowly shook his head and added, "I think I owe some pay back, nothing hot headed, mind, it needs to be thought out, revenge is a dish best served cold."

It was just the sort of thing that Daniel needed to have said but couldn't think of it at that moment, so he added, "Our friend here is right lads, we all know what Davy would have wanted. If anybody took liberties on the field he would simply kick them up in the air regardless of who they were. Charlie do you remember last year's cup semi when we were playing Spartans. That nasty big centre-half took you out across both knees, within five minutes of the restart he was being carried off unconscious!"

"Aye, he flew high enough for folk to mistake him for the man in the moon!"

Art stepped in to the reminiscing, "Never mind about that, what about that elbow in the mouth of the full-back of Crooks, knocked his top two teeth out, clean as a whistle."

Suddenly there was an avalanche of memories of Davy's transgressions on the field of football.

The giant again spoke and as before he managed to bring about a certain amount of thought and calm in his soft but uncompromising voice, "sounds more like an assassin than a footballer!" Everybody in the dugout were laughing at the memories and the comment, whilst just being in the depths of depression they were lifted. The team were back almost as before and it had not escaped Daniel's notice who had made it happen. "So my large friend who might you be?"

"The name's Patrick O' Donnell but my friends all call me Geordie!"

There was a sudden silence whilst everybody took on board what he had just said. Unsurprisingly, it was Ray that broke the silence, "How the hell does an Irishman end up with a nickname like Geordie?"

Geordie warmed to the invite to start spinning a yarn.

"Well my parents come from the edge of the Slieveanorra Forest in the north east of Ireland, a little village called Loughguile, near Lissanoure Castle".

Ray rolled his eyes at Daniel has he realised he had started what could be a long story which covered Geordie's entire life, "Cut the shite," injected Ray, "just tell us the bit about your name".

Totally unfazed by the remark, Geordie continued, "My parents were poor and so devoted to their beautiful little baby boy they moved so my father could find employment in the great city of Newcastle upon Tyne working in the shipyards of Swan Hunter. I too started work there when I was old enough until I joined up with the Shields Pals as part of the Northumberland Fusiliers. We were reliefs coming up to the front line when our guide seemed to be lost. The next thing we knew we had walked right up Fritz's wire and holy hell broke loose. I think the name was a bit of a piss take of my mates when I joined Swan Hunter, but I always did like it."

Having allowed him to finish, Ray patted him on his shoulder and gave it a friendly shake, "Well, if you want to be called Geordie, I'm certainly not going to argue with you!" and with that he pulled Geordie towards him.

Together, side by side they looked like they could block the sun's rays off the earth, they cast such a shadow. "Can't think of you ever being a beautiful little anything!" added Ray with a smile.

The others started to talk to him and welcome him with a host of questions about how he managed to avoid the hail of lead, when had he arrived in France and what was he going to do now that he was the only remaining member of his section. His singular loss seemed to ease the hurt they were feeling even though Davy's death was still so recent and raw. There was something about this big man that just seemed right to Daniel, the section seemed immediately at ease with him.

At that moment, Henry walked into the dugout and was immensely relieved to hear good spirits. He straight away thought that Daniel had been the reason behind this and waved him over.

"Don't know how you did it but well done."

"I wish I could take the credit but it was our big stranger, who as well as being an Irish Geordie he unsurprisingly has the gift of the gab which seemed to be very poignant at a time when we needed it."

"Geordie!" shouted Daniel, waving him to come over to meet Henry.

Introductions complete, Daniel mentioned with a bit of suggestion thrown in to Henry that Geordie was a Lewis Gunner and seeing as they had just lost Davy, that it might not be a bad idea to allow Geordie to stop with the section in the short term.

"We are a section without a Lewis Gun and Geordie here is a Lewis Gun without a section, makes perfect sense to me?" Daniel questioned.

"Oh, I can throw a pretty mean Mills bomb as well," added Geordie.

"What do you mean by that?" the pair said in unison.

Well back in training camp everyone said that they had never seen one thrown as far as I managed to chuck it and, because of the distance, it never gave the buggers time to chuck it back!

A competent thrower could manage 49 feet with reasonable accuracy, so Daniel asked Geordie how far he throws them with accuracy.

"Comfortably 60 feet with accuracy but, if pushed, I can chuck it easily 75 feet," was the reply, but not in a boasting way. If anybody else had made that kind of a claim to Daniel he would have at first called him a liar and thought of him as a bragger. Again, for some reason unknown to Daniel he did not take this statement as bragging but he also believed Geordie.

Daniel turned to Henry, "A grenade can throw lethal fragments farther than 30 yards so he could have a killing range in excess of 50 yards, if true he would be a good addition to the team!"

"We will see in the morning if this claim is true or not, if you're up for a challenge Geordie? Following that we need to see if he is any good with that Lewis," looking at Daniel he added, "you know yourself the two Lewis's are watching our backs, we need someone who can use it as well as Davy did. Mind you, looking at the size of him he could have one in each arm; now that would be something!" He joked. "If it looks good after the test, if you want to Geordie, I will speak to Lieutenant-Colonel Pickering."

The rest of the section had been listening and they let out a cheer at this. They seemed to have taken Geordie's exploits in no-man's land as a lucky talisman arriving at just a time when they needed him to replace the desperately unlucky Davy. God rest his soul.

The section tried as best as they could to sleep, or at least rest, during the remainder of the night. This was not easy due to the incessant shelling and sporadic machine gun fire that Fritz kept up. It wasn't all down to Fritz; the allies did their bit to add to the mayhem, although due to shortages, it was not as widespread as the enemy's. Henry and Daniel sat down to write the hardest letter they had ever had to compose; a letter to Davy's mam and dad. It was Henry's job as section OC, but due to his closeness to all the team, Daniel also wanted to add his condolences in his own letter.

In the morning, as per trench orders, after breakfast they had inspection and were given their tasks for the day. Where most of the Tommies in the front line would be keeping low during the day, the Auckland Pals needed to get orientated to their surroundings. Art went to work viewing over the top with his newly delivered trench periscope and drawing the enemy positions, wire and any focal points, if any. He also drew the listening post positions that the allies had in no-man's land as these would be useful and could be used as jumping-off points and rallying points for their stunts. To call it a periscope was a little flattering, it was two mirrors that he had to fasten to his rifle. He was promised by Henry that a proper one would arrive soon if his sketches proved useful. Even now the bombardment did not abate and, if you showed yourself then Fritz had a reason to home in on your section of the line, all you could do was keep your head down and hope for the best. For that reason, it was easy to see why everybody who had spent time on the front had become fatalistic, the horrendous nature of death on such an industrialised scale meant that numerous creative ways of avoiding saying "killed" were used in an attempt to cope with it. If your number was up then you would, "cop a packet", "become a landowner", you would be "going home", "being buzzed" or "huffed", "drawing your full issue", "being topped off" or "clicking it"; anything rather than dying.

Having got the permission of Lieutenant-Colonel Pickering to carry out the test of Geordie's claims and to test his ability with the Lewis, they waited until a series of shells had fallen in their area so as it looked like they were just reacting to that and not testing something or someone. He proved good to his word. His Lewis operation and accuracy was up to the standard they had got used to from Davy with the added bonus that Geordie did not need to rest as often when using it alone. Somewhat like Ray, so long as there were magazines to feed the hungry Lewis, Geordie could keep firing. When they saw the first of the Mills flung into no-man's land they could not quite believe what they saw. Ronnie, Art and Anders who were the section bombers and considered themselves able to throw Mills bombs further than most, could not believe what they were witnessing.

"Have you ever considered playing cricket, Geordie?" questioned Anders, "You could take the bails off from the boundary at Lord's, with an arm like that!"

It was true; it was not just the distance, although that was impressive, the accuracy was exceptional.

Having seen all the proof he needed, Henry went off to make his case to the OC. It didn't take much convincing; with Geordie not having a unit and the section having a spare place it made sense. So Geordie became the first outsider to join the Auckland Pals.

Follow a session of studying Art's sketches, differing members of Lieutenant-Colonel Pickering's staff added their intelligence, pinpointing machine gun posts and other known heavy fortifications. Pickering wanted to know which section of the Hun army was facing them as, over the last days, the air reconnaissance had suggested that their front line had been relieved. Air reconnaissance was all well and good, but agreeing with General Haig's assessment days earlier, Pickering knew that the concrete evidence comes from feet on the ground. The section would conduct their first stunt the following evening giving them just over twenty-four hours to plan and prepare.

Henry had a completely different approach to informing his men to that which was standard in the British Army. Basically, the troops were told only the basic information and the officers held the details. This was understandable when you were dealing with thousands, keeping secret information away from the spies within, would be almost impossible. The downside to this philosophy was when your officers were hit and taken out of the assault the attack would lose cohesion and purpose. This was why the enemy especially targeted officers and why some officers stopped wearing their insignia during attacks. Henry on the other hand informed his much smaller section of every detail. The basis of the plan formulated by Henry and Daniel was given the go-ahead from Pickering, it was discussed in detail with the section who made suggestions. These were discussed and debated, some taken on board, some not. The outcome was that everybody going on the stunt knew every aspect of the plan and if all but one failed to survive then they could bring back the intelligence.

Daniel had taken bearings from their start point to the listening posts on to the selected cover points where the Lewis's were to be set up and on to the wire where the forward cover would set up. He had estimated distances between each point but knew this would only be a guide as the ground was so pockmarked from shelling, what should be 15 yards across open ground actually became twice that distance. Daniel had even taken bearings off the stars, having located the North Star, Polaris, earlier just in case it was a clear night.

Finally, all was ready and there was nothing left to do but rest and wait for the off. They tried resting and some were lucky enough to sleep. Not Daniel; he wrote his customary letters to his parents and of course to Marie. He went over the plan time and again. He had studied the terrain so much that when he closed his eyes he could see the ground spread out before him. When sleep did sneak up on him he was woke by the other inhabitants of the dugouts, rats that had absolutely no fear of humans. They would very happily run over their roommates' bodies and even faces if that was the route they wanted to take. And still the shelling went on.

Two hours before the off at 9.00 p.m., the section "stood too" and had inspection. They only took the bare essentials not like the normal approach for attacks where Tommies were expected to "race" across no-man's land loaded like pack horses. Theirs was a mission of stealth and nothing should hinder their progress and, besides, they hoped to return to whence they started if all went to plan. They had a meal of stew made from bully beef, bread and jam with sweetened tea to give energy. Finally, they went over the plan one last time with each member of the team going over his role. The last thing to do was for Henry and Daniel to brief that night's sentry so they knew to expect their return.

At 11.00 p.m. on the dot the section slithered out over the parapet and made their way in single file through the allied wire and up to the listening post. The dark silence was tangible; it was hard to believe that so many combatants waited to slaughter each other just a few yards in either direction.

Daniel took his bearings and led the way forward with Henry close behind. As his uncle had coached, he took notice of everything and anything out of the ordinary which could be used as a guide on his way back, a shell hole with the remnants of a light artillery wheel, a shell hole with the bloated remains of a dead horse, a tree stump, anything. They deposited the Lewis's at the agreed points with Fouller, Ronnie and Anders in support and struck out for the German wire covered on both flanks by the Lewis's. At the wire, as practised and planned, Kenny, Jack and Tommo cut the wires and set up to give further cover. Once through the wire, Daniel with Charlie went east along the wire for thirty yards and Henry, Art and Lazzer moved west the same distance.

As they crawled along, feeling rather than seeing, Daniel and Henry used their outstretched arms ahead of them to reach, pull them up the full arm length, each arm length being approximately one yard. At the estimated correct point, both teams moved due north until they hit the enemy trenches either side of the machine gun post identified by Pickering's staff from Art's sketches. Both teams dropped into the trenches and moved to converge on the machine gun nest which was set in a fortified nest slightly ahead of the rest of the firing bay in the front line trench. This position gave them their clear arcs of fire that allowed unrestricted slaughter. During the entire time, their progress was intermittently disturbed by the machine gun which kept spasmodically firing at nothing in particular. It took nerves of steel to keep going and not to panic thinking they had been spotted, but they did and, inch by inch, they got to within a few yards on either side of the nest and waited checking their watches to see how their progress matched the plan.

The idea was to await Henry's signal, which was to fire a Very light into the nest and follow up with overwhelming force, overpowering the team who were manning the guns. They intended to attempt to take two prisoners so the others in the nest were to be disposed of by use of the bayonet at close quarters. The thrill and excitement had Daniel buzzing, he had not felt anything like this in his entire life, his adrenaline was coursing through his veins and his heart beating so strongly Fritz must be able to hear it. They inched further on, suddenly there was a distant voice from behind them, there was the flash of light as a curtain was drawn back and the contents of a pipe was knocked against the support of the dugout. It was a lucky break. Daniel signalled to Charlie to go towards the light and give them two Mills bombs when Henry gave the signal. The seconds seemed like minutes and the minutes seemed like hours but finally there was a whoosh as the Very light lit up the machine-gun post, a scream as it hit some unfortunate and Daniel and Henry was in amongst them, bayonets giving payback for Davy. Behind, the Mills bombs went off and

Daniel pressed his bayonet point against the neck of the only remaining gunner; they had been a little bit over zealous with their payback! Fritz was very compliant when he saw the result of Daniel and Henry's handiwork with his colleagues. Whilst staying as low as possible they ran directly to the gap in the wire being directed by the low pitch whistle that Tommo and Kenny had agreed upon. There seemed to be a secondary explosion from the German dugout where Charlie had lobbed the two Mills bombs, for this was much more powerful than two Mills could create even in a confined space. This was perfect; it seemed to create enough confusion within the German line for them to possibly consider that there had been some sort of accident, because, for some reason, no shots were fired until they had withdrawn behind the listening post. This meant they had a shallow trench to follow back to their lines and to safety before the lead started to fly. Just as predicted, Fritz had not caused any bother once out in no-man's land, he obviously didn't fancy his chances against his own machine guns!

Pickering had come out once the explosions had happened and the sentries had informed him they were returning. Fritz was delivered to the lieutenant-colonel by Henry with a formal military handover. Pickering could not help but show his delight with the success of the mission and the justification of the investment of equipment and time that had got this result. Haig would be over the moon with him! This was the start of something special as far as he was concerned and it would cement his next promotion.

"Excellent work, Captain Neville, you can brief me about the mission in the morning when you have all the information from your lads. In the meantime you can go and check on them and I think a double ration is in order, don't you?"

"I certainly do sir, thank you and see you in the morning," with that he saluted and was gone, back to the lads.

In the dugout there was a great joyous commotion as everybody discussed what they had done and "how it had gone like clockwork!" and "Old Davy would be proud of us!"

"Okay, okay keep it down or you may as well give Fritz an invitation to drop a few tons of whizz-bangs on us," warned Daniel trying to get some organisation to the debrief, "nothing is perfect and if we are not to end up keeping poor old Davy company for the rest of the war then we need to improve every time we go out, and believe me they are not all going to be as easy as that."

It was generally agreed that the two-stage cover of their withdrawal was good and gave plenty of covering fire opportunities if needed, but depending on the target more men at the sharp end might be needed, so that would require less left for cover. The idea of the secondary diversion was a definite bonus and needed to be a consideration.

"Aye, thought you might like that idea of mine," boasted Charlie, pretending he had planned it all along.

"Bloody good idea," agreed Lazzer, who had always been a little bit gullible and actually believed Charlie until the others started to berate him for his stupidity. Lazzer, as usual, took it in good spirits (he had had plenty of practice over the years!). But it all pointed to a group of lads who, regardless of just losing a close friend, had very buoyant morale. That was very pleasing to Henry and Daniel.

The two wanted to work out how they could get hold of an explosive device which worked on a delayed fuse, creating a diversion just as had happened accidentally back in the German trench. They could not use a standard industrial fuse as that would be too visible and obvious.

Daniel with his knowledge of explosives from his days in the pit suggested that he and Ray would see what they could arrange whilst Henry gave his full report to Pickering the following morning.

That morning the trench was all talk about this "special team" that could ghost through enemy lines and this gave Henry's eye for a dramatic idea. To strike fear into the Hun lines they could leave a calling card every time they went in. But what was readily available and suitable? Following his report, he returned to the dugout and the lads unwittingly provided the answer. They were playing cards and, on the table having just left Kenny's hand, was the Jack of Clubs.

"You're a bloody marvel, Kenny!"

He never looked up, but without any hesitation replied, "I know it, it's just the rest of these fools who have never realised it!"

Meanwhile, following a somewhat hairy trip down the communication trenches, where it seemed that Fritz was dialled into Daniel and Ray for the entire journey, the pair finally got to the forward artillery batteries where Daniel sought out the OC and explained their requirements. This was something different to get your teeth into so the captain was more than helpful.

"The No 54 is organized on a time or percussion system, selectable by removing a safety pin marked with a 'T' or 'P' respectively."

Ray lifted his eyebrows up to the sky and under his breath whispered, "Just what we need, a bloody professor!"

"Removing the 'T' allows the activation of the movements of the time system pellet firing the time ring powder track, or 'P' the percussion pellet that would enable the inertia block movements at arrival, under the action of the shell departure shock. The time behaviour however is limited to sixteen seconds. If you were to leave this in a bag of Mills bombs it could go up quite nicely. I dare say if you leave a few 303s in there it might give a further distraction, Fritz will hear allied bullets amongst the explosion; he'll think he is being attacked."

"And if that is to the rear of his position," added Daniel with a smile, "he'll think the attack is coming from there, allowing us valuable time to make our escape."

Daniel thanked the captain for his help and explained that the conversation should be kept secret and that Lieutenant-Colonel Pickering would be in touch shortly.

"Anything to help the PBI said the captain." The artillery used PBI to describe their colleagues in the infantry; Poor Bloody Infantry.

Daniel got several of the 4.7 ins shells with the No 54 fuses delivered to their dugout. He dismantled the fuses just as he was shown by the captain and then emptied the charges into a few spare socks he had managed to get sent from the regimental quartermaster sergeant. This in itself was a statement of just how pleased Pickering was with their initial success. It must have been painful for the RQMS to allow the issue of socks without all the formal paperwork, but with Pickering and ultimately Haig behind the request it was not going to be turned down. The charges were emptied out and subdivided into the socks and then, just like in the pit, to stop the charge falling out of the socks (or the dynamite falling out of the hole that had been drilled into the coalface) covered in grease. This combined with a couple of Mills and 303s ammunition were all placed into sandbag sacks. Again, a test was carried out following a close bombardment by Fritz and sure enough it seemed to have the desired effect. Daniel would have liked to put more Mills and 303s into the sack, but they had to be carried and after all, they were only being used as a diversion not to actually kill anybody! If that happened it would be seen as a bonus.

During this delicate operation, the dugout became unsurprisingly deserted, Ray explaining, "Danny, we all love you to bits, but we have no wish to be in bits you mad bastard!" and with that the whole group starburst out of the dugout.

While they were out and about they took the opportunity to see where the other Auckland Pals had been posted. Since arriving at the front they had been immediately wrapped up in the preparations for the stunt or sleeping. Following the success of the test, they returned with news for Henry and Daniel. Apparently their fellow Auckland Pals had, to a man, been shipped out to a place called Messines, just east of Ypres were their skills from the pit were being put to use or at least that was what a sergeant from the Yorkshire Regiment had told them, it was all a bit hush, hush.

The lads had only been in the line a short period of time but, following their mission and the crawling about in the mud, they had already taken upon the appearance of troops who had been up there for weeks. It was Anders who had first started to chat but, within hours, everyone was scratching as the fleas and lice made a meal of them. Within the norm or trench life, these little devils rated worse than the rats. In fact, Ronnie who had caught one rat in a homemade trap to keep as a pet decided that if he could train Gerald to eat the lice eggs that were laid into the seams of their clothes, Gerald would become an integral part of the team!

"Great idea Ronnie, you always were bonkers!" was the encouraging comment from his mates.

Nonetheless, Ronnie was happy with his pet rat, Gerald, until a few days later when Gerald gave birth to six baby rats and he became Geraldine!

Between stunts, the section took their share of the burden of trench routine carrying out fatigue duties during the night. This would include bringing up supplies from the rear, sentry duties and going into no-man's land to repair the wire and picking up some of the corpses for burial. The night time work was by far the more hazardous with Fritz looking and listening for any activity out of the ordinary so his machine guns and artillery would have a suggested target to bombard. They could do this at any time during a twenty-four hour period and it was unbelievably mentally wearing on the troops. You could never actually relax and think you were safe and even, as tired as they were, sleep was never as refreshing and reinvigorating as you needed and as time went on morale was sapped. Relationships within the trench could get strained over the most innocuous issue. NCOs and officers had to keep on top of this powder keg. Within the normal section, platoon daily interaction had to maintain a high level of discipline constantly. This was one area that the lads benefitted from, being so close and having known each other since childhood, regardless of what happened, they remained mates and just sorted issues out between themselves without it getting out of hand. This certainly made Henry, Daniel and Ray's lives a lot easier than other officers of all ranks.

Another part of the trench routine was night time patrolling of no-man's land and entire nights in the listening posts. With their skills and new found fame the lads got these details regularly and it actually got them even more familiar with the terrain across their particular part of the front. Subsequent stunts however were a little more mundane, if there was such a stunt into no-man's land. They did come across a Fritz patrol during one of these missions. It was in one of the wider areas of no-man's land and when the German patrol looked directly at two Lewis guns carried like toys by two giants the whole patrol threw their hands up in surrender without a single shot being fired. The cap of the German captain was removed; the newly adopted calling card attached and left hanging on the German wire for the entire enemy line to see come daylight. Another patrol had the lads almost up to the German trench and inside the German wire where they stayed there for a couple of hours listening to conversation within the trench. Several calling cards were left across the front of the trench to let Fritz know he had received a visit. It was Henry's wish, he explained, "to cause paranoia in the German lines and the calling cards were a way of focussing Fritz on being hunted."

Ypres Salient
Gravenstafel

It was in the second week of their first deployment into the front that Henry got the call from Lieutenant-Colonel Pickering for the briefing of their second real mission. On his return to the dugout, he called everybody together to discuss the stunt and get views from the lads.

According to the latest ariel reconnaissance there was a strange build-up of a different type of artillery shell in large numbers, remote to any artillery batteries that Fritz had in place. These shells had appeared to be under the command of people in white laboratory type coats which meant one of a few different possibilities.

"They had obviously been far better concealed than anything before and HQ have to know why. Or, these shells were being stockpiled and kept away from any other ordnance dumps and HQ have to know why. Or, it is something new and so far never experienced on the battlefield, especially if it needed boffins to look after it and you guessed it," explained Henry, with the rest of the lads joining in, "HQ have to know why."

"This stunt will require us to move from Hooge where we have been for the last week or so, a little further north to between St Julien and Gravenstafel. Our objective is approximately one mile behind enemy lines at a place called Goudberg where this siting took place. We are to move up to Gravenstafel and meet up with the 10th Battalion of the 2nd Canadian Brigade, Canadian Expeditionary Force (CEF). The other part of the line is held by French Territorial and Colonial Moroccan and Algerian troops of the French 45th and 78th divisions. Our contact is a French Canadian Colonel called, Dupuis. We need to travel tonight, rest and plan tomorrow during the day and move out on the stunt the following night. I am expecting this to take overnight so we will have to reach our objective, lay low over the following day, observing whatever we can and return the following night. There is a wood east of the dump which could make for good concealment while we conduct our observations. This is going to be a challenge lads; we never trained to be out as long as this. We have only practised quick hit and run stunts, however the only difference is the timescales we need to be focused over. The skills required are just the same and we all know we have them in abundance!"

There was silence from the lads, as the mission sank in. It was not a silence born out of fear or concern it was a silence of absorbing the facts and starting to focus on their role. There was also a little bit of pride in that they were being moved so far especially for this mission, because they had done such a good job previously they were seen to be a team with special skills that could not be found any closer. There was a steady nodding of heads, questions and suggestions of what they needed and how best they could flank the German line. It was with huge pride that Henry looked towards his friend, smiled and nodded, accompanied by a wink of his eye.

When darkness fell, they set off back down the communication trench. They were laden down with all their equipment which included a few of the delayed explosive devices in their sandbags. At the end of that trench they got to the open ground near a bombed out farmhouse where they met up with a guide who was to take them all the way up to the Battalion HQ of the CEF. The journey was uneventful and they were far enough from the front line that it allowed them to talk so that helped pass the time as they marched into the darkness. They had been following a dirt road so navigation had been relatively easy. There were no junctions until the point where the road met another leading from St Julien to Gravenstafel. Heading off into the devastated village where there was nothing standing higher than a single-storey building but that was only a pile of debris, they came to a cleared section around an old winery. Although the building was nothing more than a heap of rubble the clearing led to a basement that was being used as the CEF HQ and, as well as the CEF HQ staff, the room was lined will barrels of wine. The guide took Henry to meet Colonel Dupuis and with the introductions complete, the colonel was about to start the briefing when Henry signalled to Daniel to come over. Introduced him and explained to Dupuis that he was a vital part of his planning team so it would be better if he heard all the information direct. Basically the no-man's land was reasonably well known but beyond that there was just what the Royal Flying Corps had passed on which Henry and Daniel already knew; fields and hedgerows leading to the wood overlooking the dump. From HQ the guide took them straight up the communication trench past the second line support trench and into the front line. The captain he was handed over to explained that they were expecting something because this had been the first night of their deployment to this sector that Fritz had been so quiet.

"Usually Fritz manages to make a nuisance of himself most of the night, they must be up to something? I think, as I understand it, that's where you come in."

"Yes and we need to be off tomorrow night so I will need all the intelligence you have on the area immediately in front and beyond their lines," requested Henry pointing towards the enemy, "you may be right about something happening because the top brass seem very keen for us to get on with it."

Due to the short notice of the mission, there was nothing available for the lads to shelter in so they had to huddle together in the bottom of the trench trying to keep warm. Just to add to their misery, it started to rain steadily. The trench had at least four inches of water in it and that steadily increased in depth as the night progressed, thus the lads were thoroughly miserable when "stand too" was called at 5.00 a.m. that morning. They went further down the communications trench to get breakfast leaving Art with his newly delivered periscope to start sketching the immediate ground between the two front lines, with whatever he could include on the distant horizon. Ronnie brought him his breakfast with a large mug of tea that had a rather unpleasant petrol flavour due to the water having been transported in fuel containers. However, it was hot and wet so he did not complain, as Art saw it, it was a waste of time complaining anyway, nobody took any notice, his philosophy was keep your head down and get on with it! Within the hour, the sketch was complete and Art apologised to Daniel as he handed it over.

"Sorry Danny, with the time available that's the best I could do."

Daniel looked at the sketch and could not believe Art was apologising, "Art it's a bloody masterpiece, when all this stupidity is over you need to think about doing this for a living. You have a real gift and it beats working in a hole in the ground!"

Daniel took the sketch away and found Henry in the Canadian captain's dugout that acted as his section HQ. Colonel Dupuis and his opposite numbers from the French 45th and 78th were poring over a series of maps that the French had come forward with, not having shared them with the Canadians before. On seeing Daniel, Henry introduced him and asked him to get Art back so he could copy the relief map of the area and relate it to what he had drawn from, then he wanted Art to draw a map of their proposed route. By lunchtime, Art had finished and, whilst waiting, Henry had explained his route and the plan asking Daniel to butt in at any time if he had any better suggestions. There were some surprised faces on the other officers as this captain allowed his sergeant and even the private to question and suggest alternatives. However, as the three fired ideas back and forth and a plan unravelled before them even the old traditional officers amongst them started to see the process actually worked and, far from undermining the young captain's authority, he seemed to have total respect from his men. Mid-afternoon saw the plan agreed and Henry, Daniel and Art left the dugout to meet with the rest of the lads. They had stayed down where the breakfast had been served prior to it being carried up to the front line. The cooking ranges were built on the back of carts so they could be transported and when two or three of these were parked together they gave off some considerable heat. The lads had taken advantage of any extra food available and the heat so were well fed and rested. Art did some catching up and Ray brought plenty of food for Henry and Daniel as they went over the plan. Once beyond the German line, there were so many unknowns that the plan had to be fluid at that point, but unless an opportunity presented itself, the plan was observe only and return unseen. Easier said than done! At 4.00 p.m. Henry and Daniel tried to get some sleep, just as before the last stunt, Daniel wrote to his parents and to Marie. He kept the information very general, he knew it would be censored anyway, but would not want to worry anybody of the nature of his duties. He managed to get a few hours' sleep prior to Ray waking him at "stand to" and they were first in the queue for their meals. So it was a revitalised team that set out on the evening of 19 April 1915. The trench system was splintered between the Canadians and the French, plus, reports and Art's observation sketches suggested this was replicated on the German side. It was one of these gaps they aimed for, to slip through hoping good old Fritz had taken his eye off the ball, whilst concentrating on the other matter, if indeed he was up to something. Following the story of the Jack of Clubs calling card, the section had been nicknamed the Knaves by the other units and it was with a certain amount of awe that others mentioned them.

The two sections of broken trench that faced across no-man's land had an old water course, possibly a drainage ditch or possibly a natural stream joining the two lines like an umbilical cord. Due to the shelling you had no idea that this existed until you viewed a pre-war map, following this you could actually make out a slight depression that would give limited cover from either flank. The 20 April 1915 was a miserable rainy night that saw the Knaves set out along this old ditch heading towards the German lines with the CEF protecting one flank whilst the other flank was held by French Territorial, Colonial Moroccan and Algerians. Although they needed to be in the cover of the small copse before daylight, the first section of the route would be the most dangerous and the slowest. In single file they inched forward, bayonet in hand. The reports had been correct; at that point the German lines were not complete but just a series of shell holes. However, this brought with it its own difficulties. In a regular trench you could predict to a certain extent where you were going to possibly run into good old Fritz, unfortunately in this situation it was quite possible that good old Fritz didn't know exactly where all his men were. Just prior to getting up to the area where Daniel, who was as usual on point, estimated the enemy line to be, allowed all the team to group up by moving slightly off to the right into a large shell hole. This made it possible to set up the Lewis's to cover the section's move through the line. Once beyond, they in turn would cover the Lewis's as they came through. This had been discussed prior to moving off so it was not necessary to discuss this further when it happened. They took a couple of minutes to have a breather before doing anything as they first slid into the shell hole and it was this silent breather that allowed Daniel to hear a very low-pitched whisper of German voices. Daniel immediately made sure everybody understood the situation and moved over for a closer listen. In the very next shell hole were a couple of German sentries quietly talking; Daniel signalled to Ronnie to drop his pack by demonstrating himself and showing only the bayonet he now carried. With further listening, Daniel signalled to Ronnie that there were only two to take care of and the two men got side by side on the parapet of their shell hole, where as one, they moved over and slid belly first into the enemy. The trench had been deepened but each side was still very sloping so both men had a gentle if rather frightening slide, where they got to their feet in unison and stuck their bayonets with an upwards thrust into the stomachs of the two mesmerised Hun sentries. With their second hand covering the enemies' mouths as per their training, they despatched their prey with frightening professionalism, there was still a lot of payback owed for losing Davy! As they were about to slide back into the original shell hole, where the others awaited them, they were stopped by Henry's hand passing them a calling card!

With their rest over and the Lewis's in place, they moved through the lines sometimes within what seemed like a few feet from the sentries. They set up in yet another shell hole in the rear of the German lines covering Tommo who retraced the route to guide the two Lewis's up. When this was over they made their way to a broken down boundary wall around a field that would give better cover and allow more rapid progress. They had to get to the diagonally opposing side of the field prior to following a hedgerow up to the copse; they had to move from one side of the wall to another a couple of times to ensure they stayed on the blindside of the cover but eventually got to the copse just prior to daybreak,

"A little too close for comfort," Henry whispered as he sank down next to Daniel.

Obviously, there was no cooking or heating of water for tea so it was "iron rations" of hard biscuit and bully beef with a watered down rum ration to wash it down. On an hourly rotation, they took turns in watching the ammunitions dump where there was a constant coming and going of a full range of ranks including civilian types wearing white coats. To their consternation, Fritz started making a second dump of shells adjacent to the original stack, but unlike the other one, this was on the reverse side of the copse from the allied lines. Every time a new load arrived, several troops with very peculiar hood-like masks came out to unload and everyone else disappeared always to the same place in the westerly corner of the field where the boffins in the white coats had their tent. Occasionally during a delivery one of these boffins came out also wearing a hood-like mask.

It was mid-afternoon whilst Art was looking back towards the German front line that he pointed out what could only be a mine entrance halfway between them and the trenches. This he sketched and referenced to three fixed points so the artillery could get a fix on it later.

Henry had decided that they needed one of the boffins with a mask to take back and, if at all possible, one of the shells so all could be thoroughly interrogated and investigated. At around 6.00 p.m. another ammunition delivery arrived and one of the boffins came out to inspect it. Picking up a shell he proceeded to walk around the rear of the copse to the original ammunition dump and began talking to an officer who was clearly not comfortable being close to the boffin as he kept hold of him at arm's length every time he brandished the shell. Henry got Geordie and Ray to accompany Daniel down the hedgerow where they hoped the boffin would return. It was the obvious route between the two dumps, so it wasn't at all surprising when the boffin came back the same way. Neither was it surprising, bearing in mind the way the officer had reacted to the presence of the shell, that the boffin was unaccompanied. He walked, talking to himself whilst looking down at the shell he was still holding in his hands. The three waited on the opposite side of the hedgerow and as the boffin came to the gap, Daniel gave a whistle to catch his attention. He looked up directly at Daniel and saw Ray stood alongside him. Ray's right hand shot out like the piston from the stream engine that drives the pit wheel, there was the gristly, bone crunching noise of hard fist hitting face and the boffin's head shot backward at an unenviable speed. Geordie was there to catch him and throw him over his shoulder with the kind of ease that suggested it was only a sack of rags. He was taken so quickly, barely a minute had passed from the whistle to the three returning to the corpse. He was knocked out as cleanly as if he had been anaesthetised. Geordie dropped him at Henry's feet. The shell was placed in a sack for ease of carrying.

"Now tell me you haven't killed him!" pleaded Henry in mock desperation.

"Nothing more than a love tap, it was," replied Geordie, with Ray smiling his agreement.

"With love like that, I'd hate to see your hate taps!" chuckled Daniel.

"We need to be in a position where we can move out quickly if our friend here is missed. With a prisoner, we need all the time we can afford to get back tonight."

At the front of the copse was a partially intact shepherd's hut which would give a quicker route back to the boundary wall of the field where they had started from after first passing through the lines, so Daniel suggested that, "If we drop out of the copse during dusk and use the blindside of the hill to get to the hut we can wait until full darkness before moving direct to the point where we can return through the line. We will be exposed a little bit but it will save us a couple of hours if the trip outwards is anything to go by! Besides, they won't be watching people coming from this direction as closely, will they?"

At 11.00 p.m. they moved out and, using a couple of kitchen wagons as cover, they got to the rear lines very quickly. In the time they had been gone, the support trench was almost complete, it was very dark and the Germans were working across the area, finishing off the far end parapet with sandbags. Their main focus was there and it was the section that was complete that was the least occupied. The few Germans in the trench were busy digging out their own shelters and paid very little notice to a group of people coming up from the rear. One at a time, the section jumped across the support trench and sank down into the depression that was the old water course. The boffin who had come round and could understand English had been threatened with Geordie and Ray. One of his socks pushed in his mouth and tied in place with his other sock, the hood-like mask was then put in place. The rest of the white coat was left in the shepherd's hut with the usual calling card. Tommo and Lazzer had the task of marching the prisoner, however when it came to crossing the support trench it was Geordie and Ray who threw him from one to another over the section of trench which was about four feet wide by this stage of construction. The plan from here was a simple retracing of the route they had arrived by. The Lewis's went first with Ronnie and set up their cover positions, then Ronnie came back to guide the others. Daniel had stayed back to plant the No 54 "sock bombs" and a few Mills bombs in the kitchen wagons. When Ronnie had returned and they had started moving out under the wire the usual whistle signal was used so that Daniel set

119

the fuses and ran, jumped the trench and followed the others knowing he only had 16 seconds until things started getting interesting! As the explosion erupted in the rear of the German lines they speeded the crawl up so they were just on their hands and knees and making rapid progress across no-man's land. This was the pre-arranged signal for the artillery to open up with a bombardment to keep Fritz's head down. German machine gunners started strafing the darkness, their sweeping motion suggesting that they had no real obvious targets. Even the Very lights didn't manage to show them their targets. Within twenty yards of the Canadian front line, they started to call out the password to their comrades, the boffin made a bolt off to the left, still blindfolded but wanting to at least try something to make this kidnap unsuccessful. He didn't get very far because Lazzer was up on him like a flash. There was a sickening thud and a large expulsion of breath as Lazzer lay prone over the boffin who had started to scream. Henry got to Lazzer and under the Very light could see he was dead. Lazzer had been hit by several simultaneous bullets. Half his head had been removed, as had his right arm at his shoulder. The boffin was covered in Lazzer's blood and brains. The two Lewis's had reached the trenches and set up covering fire from the sides of the returning section, trying to draw the fire from their mates. Henry pushed Lazzer's limp body into the depression for Tommo and Ronnie to drag back to cover and got the boffin by the throat. Still blinded by the blindfold, he was a nervous wreck and very meekly allowed himself to be guided into the Canadian trench by Art. Daniel was shuffling past Henry whilst he returned into the depression when he heard Henry shout out in pain, spinning round and landing on the back of Daniel's legs.

"No!" screamed Daniel as he spun round to see his friend roll to one side and on to his knees.

Henry was clutching his left upper arm with his right arm. Without thinking, Daniel pulled Henry back down flat so he was out of direct fire.

"Henry! Where are you hit, can you still move?"

"It's my upper left arm; I can run for it, I just can't use my arm to crawl!"

"OK, roll on to your back and I will drag you. If you stand up in this you won't stand a chance," this wasn't a request from Daniel and Henry knew he was right, so he just did has he was told.

Inch by inch, foot by foot and yard by yard they moved to safety with a major fire fight going on above them. Daniel moved himself across the ground on his back then reached back down between his legs and felt for Henry's collar and pulled hard to bring him towards safety. They could feel the pressure waves from each bullet that passed inches above their heads. Meanwhile, the others were digging a gap into the parapet so they would not be exposed to any sniper or machine gun when at last Henry and Daniel reached the trench. After what seemed like an eternity, two mighty hands had his shoulders and pulled him into the trench. He was in Ray's safe hands and, as he looked back, he saw that Geordie had Henry. They both looked at each other and the relief was culpable and then the anguish hit them as the realisation of the loss of Lazzer took effect. They both looked around at the broken rag doll that was Lazzer. To cause that much widespread damage to a human body he must have been hit by the two machine guns, one on each flank almost at the same time. Not only had he had his arm blown off at the shoulder and the same half of his head obliterated but he had caught it in the gut too. In the process of recovering his body, these injuries had given up their contents and his intestine had spilt out on to the floor, covering them with mud and grime. Ray was trying his best to hide the sight from the rest of the section whilst at the same time keeping the corpse out of the bottom of the trench which was knee deep in a treacle-thick soap of human excrement from the overflowing latrines and thick Flanders mud which had a thousand decaying bodies adding to its very peculiar putrid aroma. Geordie saw the plight of his mate and also lent a hand; together they made a very efficient screen and managed to get the body placed on the firing step.

Captain McMullen of the CEF had arrived and hardly acknowledged the death of one of the section; it was just an everyday occurrence on the front line as far as he could see.

"Colonel Dupuis compliments, Captain Neville, he would like your report as soon as possible and to see your prisoner and anything else of relevance."

Henry looked around wanting to see to his lads but realised that duty had to come first.

He turned to Daniel, "Danny I'm going to need your help, and you Art. Ray can you see to Lazzer and get his pay book, get stretcher bearers to take him away and find out where he is to be buried."

Ray didn't need to be asked. He wasn't about to let anybody else look after the body, without looking back he answered, "No problem and as soon as you have given your report you need to get that arm sorted or you will be losing it in these conditions!"

"Yes, of course you're right; I will get it tended to as soon as I leave the colonel".

Captain McMullen looked at Henry's arm clasping his other and the blood oozing between his fingers, "Private Finch" he said to his batman, "get the battalion medical officer to the colonel's HQ immediately, explain what's happened he knows the importance of this!" with that there was a swift salute and the private was gone. "This way Captain if you please."

Daniel followed with the boffin still wearing the hooded mask in front of him. He had been the cause of another death within the section. He wasn't taking any risks of losing him, he had better have been worth it. In his back pack was the sack holding the new type of shell they had recovered.

In the colonel's HQ the mask was removed from the boffin and there was a gasp at the extent of the damage to his face.

"Put up a bit of a struggle, did he," this was more of a statement than a question, by the colonel.

"Not after my sergeant subdued him sir."

"What in God's name did he subdue him with? A cricket bat!"

There was low laughter from those present when the boffin silenced them, "It was totally unnecessary, I would have come without any violence, I do not agree with the use of this," he pointed at the shell that Daniel had placed on the table, "it is totally indiscriminate and inhumane."

"What is?" asked Dupuis, beckoning the boffin to sit and pouring him some whiskey into a mug.

"I don't suppose there is a chemist amongst you who could understand the slightest thing I am about to tell you?"

At that moment the medical officer, Capt. F.A.C. Scrimger arrived to take care of Henry's arm.

"Ah! How good's your chemistry Scrimger?" boomed Dupuis.

"Got my PhD before studying medicine," was the rather defensive answer, "why sir?"

"Because our friend here," Dupuis offered his hand to the boffin, giving him a chance to introduce himself, at the same time filling his mug up to the top, "is about to tell us about something that he finds indiscriminate and inhumane."

"Dr Gerhard Shlinger, at your service, gentlemen." He was another for the theatrical, as he paused for effect ...

"On the 22 April 1915, the German Army will release 200 tons of chlorine gas that is to be deployed in over five and a half thousand cylinders opposite your lines, north of Ypres. The gas is visible and has a distinctive smell, like pineapple and pepper combined. The poor devils that are downwind of that release will experience pains in the chest and a burning sensation in their throats and eyes. They will eventually be unable to breathe and die of asphyxiation, those not totally overcome will be unable to put up much of a fight, the chlorine will also burn exposed skin, this is why I call it indiscriminate and inhumane."

There was silence in the dugout. Daniel considered the fact he had just carried this deadly gas cylinder under heavy gunfire for hours and the colour drained from his face!

"That is tomorrow for God's sake, get on to Canadian Division HQ and let them know we have an idea that something is going to happen tomorrow. Gentlemen, suggestions please?" asked Dupuis sounding slightly flustered.

"If I may make a suggestion sir," requested Henry whilst Scrimger bandaged his arm.

"Of course man, let's hear it, don't be shy".

"Well if what Dr Shlinger says is true, the gas needs to have the wind in the correct direction?" Henry looked for the nod of agreement from Dr Shlinger, he got it, "Then we do not know if the wind will be in the correct direction tomorrow and if it does then when the gas cloud moves over us we must move to the side of it and as Fritz follows up we will enfilade them from the flanks. Is there anything we can do to protect our troops from chlorine?" he asked both Shlinger and Scrimger.

Scrimger had been thinking about this whilst dealing with his patient, "Well urea breaks down some of the worst effects of chlorine, urine is diluted urea, so if we piss on rags and breathe through them it should relieve some of the most dire symptoms. You will need some sort of goggles to protect the eyes and all skin, including hands should be covered. The men's throats and mouths will have a metallic taste if they get a dose, this could be the only early warning they get prior to being overcome," he was firing ideas out in a stop-start fashion and Dupuis had got his orderly to make notes.

"This counter measure will only have minimal affects you must stay out of the cloud," insisted Shlinger,

Someone came in from outside to inform the group that, at the current time, the wind was blowing south east, straight down no-man's land and therefore very hard to see Fritz using it at dawn. That was good news, they had a little time. The shell, or as they now knew it, the gas cylinder with the gas hood was taken by runner to Division HQ for further analysis and Dr Shlinger started his journey under guard back to Army Intelligence HQ for further interrogation.

"Sterling job you and your men did there Neville, any casualties beside yourself? This information will be invaluable, bloody good show!"

"Yes, one dead, a fine man, irreplaceable!" he replied, remembering and recounting the events in his head.

With this in mind he slumped down in the chair that Shlinger had just vacated and shook his head.

Daniel brought the conversation back on track taking some of the focus off Henry, who had started to look very tired with the effects of the pressure of leading the stunt, Lazzer's death and his own injury.

He pointed out on Art's sketch where the entrance to the mine was and added, "What happens if they are mining under us to release the gas right up close, we may want our artillery to give this some special treatment?"

"Brilliant! Your boys are a font of knowledge and good suggestions; it will all be in my report back to HQ. Neville, you can count on that, go and get that arm sorted out properly at the dressing station. Take all your boys back there for a few hours' rest but we will need all the help we can get back here when or if the wind changes."

Dupuis then shouted an order to the signaller to get the Artillery Batteries to concentrate their fire around the area identified on Art's map. Within moments, the barrage was pounding the German line and as far as the lads could make out not far off the mark!

Henry, Daniel and Art made their way back to the section to meet a group of very dejected soldiers. Lazzer's body had been removed and the whole group sat on the firing step where they had been left nearly two hours earlier. It was still very dark but Daniel could see the faces with the stares that looked a thousand miles into the distance, unable to focus on anything and he knew that had to change, quickly.

"Right, we need to get Henry down to the dressing station and then find some food and re-supply before we return here to put it up Fritz, we've got more payback to dish out!"

"Too bleeding right we have," growled Ray.

"That'll be right," added Geordie.

Heads started to nod and the murmurings became stronger, expletives were exchanged describing what was going to happen next time each of them came face to face with Fritz.

Checking it was only the lads within earshot, Ronnie said, "Away then, Henry, we will have to take care of you again, some things never change!"

There were a few light chuckles as the lads moved off down the communications trench making their way to the dressing station. Fritz had started to answer in kind the bombardment from the allies and this grew in intensity following a rather large explosion from the area where the mine entrance had been located.

Considering it had been quiet over the previous few days, there were still plenty of customers for the medical staff at the dressing station. Scrimger had returned but was now busy on the phone pacing up and down, very animated, barking out all his chemistry knowledge to his audience on the other end of the telephone line, "Yes, cotton pads soaked in their own urine, well it doesn't have to be their urine, but I think they would prefer their own, wouldn't you? Oh! And we need goggles from the transport corp., as many as you can get."

Just to the left of the dressing station was another large marquee-style tent that held some of the seriously injured awaiting for the transport to the rear. Out to the rear of that tent were row upon row of dead bodies that had not been able to be helped by the medical staff. This looked like a sea of khaki, but the thousands of unmoving ripples were not waves but each a dead body. The whole area had the smell of blood, ether and petrifying gangrene. At the rear of the open air morgue were wagons of amputated limbs waiting to be taken away with the more complete bodies. This was a brutal perversion of humanity. How could one civilised race do this to another, thought Daniel, at the same time realising that this scene was being replicated hundreds and hundreds of times up and down the Western Front, on both sides, and this a quiet day!

The moans and shrieks of injured and dying seemed like the chorus of the condemned and Daniel knew, although his friend needed to be treated, the rest of the section did not need to see more misery following losing Lazzer.

He called Ray over, "Apparently the hospital kitchen is over there," he pointed in the direction of a smaller tent, "the entrance is on the other side so you can eat without looking at the dead! Nice of them to be so caring, don't you think? Go and get them fired up, sometime tomorrow the balloon is going to go up and Fritz is going to come knocking!"

Scrimger came over when he had finished his animated conversation.

"Nurse, come over here and tend to Captain Neville's wounds please, I quickly cleaned and bandaged it at the front, but it will require a more thorough job before I close it up." Turning back to Henry and Daniel, he added, "It will need stitches and is going to hurt like the devil. I know this is wasted, but my advice is you rest up for a couple of days to regain your strength, you have lost a lot of blood and it's got to have weakened you."

"Thanks Doc. However I think Fritz will have something to say in a few hours so we need to get back up to the front."

Henry could feel Daniel's stare burning into the back of his head, so without turning round asked him, "OK mother, and you would do exactly what? I'm sure you would have your feet up for the next couple of days!"

Daniel looked towards the roof of the tent in exasperation. His mind was taken off the issue of Henry when he realised that even the roof of the tent had blood stains on it. In fact, looking around the area that housed the operating theatre tables, there were coagulating pools of blood which intensified the thick, choking, sickly smell of the area due to the extra heat and lack of fresh air that was blowing outside. Some staff had started to clean the area when Daniel noticed Scrimger looking at him.

He must have realised what was going through Daniel's mind because he explained, "We just had a bit of a rush before you got back. They had sent a patrol out further down the line to act as a bit of a diversion. We send one out every night and they didn't want Fritz to think something was amiss so this lot went out," he pointed to the men at the other end of the tent, laid out on camp beds, they were a sorry collection of pain and misery, "unfortunately they got badly shot up," pointing up to the roof of the tent, he added, "that's what arterial bleeding can do!" His face softened when he saw the surprise on Daniel's face. "Why don't you go and join the others, get something to eat and have a bit of a rest? It's pointless both of you going without, besides he's going to be needing you more than ever, if things are to kick off. Don't worry," he reassured Daniel, "me and my staff have done this sort of thing before!"

With Henry adding his support to the idea, Daniel reluctantly left the tent to join the others. Considering what he had just seen and all that had happened over the previous few hours, he ate well and caught a couple of hours' sleep until Ray gave him a gentle nudge to wake him at 5.00 a.m.

"Stand to, Danny," what time do you want us to head back up?"

Daniel felt surprisingly well and his appetite set up by the smell of bacon now permeating from the kitchen, "We'll get a good breakfast and see how Henry is and take it from there. We need to get stocked with iron rations, if those bastards are coming, it maybe some time before we get back to a kitchen for real food. The wind is still coming down from the south east, but it feels like it has dropped a fair bit. I don't thick Fritz is going to use his gas in the next few hours. Get them ready to move for 9.00 a.m. I will take Henry some breakfast; give me a shout if I am needed."

Ray placed his big hand reassuringly on Daniel's shoulder, "Leave it to me Danny, I can sort this out, you don't have to do everything, but if you try to, you are going to disappear up your own backside. We all need you at full fitness, so let us all help when we can."

Daniel smiled back at Ray and simply answered, "Thanks," and turned towards the dressing station.

Henry looked very pale but seemed to be in good spirits, "How are the lads Danny?" was his first question when he saw Daniel approaching, "And how are you?"

"All fine and we will be ready to move off back up the line by 9.00 a.m. with full provisions and full bellies! Have you eaten yet?"

"Never stopped, they've been feeding me every waking moment," Henry pointed a sideways thumb at the nurse who was tending his needs, "This is Jane, Jane this is Sergeant Daniel Byrne," he introduced in exaggerated formality.

"Pleased to meet you Jane, I'm sure that my commanding officer has behaved himself and not been too much trouble through the night?" Daniel quizzed her with mock sternness.

"He has been a total gentleman," answered Jane coming at once to Henry's defence. "It's a real pleasure to look after one of our famous Knaves," she purred.

"I am pleased to hear it. However, take my word for it he does take some looking after, so I will send Geordie over to help him get ready, if you want to meet another Knave, you will, pound for pound get your money's worth with Geordie!"

Daniel winked at Henry and left. Just as he exited the dressing station, Scrimger was heading towards the kitchen. They got some breakfast together and Scrimger asked Daniel if he had asked Henry if he intended returning with the rest of the section.

"To be honest with you, the thought never even crossed my mind. I shouldn't think he has given that the slightest consideration, has he said anything to you?"

"Oh yes, let's just say, wild horses are not going to keep him from leading you lot. But just a word of warning, it'll be a couple of days before he's back up to strength and that's if he does rest, it could be even longer depending on the circumstances."

"We'll look after him Doc," said Ray over Daniel's shoulder. He pushed two large mugs of sweet tea towards the pair and added to Daniel, "the Doc has got us some goggles and gloves from the Transport Corp with mouth and nose masks made from bandages and dressings. Apparently we have to piss on it before we tie it in place!" This final bit of information was emphasised to show his disgust.

Daniel couldn't help but laugh and, remembering the overheard comments from Scrimger over the telephone, he helpfully suggested, "If you feel that it is not appropriate to piss on your own mask, then as a friend I am quite prepared to do it for you!"

Ray looked at Daniel and then at Scrimger and back to Daniel again. He shook his head, murmured, "Bloody weird!" and left, heading back to the section, shaking his head in disbelief as if he was struggling in reconciling the idea of placing a facemask covered in his own urine over his nose and mouth.

Daniel turned to Scrimger and thanked him for the equipment.

"No need to thank me, it's the least I can do. If it wasn't for you lot when the injured started to arrive we would have no idea what was affecting them. I can't say there'll be anything we can do, however we will be a little better prepared. Now, remember keep all skin covered, goggles on and masks well wetted, but remember what Doctor Shlinger said, staying out of the gas cloud is the only real defence!

At 9.00 a.m. they were ready to head back up the line. Henry appeared, but he was without Geordie, when asked he smiled and replied, "Who could credit it. She must be eight stone wet through and he the size of a mountain, and

131

could probably put her into his pocket for safe keeping. Within two hours they haven't stopped swooning at each other. I gave him ten minutes to say his goodbyes in private."

"The dirty, lucky bastard!" groaned Ray, he turned to the others and added, "see if I was not babysitting you lot that could have been me!"

"Not with a face like that it couldn't!" replied Ronnie ducking behind Anders so as not to give Ray an easy target.

The easy banter and laughter showed everybody that whatever they had been through they were ready to face Fritz head on.

The Battle of Hooge
The Second Battle of Ypres 1915

The ongoing bombardment was getting heavier as they negotiated the communications trench between the support and front line trenches. Throughout the night, the sappers had been working like Trojans to get the front trench completed to give the troops some chance of defending the position. They had fully connected all the individual shell holes that small groups of troops had made their own by digging down to a depth of five to six feet and adding another couple of feet with sandbags on the parapet, these had been brought in on a truly unimaginable scale. They must have taken the whole beach from Le Touquet, mused Daniel to himself. The sandbags were arranged in a castellated fashion to allow some protection from the flanks however this did restrict your ability to move your rifle from side to side. A firing step had been cut in the side of the trench which faced the enemy and every now and again a small dugout had been constructed by the troops themselves. The sections that the sappers had constructed to join the shell holes were all staggered, so as to create firing bays and to stop a single blast travelling all the way down the trench. The construction work had only just been completed and the digging had uncovered many corpses that had been previously buried and were in different stages of decomposition. One rather macabre example of this was the arm of a German soldier that was sticking out of the side of a trench perhaps three feet from the trench top. It was being used as a hook for hanging different paraphernalia such as coats and had a sign attached asking those passing to "give me a hand here!" The freshly uncovered corpses really did make the place stink and the slime from that decay lined the trench walls. Daniel looked around the men who inhabited this section and then again at his lads and they did not seem to care or react to these conditions. Just what depths will a man descend to before he can no longer reason right from wrong and therefore fail to recover a sense of normality when hostilities come to an end, wondered Daniel, at least while he was questioning the mayhem he saw before him, he thought there was still hope for himself!

On arriving at the CEF Battalion HQ they had been ordered to the front close to a village of St Julien and surrounded by Canadians. They were with the 1st Canadian Division and had become just another section of the PBI (Poor Bloody Infantry). In a mass attack, it was all hands to the pump and even the famous Knaves became normal foot soldiers. Your life was in the fickle hands of fate, who would decide if you or the bloke next to you caught a packet and therefore in a few months' time your semi-decomposed body could be being used as trench furniture. They were positioned next to Lance Corporal Frederick Fisher of the 13th Battalion CEF's machine-gun detachment and, along with their two Lewis's, could throw some serious lead about. The village of St Julien was comfortably in the rear of the 1st Canadian Division's position on the 22 April and many of the division's supplies and transport was stored there, so it was an imperative that they withstood the German attack that everybody, thanks to the Auckland Pals, knew was coming. The other side of the village was held by French Colonial troops from Martinique and this was a concern to Colonel Dupuis and why he had massed machine guns over on that side so they could also assist the French Colonials if required.

By mid-afternoon, it was clear that the wind direction had changed and was blowing towards the allied front line. Would Fritz attack now or leave it until the next morning? It had been reasoned by the powers that be, that the attack had to be during daylight. They had learnt from Dr Shlinger to expect the forming of a grey-green cloud and this was part of the German strategy to follow this cloud but, to do this, Fritz himself had to see it. So a night time attack ruled this out.

However, regardless of their logic it was at 5.30 p.m., in a slight north-easterly breeze, the gas was released, forming a grey-green cloud that drifted across positions held by French Colonial troops from Martinique and, in a moment, death had them by the throat. In the gathering darkness of a truly awful night, they fought with their own inner terror, running blindly in the gas-cloud, and dropping with breasts heaving in agony and the slow poison of suffocation mantling their dark faces. Hundreds of them fell and died; others lay helpless, froth upon their agonized lips and their racked bodies powerfully spewing, sick, with tearing nausea of short intervals, in between gasping for breath. Their fate was sealed; they too would die later – a slow and lingering death of unspeakable agony. The whole air was tainted with the acrid smell of chlorine that caught at the back of men's throats and filled their mouths with its metallic taste. It was unrealistic to expect the French Colonial troops, or anybody else for that matter, to stand. They broke ranks, abandoning their trenches and thus creating an 8000-yard gap in the allies' line.

Up to this point, the gas had only affected the colonials from Martinique, but eventually the same grey-green cloud started to appear in front of the section defended by the Auckland Pals along with the 1st Canadians. For some reason, the cloud was swirling and broke up in the wind.

The lads had put on their protective goggles, masks (freshly urinated on) and gloves. The few spare pieces of equipment they had got distributed on to Lance Corporal Frederick Fisher's machine-gun detachment, whilst the rest of the division were told to urinate on to their handkerchiefs in a hope to give protection. When the gas arrived at the allied front-trenches, these soldiers also began to complain about pains in the chest and a burning sensation in their throats. It was the turn of the Canadians to realise they were being gassed and many ran as fast as they could. An hour after the attack had started there was a further 1500 yards (1400 m) gap in the allies' line and not a German shot had been fired. Daniel looked across no-man's land and his visibility was hugely compromised. All peripheral vision was gone, he could only see what the goggles allowed. The German soldiers themselves seemed apprehensive of the chlorine, few were moving forward and the delay enabled Canadian and reinforcing British troops to retake the position before the Germans could exploit the gap. That did not seem to be the case over with the Martinique line. There were no reserves to retake the line and that small trickle of German troops in the line began to increase and, without check, a bulge in the line started to appear which stretched behind the Canadians into St Julien.

Henry took the initiative and, along with Lance Corporal Frederick Fisher's machine-gun detachment, the Auckland Pals dropped back to the village outskirts where they started to attack the so far unopposed German advance. Enfilading the German advance was easy, due to the fairly narrow width of the advance, which was actually only the width of the village. They managed to reach the village centre and set up strong points which gave clear lines of fire down the streets all the way to the new French Colonial front line. With both allies and Germans in the village for once, the artillery left the front lines alone and concentrated their bombardments on the rear, supporting line, and oh how they did. The incessant artillery barrage continued like the thunderstorm from hell, almost as though like a child who had been thwarted and had decided they would cause mischief elsewhere.

A hastily convened meeting between Colonel Dupuis and Henry had resulted in a plan being formed. With Canadians holding the line just to the east of St Julien and the French Colonials having dropped back to the south-west of the village, the Canadian machine gun detachments had no option other than to force entry into the village and to set up alternating defensive and offensive positions depending on the cover they could find. The machine guns alternated by facing the attacking troops whilst the others hit the rear of the German vanguard. This covered a diagonal line from south-west to north-east following Sint-Juliaanstraat connecting the colonial line that had eventually been reinforced by French regulars following the dispersal of the chlorine gas by the swirling winds and the steadfast Canadians. More Canadian machine guns from their front line could enfilade the German flank across the barren approaches to St Julien thus slowing down the flow of troops entering the village and assisting Lance Corporal Fisher's cause. Unbelievably, communications had been almost immediately re-established when the French Colonials halted their retreat, so French machine guns set up to face into St Julien creating a tightly packed line of machine guns across the village that set up a deadly killing zone which effectively cut off the German vanguard. At its worst, the rift in the allied front line had been almost 9000 yards and this had been funnelled down to the width of the village. Every German soldier south of Sint-Juliaanstraat was now stranded and this area has been sectorised and the Auckland Pals split up into two small units with Henry and Ray with his Lewis gun heading up one group, taking the western sector and Daniel and Geordie with his Lewis taking the rest of the Pals into the eastern sector. They were to go house to house clearing old Fritz, flushing out the vanguard, who, while ever the wall of machine guns held were without support. A few brave German souls tried to push forward out of the village and beyond but with the south side of the St Julien approaches being as bare of cover as the north, both the Canadian and French had enjoyed shooting fish in a barrel when they tried to make their breakout.

Henry and Daniel's units gave each other a workman-like nod as they set off into the different areas. Daniel had been very impressed by the speed and authority his friend had shown because the plan they had adopted was predominantly his with just a few contributions from Colonel Dupuis and his staff, although it was clear that they thought it was all of their own work. Obviously, Henry had learnt a lot more than just soldiering during his intelligence training.

Each unit nominated a scout to head up the team and check street by street for positions held by occupying German troops. This had to be done by sight as opposed to hearing due to the ongoing artillery bombardment which was so savagely heavy it made the whole ground shake like a mighty earthquake, the big difference was that earthquakes end! No pit explosion ever sounded like this. Tommo was acting as scout for Daniel and entering a street that faced towards the rear of the Canadian lines. Tommo reported that there was a couple of houses where he could see heavy fire being directed towards the Canadians from the first floor windows, rifle fire was spitting lead in the direction of the allied line with the Canadians answering in kind. Daniel and Geordie entered the first house from the opposite side checking the downstairs room by room, to Daniel's amazement there were no sentries posted. This confirmed Daniel's original assessment that Fritz was firstly unaware he had been cut off and that his total focus was on the enemy they now faced and had taken their eye off any other ball! They poured concentrated fire down on to the Canadians from the same room which took up the whole of the rear of the house. This gave Fritz a good arc of fire, but unfortunately for them, put them all in the line of fire for a well-placed Lewis gun.

Step by step, Daniel ascended the stairs, staying close to the wall so as to minimise the creaking of the stair boards, it felt to Daniel that he was making enough noise to wake the dead it didn't seem possible that old Fritz wouldn't hear him. Three steps from the top, a stair let out a groan of complaint under Daniel's weight. His heart was beating to a point where he expected it to burst out of his tunic at any moment; beads of sweat sprang from his forehead and streamed down his face. He froze, waited and still the torrent of rifle fire carried on unabated. Having gained the landing, he covered the door, pistol in hand and a couple of Mills bombs at his feet and beckoned Geordie up. Tommo followed and the others set up cover from the ground floor. There was, in actual fact, so much noise from the incoming and outgoing fire fight they probably could have herded cattle up those stairs without being discovered, but they weren't about to take a chance. Things were deadly serious and those who took foolhardy chances could be placed into two brackets; alive and very lucky or dead!

With Tommo on one side of the doorway and Daniel on the other, they gently pushed the door open to see so many German troops that not all could get to a window to shoot, some just reloaded the weapons for their comrades. Quickly, they both rolled a Mills bomb along the floor between the German feet and ducked back out of the room shutting the door and taking cover at the side of the doorway. The door splintered outwards followed by a tongue of flames. In such a confined space, the noise was deafening even by front line standards, with their ears ringing they stood behind Geordie who unleashed a hail of bullets from the Lewis. He painted his deadly stream of lead down the window-side first then up the rear of the room. They looked across the remnants of the room. Death had been delivered with total indiscriminate ease, scything victims down like felling storks of wheat during harvest, so easy, so uncompromising. However, the firing had not stopped and it was only then that, to his horror, Daniel realised he has missed another room at the end of the landing, where a fanfare of staccato shots rang out. He suddenly realised that he could have led all of them to their deaths by not taking in the full picture when he ascended the stairs. However, this was no time to consider what might have been, it was time to act upon his good fortune, the fire fight was still so strongly contested between the Canadian and German protagonists that nobody seemed to have realised what had just happened. All three moved slowly along the landing to the second door that had been completely overlooked until then. Each foot placement seemed to echo and the fifteen yards seemed more like one hundred to Daniel, his heart again pounding like a drum. They set up in the same way and carried out the same procedure with the same deadly result. When the dust settled, they counted twenty-three dead between the two rooms. Daniel had Geordie cover the downstairs from the top of the stairs with his Lewis, he was damned if he would get caught as Fritz had allowed him to catch them. They started examining their handiwork gathering intelligence about which unit these troops belonged to and, on finding a German *Hauptmann* (Captain), Daniel took a look through his personal correspondence and belongings. Hauptmann Franz Kline was from Hamburg and very dead. He had set up a defensive wall in this area when he realised that his troops had been cut off. Unfortunately for the Hauptmann he had made a fatal mistake of using all his men for assaulting the Canadian line and in his haste had forgotten to post sentries. Another mistake he had made was to bring with him his battle orders and a map showing not only the German objective but their defensive strategy in case of counter attack, this showed quite clearly where the gas shell storage depots were, highlighting them for heavy defence. Amongst his other possessions was an Iron Cross, First Class, which was attached to his tunic under his overcoat, a hip flask which was engraved with the imperial eagle with the inscription of: XII (1st Royal Saxon) Corps 23rd Infantry Division presented by, General der Infanterie Karl d'Elsa. Daniel took a smell at the contents, there was the unforgettable smell of schnapps, which Daniel took a pull on and passed it round his men ensuring he got the flask back. This, and a rather handsome wristwatch, would make very nice trophies. He took a few letters from inside his tunic that he could hand over to the Intelligence Section and his forage cap and insignia, and then started to look around to see what their next move was to be.

As Daniel looked out of the window, he was nearly shot as waves of bullets hammered into the house from the Canadian lines. Obviously, their allies had not realised that all firing had ceased from this house. Daniel took Art's periscope and surveyed the scene outside. Down in the garden of this and the neighbouring house behind a solid stone wall were many more of Hauptmann Kline's troops and they were putting up a stoic resistance to all that the Canadians threw at them, there was also heavy resistance from the neighbouring house. Daniel left half his unit in the two rooms that they had just cleared and took Geordie with his Lewis and the others to clear the house next door. By the time he had left, it had become clear the Canadians had realised that the danger from this house had subsided as their attention now was directed much greater at the wall and house next door. With this in mind, Daniel took his few troops into this house; surely these Germans would not be as careless. Daniel, Tommo and Geordie moved around the opposite side of the houses to where all the action was happening. They used the cover of the hedgerows to navigate their way unseen until they were at the door into the second house. It appeared that the defensive position was similar to the first house, all the fire appeared to be from the opposite upper floor. He inched the door open only enough to see two sentries who this group had had the good sense to leave downstairs. However, with all the action happening at the other side of the house these two had all their concentration fixed in that direction which gave Daniel time to quickly dart inside the house and move behind a chair where he despatched the two foe with three shots from his Mauser pistol. He had actually only winged the first one so had to finish him off following the fatal shot to the second sentry. Unfortunately, this alerted another sentry who until then had been unseen at the top of the stairs, he took up position to shoot Daniel. He was obviously totally focussed on Daniel because his positioning left him in full view of Tommo, who squeezed off a couple of fatal shots. However, this was having a snowball effect because the more shots that were needed to deal with each German more Germans were responding. Two came to the door of the room where most of the noise had been coming from. They were cut down by a scything blanket of Lewis gunfire and, following this torrent of lead, ran Geordie screaming like a banshee, who on reaching the top of the stairs, let fly with everything the Lewis had into the now open room. Closely on his shoulder were Daniel and Tommo who, as they ran, prepared their Mills bombs for delivery of even more destruction and mayhem. In an adrenaline-fuelled moment it was all over and another cluster of Germans lay dead all around. They checked the rest of the house for further unwelcome guests and when satisfied that the house was clear and the hail of Canadian fire had started to be redirected on to the walled area they set up in the window facing the rear of the German defensive line behind the wall. Following Daniel's signal, a shrill blast on his whistle, two windows from both houses poured lethal fire down upon the unprotected rear of the enemy. There was nowhere for them to go. To their front the Canadians and to their rear the Auckland Pals, the fire was so frenetic that even if Fritz stood up to surrender he was shot down, for the few that tried to run the outcome was the same, death. No mercy was shown, the Hun had demonstrated with the release of the gas what they were capable of and, for that, it didn't even enter the heads of Daniel and the Auckland Pals that shooting fellow soldiers in the back was anything other than necessary. This was war, it was horrific and tragic but to survive it, you could not afford to have any sympathy for the enemy.

Grey-clad storm troopers of the 23rd Infantry Division, 1st Royal Saxon Corps lay around like dozens of broken puppets, a seething mass of mutilated, dead and dying. It was a sea of molten bodies, some still moving in their final death throes and finally the chorus of anguish and pain faded.

The Canadians from the line came forward and a runner despatched to deliver the intelligence to Battalion HQ. Their thanks and congratulations to the Auckland Pals were heartfelt and the Knaves' reputation had grown another chapter.

In the other sector, Henry's scout, Ronnie had identified that the bulk of the resistance were trying to force their way back through and around the village square by overpowering the Canadian machine gun detachments under Lance Corporal Fisher. They had taken a very heavy toll on the attackers who had been driven into a cluster of three houses that stood alone, facing across the square directly opposite the line of machine gun emplacements. This was just to the west of where Henry and his group had set off from, leaving Daniel's group to their own business. Henry used a different tactic to Daniel; with Canadian machine guns holding Fritz from the front he used his Lewis gun and any other firepower the group had at hand to seal the rear lane. He got Anders and Ronnie to fire their rifle grenades to smash through the buildings. A thunderstorm of number 23 Mills grenades destroyed the wooden houses and their incendiary effect left the houses as a blazing inferno. Fritz soon realised that they had a choice of either having their protection becoming their crematorium, facing the firepower that now surrounded them or surrender. It was a true testament to the courage, fighting spirit and mettle of these storm troopers, that not one took the option of surrender!

With the resistance in the village diminished to the odd pocket and communications with the French having arranged for their troops to enter from their flank to meet the Canadians entering from their side, the allies started to push the frontline back to the perimeter of the village. By evening, the allied counter attack had returned the front line almost to the starting point prior to the German gas attack.

Henry had got the whole section back together in the square where he delivered his debrief and listened intently to Daniel's own explanation of his section's action. The Pals started off for a requested meeting with Colonel Dupuis. They moved off in single file aware that the village was not completely clear, so they had one Lewis front and back with Tommo acting as scout up ahead. Cautiously, they moved down the Sint-Juliaanstraat towards the Battalion HQ within the Canadian lines. They were opposite a school building when a series of shots rang out; everyone took cover in the gardens of the adjacent houses with all firepower being brought to bear on the school. It wasn't until Daniel had got to cover, he looked back to see his old friend, Henry lying prone at the side of the road.

"Ray, Geordie, plenty of covering fire, keep those bastards' heads down," bawled Daniel as he hurdled the wall he was protected behind and ran towards his old mate. He could see he was moving as he approached.

"Get back Danny, I can take my chances here, there's no need for you to get it also," he knew he was wasting his breath, just has he knew if the roles had been reversed he would be doing the same.

"Sod off, Henry, you must be kidding if you think I would dare face Catherine after leaving you out here, when I promised her to look after you! Where are you hit?"

"It feels like my lower leg is on fire. I think it hit the floor before hitting me, I heard it before I felt it."

Daniel had hold of Henry under his arms and dragged him backwards towards the walled cover he had just left. The torrent of bullets from the Lewis guns peppered the school building which seemed to have made Fritz less interested in firing at Henry and Daniel. On reaching the wall, both were unceremoniously hauled over the wall like rag dolls by the others.

"Shit, Henry! Have you got a lead magnet in your pocket?" chuckled Ray when he realised that Henry wasn't too badly injured.

"It's very good of you Captain, stopping all the bullets for the rest of us, we'd better get you back so as you are good to go next time!" agreed Geordie in his sardonic Irish brogue.

Stretcher bearers had been close at hand following the end of the main fighting. They dressed Henry's wound as Daniel caught his breath, and a detachment of Canadian Infantry had taken up the fight by storming the school on behalf of the Auckland Pals whilst they had assisted with a withering covering fire. Unfortunately, this did not mean there were no further injuries incurred by the allies. Two of the Canadians were also hit, one shot through the neck and head, and he would have probably been dead before he hit the ground and the other shot in the shoulder, was sitting on the ground holding his own field dressing to the wound and pressed it against the pumping blood. The rest of his colleagues made their entry into the school using good old brute force of boot and shoulder. The building was cleared room by room and no prisoners emerged when the Canadians came out.

Henry was still giving orders from his stretcher ensuring his section followed him back to Battalion HQ to give his report to Colonel Dupuis. His report was concise and, considering the blood loss, very lucid. He also highlighted with the colonel the requirements for his section to be re-supplied, fed, watered and rested before being allowed to return to their own battalion. During this time, Daniel was by his side and it became clear to him that due to the previous wound and blood loss not having had time to repair and this latest injury, his friend was in a bad way and only grit and determination drove him on. That was until he had completed his report when he fell back on to the stretcher unconscious. Daniel surmised that these injuries were going to take quite some time to recover from. He asked the colonel if he could see to it that the Knaves' calling card along with the Hauptmann's cap and insignia was fired over into the opposing trench, just to let them know who had helped repulsed their attack and delivered the coup de grâce.

"It was what Henry would have wanted to do if he were here," explained Daniel.

Unsurprisingly, Geordie volunteered to go with Henry and ensure he got to the correct dressing station, somewhere where they knew of his previous injuries and where a certain nurse was waiting!

Daniel and the rest of the section gave Geordie a few coarse words of encouragement and made sure he knew to meet them at their normal battalion HQ the following day, and then they traversed the communication trenches back out of the network of excavations where they followed on to the kitchens and the Canadian quartermaster. The story of the Knaves had quickly spread throughout the battalion and even the quartermaster did not begrudge them all the supplies they asked for. There was a derelict barn nearby which only had a part roof in place and some mouldy old straw on the floor, but that night it felt very welcome to a cohort of weary soldiers from Co. Durham. Meanwhile, the battle for St Julien continued unabated with the Germans throwing wave after wave of further attacks at the line. On that morning, the Germans released another cloud of chlorine, towards the re-formed Canadian line just adjacent to St Julien. Yet again, word was passed among the Canadian troops to urinate on their handkerchiefs and place these over their noses and mouths. The counter-measures were insufficient and German troops took the village. Over the next days, the York and Durham Brigade units of the Northumberland Division counter-attacked, failed to secure their objectives but established a new line closer to the village. Later on in the month, the Northumberland Brigade attacked again and gained a foothold in the village but were forced back with the loss of close to two thousand casualties.

However, oblivious to what would unfold when they left Daniel led the Pals away the next morning following a hearty and now almost traditional breakfast of bacon, bread, jam and coffee. They set off back to their battalion HQ which, after a few detours, they found had been moved to a place called Oost Bellegoed which was on the Zonnebeek to Ypres road or Leperstraat. There they met Geordie who amazingly had had far less problems in finding the new HQ than the rest of the Pals had. Luxuriating in being centre of attention, he settled down as though he was about to spin one of his yarns. Henry had been treated initially by Dr Scrimger again, who had shipped him off to a hospital at Calais for a full assessment and treatment. However, he was very coy about his success with his nurse, Jane Holiway, but it was clear to all that he had had a very agreeable evening being the bodyguard for his captain!

It was now early May 1915 the to-ing and fro-ing of the German offensive was still going on and it was spreading across the Salient. Word had been received from Henry that he was okay and in the hospital in Calais but was out of action for the foreseeable future. Catherine had moved up from Château de Noyelles where she had remained with Marie and Marie had travelled too! Daniel had taken charge of the section and they had a few excursions into no-man's land to gather intelligence and had managed to bring back a prisoner. Lieutenant-Colonel Pickering had not requested a replacement for Henry because, as he had explained to Daniel, the success of the section was down to the closeness of the team and bringing a stranger in charge could damage that chemistry. However, having lost a couple of the unit, killed in action and with Henry convalescing the section needed to get a couple more recruits and where better to get them from than the rest of the Auckland Pals who they had not seen for some time. Daniel was tasked with taking his section for a week's rest into the rear and searching from the other Auckland Pals for a couple of replacements. Daniel already knew who he would want and, with written orders from the lieutenant-colonel, sent Ray off to have them transferred. The rest took transports back to an area just outside Calais called Merck where they had a very short journey into Calais, to make the most of their rest time and allow some short induction to the new members of the Knaves. Daniel couldn't believe his luck, not only could he see how his old friend was doing but he could meet his beloved Marie once again.

The section was billeted in a series of houses and, for the first time in many weeks, actually had beds to sleep on. They bathed and had their uniforms cleaned and pressed, the hot iron made short work of the lice eggs that their unwanted tenants laid in the seams of their clothes. It was like being reborn and the lads hit the town in style. Daniel on the other hand had other plans, but was surprised that Ray insisted in coming along to see Henry, promising to meet up with the others later and, if not, catching them the next morning at breakfast before training the new recruits started. Daniel had sent word to Marie, Catherine and Henry that he would be visiting the hospital and hopeful of a full reunion. He was anxious of the reply he would get. Of course he expected a positive response from Catherine and Henry, but how would Marie react? They had written several times to each other and each time they had conveyed their deep love for each other, but was that just Marie pitying a soldier at the front? This would be the acid test, that what they had experienced at Château de Noyelles, what seemed a lifetime ago, was still there. Daniel knew from his side it was stronger than ever, in fact not a day had gone past without him thinking of his beloved Marie. Daniel had faced bloody death on many occasions and had comrades killed in front of him but the thought of Marie not reciprocating his feelings truly filled him with dread. A fate worse than death.

Ray and Daniel were walking down Hospital Lane, all the way from where the transport had dropped them off nearly a half a mile away. Daniel had been quietly dwelling on his insecurity.

"What's up with you?" quizzed Ray, "You haven't said a word all morning and I can see the tension in your shoulders and your walk, you're like a cat on a hot tin roof!"

Daniel couldn't hold back his doubts any longer; he needed a release, so the pressure in his head and heart could be relieved. He stopped, turned to Ray, gripping his upper arms and looking into Ray's eyes with almost maddening panic.

"What if she isn't there? What if she has just been humouring her soldier friend on the front? What if she doesn't feel the way I do?" It flowed like a gush of water out of a hose that had been held back by someone's thumb.

There was a moment's silence whilst Ray took on board his friend's dilemma and he simply said, "Why would she? You had a very special time together; she has sent you loads of letters when she didn't have to, she wouldn't have if she wasn't smitten with you. Christ almighty, Danny, pull yourself together before you see her or you will scare her off with those wild eyes. You damn near frightened me there!"

There was a further pause and he added with a hint of Ray-style humour, "Besides you're a good looking fellow and if I was a woman I would fancy you." With that, he released his arm from Daniel's grip and gave him a friendly light punch on the arm, "Come on, we don't want to keep anybody waiting."

It allowed Daniel just a little reprieve from his self-doubt and they entered the hospital. They were expecting to go to the reception to find out where the patient could be found. But as they entered through the main doors there was a high pitched, excited voice shouting, "Daniel!"

In a flash, Marie was in his arms and kissing him, without any concern for onlookers, she cried, "I've missed you so much and been worried sick every night when I think of you."

Ray moved off and whispered discreetly, "Aye, she looks like she's not so bothered about you!" With that he went to see the matron to find his way to Henry, it was obvious those two would be some time!

Marie was crying with joy at being in Daniel's arms once again and explained how she had been having such doubts that he would not want to see her again and that his letters were only designed to humour a silly girl, that his invite to meet was only politeness due to Catherine staying with her.

They made their way outside where a bench seat was positioned at the side of the entrance. Daniel was laughing and, as he did, the tears welled up in his eyes and proceeded to tell her about his doubts and even the little panic attack he had just had that required Ray to snap him out of it.

"Where is Ray?" he asked looking around, "I must introduce you" and as he said the words he knew good old Ray had made himself scarce to allow them time to themselves, what a good mate!

"I think your friend is giving us time to reintroduce ourselves," whispered Marie as she gently placed her hands around Daniel's head, pulling him towards her and kissing him deeply and passionately.

Although rather self-conscious of the surroundings, Daniel was powerless to object, not that he really wanted to. He had waited and dreamed of this for so long, he was not going to allow the British stiff upper lip to get in the way, besides, when in France!

Eventually, they got up and started making their way down the corridor to ward seven where Marie had left Catherine and Henry. Stood there at Henry's side was Ray eating grapes by the handful.

"See you found the food then?" he smiled as he looked around.

"I was going to stop and help you but I guessed you had that battle covered!"

Daniel was back to his confident best and was beaming with pride with Marie on his arm, he moved around the bed to greet Catherine and at the same time saw that Annette was there.

"Annette, it's great to see you again," said Daniel moving over to greet her and set about introducing Ray to the three ladies.

Marie explained that Annette had joined them in Calais as they had taken lodgings for the duration of Henry's convalescence and, with Henry allowed to leave the hospital for short spells, that she expected everybody to dine at the house in Rue Mollien where there was more than sufficient room for all to stop the night, including Ray if he didn't have anything else planned?

Ray was a little taken aback by this very generous offer but also remembered his promise to the lads.

Before he had time to answer, Daniel had guessed his plight and answered, "Of course he would, he did promise once he accompanied me to see Henry he would meet up with the lads and keep them right for the training. We need to start with our new recruits tomorrow, but let's face it Ray, you will never find them now and if we don't make an early start tomorrow there's nothing hurting, besides our commanding officer is with us!"

"Quite so!" agreed Henry, "And who are these new starters?"

Daniel looked at the still pale face of his old friend and held out his hand, "It's great to see you in good spirits, how's the paper cuts doing?!"

"They would have been a lot worse if you hadn't got me out of there," he replied and turning to his audience, continued by adding, "not once but twice in a matter of days! It's strange how things happen; a second generation when a Byrne has dragged a Neville's backside to safety!"

"I just couldn't face the paperwork or Catherine for that matter!" joked Daniel.

"Yes and you actually did say that you wouldn't want to face Catherine if you left me, when you dragged my sorry backside behind that wall in St Julien. Most of that was a blur, but I distinctly remember that and being dragged unceremoniously over the wall by this lot," he pointed at Ray.

"Not me Captain, I had the Lewis trained on that school keeping Fritz's head down, I would have treated you with a lot more respect, sir," Ray mocked coming to attention as if delivering a report.

As they all laughed, Catherine added, "Well I am glad you did, and it proved one thing that Henry said a long time ago; if he had to face the Hun then he wanted his Pals beside him! And thank God he did," with tears in her eyes she kissed both Daniel and Ray in turn.

"Come on," boomed Henry, "get me that damned chair contraption and let's get out of here, this is reason to celebrate not to worry over what might have been."

With that, Daniel looked at the wheelchair at the side of the bed and a horrible thought crossed his mind. Was his friend crippled and in need of this for good?

As had happened countless times over the years, Henry saw the look on Daniel's face and read his thoughts. "Relax Danny, it's only while I regain my strength, I'm okay over short distances but I'm still getting tired after longer walks, so if we hope to get anywhere today I need this," he pointed at the wheelchair that Catherine was positioning for him, "It'll only be a few more weeks and I will be back and be able to run rings round you, just like I could on the football field!"

With that the captain, sergeant and the corporal with three ladies took to the spring sunshine for a stroll through the streets of Calais to the Rue Mollien. Number 56 was the end of a row of town houses that looked over the Quai de l'Yser with a small area of parkland at the rear. Once inside, there was no distant battle noise, so they could leave the war behind in their memories, albeit for a short time.

Annette had arranged the rooms and apologised to Ray that he had to sleep in the spare room at the rear of the ground floor where she had made up a bed. She was stopping on the first floor in the room next to Catherine and

Henry in case they needed help with Henry during the night. This was a totally trumped up excuse for allowing Marie and Daniel the second floor to themselves. Henry and Catherine had been afforded that freedom on the previous times when he had been allowed to stop out of the hospital. But the hostess wanted her reunion with her man to be as perfect as possible and everybody else was more than willing to ensure that happened.

The men sat in the parlour and started to drink Daniel's favourite red wine, he didn't know enough about it to know which red wine was which he just knew he liked it! The ladies in the absence of staff started to prepare the evening's food under Annette's guidance.

"So you never did say who you had got as new starters, who are they?" questioned Henry when they were all settled with wine in one hand and cigar in the other.

Daniel and Ray went on to explain that the rest of the Auckland Pals had been moved to a tunnelling battalion. Following their basic training and a few weeks in the lines, they had been drafted underground where they were digging a different type of mine shaft, one that went out under the enemy trenches and was then filled with explosives that were to give Fritz a rude wake-up call prior to allied attacks. It was not what Henry had envisaged for any of the Pals but at least they were together. However, the thought of fighting a war underground did put a chill down Henry's back.

"By, they must have balls of steel for that job," he said admiringly.

"You remember young Des Douthwaite and Johnny Wilks who we were trying to get to leave Bishop Auckland Football Club to play for us? Well, we finally got them to join us, but not exactly on the same type of field as we wanted!"

"Aye," added Ray, "Smart thinkers and quick learners, they need to get above ground before they start seeing in the dark and nothing in daylight like to old timers from the pit. Besides, they never worked down the pit, they both worked as apprentice gillies on your neighbour's estate. A pair of fearless buggers them two!"

Henry put down his wine and suddenly became serious, "Due to our success, the Intelligence Section want to set up another team like the Knaves, they have tasked me to do this and then run both teams."

Daniel butted in with a question he worked out the answer to before he had finished his own question, "But how can you run two sections ...?"

Henry nodded his head recognising Daniel had realised he was not coming back to lead the Knaves and would be running both teams from a distance, he added, "I am going to mend almost totally from these injuries, but let's say, my footballing days are behind me! HQ has told me in no uncertain terms that I will not be going back out as a section leader and I am to hand the running of the Knaves to you Daniel. Of this moment, I am to offer you a field promotion to captain, in turn you are to promote down through the ranks to re-establish you section. Me, for my sins, I have got, near as damn it, a staff job at the rank of lieutenant-colonel. God help Fritz with two sections like the Knaves hunting them".

Daniel couldn't believe what he had just heard. He had gone from recruit soldier to captain in the blink of an eye. It was obviously, largely the doing of Henry, but none the less still remarkable.

"Are we that short of NCOs, Henry?" questioned Daniel.

"We certainly are in our field of work; we are the only ones! That is until I get this other unit up and running and I can't even start that until I recover a little more strength.

Besides, the way you have carried yourself with and without me in the section you are a natural, you have a natural talent and a logical mind that Eton and, to some degree, even Sandhurst seems to ignore as part of intellect!"

There was silence in the room for several moments when Ray slapped his thighs jumped to his feet and laughed, "Well that calls for a drink!" he charged their glasses raised his in salute to his newly promoted friends and with a, "cheers and congratulations" drained the near full glass of wine.

"Cheers and congratulations to you Sergeant Murray," answered Daniel with a smile, waiting to see the slow recognition dawn on Ray's face. The realisation was evident as the beam on his face got wider.

Ray dropped back into the chair and the smile was overtaken by a look of wonderment; very humbly Ray turned to Daniel, "Thanks Danny, I can't believe what has happened to me over the last months, who would have thought Ray Murray would have ever amounted to anything? And I owe it all to you."

"No Ray, it was all your own doing all you have got is exactly what you deserve and what you earned, well done mate," and Daniel shook his hand.

"Ray, when Daniel told me he wanted you as his corporal I had serious doubts, but I trusted his judgement and I can honestly say I have never made a better decision, many congratulations," added Henry.

"Coq au Vin, is simmering and will be ready in an hour or so gentlemen, I suggest you make good use of the time to make yourselves more presentable for dinner," was the none so subtle hint from Catherine and with that she disappeared upstairs.

"Well gentlemen," Henry emphasised the gentlemen with exaggerated pronunciation, "seems we have been put in our place, I know when I have been given an order and I for one am not brave enough to ignore it!" with that he followed Catherine.

Daniel got up and walked into the kitchen looking for Marie, but not finding her he headed upstairs to get ready, as ordered. He entered their room to find a roaring fire lit, in front of it was an enamel bath full of soap suds and Marie! "Daniel I've been waiting for you, I've been in here for such a long time I've gone all wrinkly."

Daniel didn't have a chance to think of an answer or even to question Marie as to how long she had been in. When she stood up displaying her immaculate, slightly golden body. Daniel couldn't imagine that anything on earth could be closer to perfection.

"It's your turn," she said stepping out of the bath, "come over here and I will undress you and wash the horrors of the war off you," she purred whilst beckoning him with her finger.

As his uniform hit the ground the weight of the war receded and his heart rate started to increase as it had so many times during battle, but this was for a totally different reason. He sat back in the bath. She saw the bruises, cuts and grazes across his whole body; Marie washed him slowly, softly with scented soap, soft sponge and her gentle hands. Just below the water line she found how excited he was to be with her again.

She smiled, "Well I am pleased that you have missed me," she tormented. Slowly she lowered her head and kissed him with the kind of passion that took his breath away, her tongue brushing over his. He responded and her hand went below the water line once again, with two gentle strokes she followed his manhood to its tip and whispered in his ear, "This is going to have to wait until tonight my darling, the others are going to be waiting," with that Marie stood up and walked towards the bed where she stood facing Daniel and dried herself off in front of him in a particularly provocative way.

Daniel shook his head standing to get out of the bath and reaching for the towel resting on the stand next to the fire. His excitement was clear to see and Marie smiled at her achievement. With the towel across his shoulders he walked towards her.

"You are the very devil of a tease Marie de Créquy, but I would not have it any other way." She got up off the bed and they stood, naked, embraced and he whispered in her ear, "And I will love you 'til the end of time."

When they got down to the dining room the others were politely making conversation and did not stop when Marie and Daniel entered, this Daniel knew was designed not to make it obvious that they had been waiting for some considerable time. Henry pretended that he had just noticed they were there and congratulated Daniel for scrubbing up well!

"Mademoiselle de Créquy, Champagne?" Henry enquired.

"Oui, s'il-vous-plaît," she replied with a small curtsey.

Ray handed Daniel his red wine, "Here you go Danny, 'fraid you just get me and a good old Durham accent, not some fancy lingo!"

"You'll do for me mate," answered Daniel with a wink.

It was Ray's idea that the men should serve the ladies seeing as how they had made the meal, that was with the slightly inconvenienced Henry excused the main task and whose job it was decided, was to keep the ladies' glasses filled. Daniel was very pleased and surprised that Ray had come up with such a very good idea and commented on his friend's domesticity when they were bringing the food to the table.

"I've been known to have my moments," was his answer.

The meal was so superior to anything Daniel and Ray had eaten in such a long time. They complimented every bite they took and the evening passed off with pleasant small talk, all ensuring the war was never mentioned. The ladies even tried to show interest when the subject of football was brought up rather than risk spoiling the friendly, comfortable atmosphere that prevailed. After the meal, Henry and Catherine retired early with Henry looking rather drawn and tired. Marie and Daniel excused themselves and went for a walk along the Quai de l'Yser, a stretch of water that ran through the town into the harbour and bordered the small park at the rear of the property. It was a warm evening for early May with a cloudless night, looking out across the English Channel the stars were at their magisterial best, like thousands of diamonds twinkling in a celestial tiara. Unfortunately, looking in the opposite direction and accompanied with a demonic booming was the light display of the Western Front. The couple did their best to ignore this intrusion into their time and space and talked of the château, the farm with Annette's parents. Marie wanted to know about Daniel's parents and what he had told them about her.

After a short while the competing bombardments started to impinge a little too much and with a slight shiver Marie asked, "Is it as truly dreadful as it seems when all that is falling around you?" there was the obvious nervous concern of somebody who had lost loved ones and still had another love in harm's way.

"I wouldn't really know," lied Daniel, "with the special sort of work we do we don't get amongst it very often, it's the Poor Bloody Infantry that get it," and he explained how in the army they had shortened this name to PBI, he further had to explain that it was English humour.

However, with the magic of the evening losing ground to the ill noise of the war they retreated back to the house where they found the table cleared and nobody around so they ascended the two flights of stairs to what they both had been longing for since that last evening at Château de Noyelles.

Daniel sat on the end of the bed and Marie climbed on to the bed behind him and started to massage his shoulders and back. She helped him off with his shirt and continued the massage, again she traced her hands across all the scars and imperfections of war that to Marie made this man all the more appealing and desirable if that could be possible. Moving her hands down his back and around to his chest he turned to face her, gone was the mischievous tormenting look of before, the desire of a woman longing to be loved by her man was plain to see and Daniel had no thoughts of disappointing her. He unbuttoned her blouse and eased it off her shoulders, leaving a matching small black choker with a small diamond at the front around her neck and lacy bra. He stroked his hands across her breasts feeling her hard nipples beneath the delicate lace; she gasped and tensed with anticipation as though an electric shock had just charged her body. Bending forward slightly, he reached round and unclipped her bra which fell forwards and down her arms on to the bed. Tenderly stroking her shoulders, he traced his tongue down from the underside of the choker, across her shoulder and down on to the tip of one of her nipples then across to the other. She sighed slow and deeply pulling him down on top of her as she lay back.

It was 6.00 a.m. when Daniel awoke as fresh as he could remember; it was if his spirit had been reborn. He thought back to the night and looked across to Marie, the reason for his revitalised state; their first bout of love making had started off wild and frenetic but by the early hours it had grown slow, gentle and beautiful. How could he feel so full of life when he could only have had a couple of hours' sleep? Obviously, thought Daniel it has to be the quality of that sleep with Marie in his arms. She was still fast asleep so he gathered his uniform and tiptoed on to the landing closing the bedroom door quietly behind him. He dressed and descended the stairs in bounds, entering the kitchen on the hunt for some breakfast. He almost ran into Annette who was taking coffee to the table where Ray sat tucking into cheese, cold meats and bread.

"What no bully? I am disappointed!" laughed Daniel.

"Oh this will do for me," beamed Ray looking at Annette. "You needn't come over to the training ground if you'd rather stay here you know Danny?" offered Ray, knowing his new captain would never hear of such a thing.

"Sergeant Murray," he replied in mock sternness, "it is not that I do not have complete faith in your ability but it is not fitting for me, as section commander not to be there on the new lads' first day of training. Besides, I should be the one to tell the lads about Henry's new role and we have to think who is to be our new corporal, I must confess, with having such a night, I haven't given it much thought, have you?"

"Funny you should say that I have only just got round to thinking about it myself," again looking at Annette as she placed some jam and croissants on the table.

"Well then, while we tuck into this we better get thinking!"

"Do you think we need to think that hard? As much as Geordie is a character and Tommo is fearless, Art is all that and so much more. Not only can he sketch the battlefield but he has a canny knack for seeing that sketch as a battlefield and pointing out features to exploit, in that respect within the section I think he is second only to you. When you or I are not there he naturally takes up the mantle of father figure and the others expect and look for it."

"A case well-made and yes you are right, that's who I would have chosen. However, he needs to want to do it and if he says yes, who takes up his role of unofficial leader in our absence. We need to start grooming someone ready to step forward, remember next time out either one of us could cop a packet!"

As Daniel had finished, he realised that Annette was still in the room and although her English was nowhere near as good as Marie's, she had understood enough to grasp what had been said. She turned and ran from the room.

"Bugger!" Daniel cursed, "I didn't realise Annette was still there, she's bound to tell Marie and I was trying to down play what we were doing!"

Ray was already getting up from the table and wiping the napkin across his mouth, which in a weird way, considering the circumstances, Daniel saw as unusual, it was only a few months ago the Ray would have thought a napkin was for getting coal dust from up your nose!

However he did and said, "Danny, leave this to me and I'll see you out front, say, in fifteen minutes."

With that he followed the route Annette had taken.

"Yes, er Ray that's fine, see you in fifteen," his voice trailed off thinking what a strange way for Annette to react and how Ray had, as had become the norm, come to his rescue.

They were in a taxi that Henry had arranged and travelling back to meet up with the lads at Merck and discussed how the training was to be conducted. Daniel, now in charge of the section, was not going to be able to carry out the section role as sharpshooter and he saw this as a major shortcoming of the section. They had machine guns, grenade rifles, bombers and signallers but a couple of sharpshooting snipers could give long distance hits as well as long distance intelligence reports. He had had this discussion many times with Henry and, to Henry's credit, now Daniel was running the section he had let the decision rest with him.

Henry had spoken to an acquaintance, a Major Hesketh-Prichard who wanted to set up a sniper school and was developing a number of sniping techniques, including spotting scopes, working in pairs and developing observational skills. Using the current British Pattern 1914 Enfield rifle with "acquired" German telescopic sights, he wanted to experiment with some students to prove his point to the top brass that this was worth pursuing.

The idea was that the two new starters with their experience of stalking would make fine stealthy trackers who should have as good grounding in field craft as Daniel, hopefully just as good at shooting as well. With that as a starting point, the major would make them into snipers in a short time. Basically, he had to. They would be returning to the front within a week's time!

They arrived back at Merck at 8.30 a.m. and Ray set about rounding everybody up. At 9.00 a.m. they were all present and accounted for and Daniel was spelling out the changes that Henry had informed him and Ray of the previous day. Art was flabbergasted to say the least to be asked to take the corporal stripe but did so with pride and a large helping of sarcastic humour from the others. It seemed to be universally agreed he was the man for the job and time would tell if there was somebody who would shine as any potential future NCO. At 10.30 a.m. Major Hesketh-Prichard arrived and set about his task with gusto. He had a passion for his plans and this was his experimental team, so he took Des and Johnny under his wing, starting with the whole section down to the shooting range on the sand dunes just north-west of Merck. He boldly stated that he believed that, despite the sophistication of the weaponry, they were not a substitute for the training, dedication and marksmanship of the sniper. It was not long after lunchtime when it was obvious that there were four people who stood out from the rest: Major Hesketh-Prichard himself, Daniel, Des and Johnny.

Major Hesketh-Prichard took his new charges away for a condensed training period with a promise to have them back within five days on the understanding that for every period in the rear trenches he got more time with his disciples. The rest of the section took their tasks from Ray to re-supply, mend and improve everything from their camouflage suits (two extra had to be made for Des and Johnny) to more timer units for their improvised delayed explosives.

It was mid-afternoon when Daniel turned to Ray and asked what he had planned for the coming evening.

"Well, actually I have been given my orders by Annette," said Ray a little bit sheepish, "I am to meet her at 4.00 p.m. at the market alongside the Les Bourgeois de Calais, which is apparently," he said looking at a slip of paper, "at Place du Soldat Inconnu," he said in his best French/Durham accent, "where I am to help her with shopping for tonight's meal."

"Oh, well then, we'd better travel back together and you can keep the taxi once he has dropped me off ..." For the second time that day, his sentence trailed off as he thought that Ray, shopping at a French market, was very strange.

Daniel arrived back at Rue Mollien at a little after 3.45 p.m. and found Marie sat in the small garden that at that time of the afternoon was quite the sun trap. Marie explained that Catherine and Henry had gone back to the hospital for Henry to have a check-up and were expecting to be back by 5.30 p.m. and Annette was shopping. Daniel was keen to show his domestic knowledge by commenting on Ray going to the market to join her and expressed his amazement at him doing such a thing and mentioned their strange behaviour at the breakfast table, but was careful not to mention what Annette had overheard. Then, he was equally surprised when Marie burst out laughing at the fact that he had not realised what had happened between the two!

"Well!" said Daniel most indignantly, "I don't think that's very correct, on the first night they met?"

"Daniel Byrne!" reproached Marie, she shook her head and smiled, "and just how different was that to our meeting and falling in love?"

Daniel was silent, sat down and nodded, smiled and quietly said, "The old devil, he's a dark horse that one."

He then spent the next ten minutes explaining what he meant, for all Marie's English was excellent, she had a lot to learn about the slang used by everyday folk in England.

"You must be understanding when Ray explains this to you. Annette says he was very worried about what you would say when you found out. I knew Annette would like him the minute I saw him, the likeness between Ray and her ex-husband is remarkable."

"Bloody hell, you mean there was another like him?" Daniel exclaimed in mock disbelief, and got a friendly slap on the arm from Marie for his trouble.

Marie brought Daniel a glass of wine which he had heard others talk about but had never tasted, having become quite the red wine aficionado. It was a pinkish colour and, served chilled, was very refreshing, exactly what the doctor ordered on this warm spring afternoon. He made a mental note: rosé wine could also become a favourite in these circumstances. Following soaking up a little sun and some small talk that could only be of interest to a young couple in love, they planned their future as they went for a walk along the beach which was a short distance from the house. They did not see Annette and Ray although they walked past the market and spent the rest of the afternoon enjoying having nobody else to share themselves with. Daniel decided that this was how he wanted to spend each afternoon after finishing with the section's training. At that moment his feeling of tranquillity was disturbed by the spectre of his return to the front, but managed to push it to the back of his mind.

They returned a little after 5.00 p.m. to find the house company present and correct and the evening followed a similar pattern to the previous. The only real difference was Ray's very awkward attempt to explain to Daniel that there was "something going on," between Annette and himself.

After the first few stumbling moments, Daniel had decided to put him out of his misery, allaying his fears, by pretending he had been aware of it all along, "Ray, don't worry it was plain to see right from the start and I have absolutely no objections unless your intentions are not totally honourable? After all, she is Marie's close friend."

"Don't worry about that Danny I never thought I would ever get such a catch, what on earth do you think she sees in me?"

This was too easy an opportunity for Daniel not to have a dig at his mate, so said jokingly, "Beats me, I never realised how blind she was until she fell for you!"

With that, he raised his glass and saluted his friend. "Good luck and the best of health to the pair of you."

"Cheers Danny!" Ray's relief was easy to see as a huge wave of relaxation rolled across his face and shoulders. Henry who was sitting down added his congratulations.

"If any more of you West lads get fixed up over here we will be taking over the country far easier than Fritz is finding it," with that he also raised his glass in Ray's direction.

Daniel immediately sought out Annette, approaching her with his biggest smile to ensure she understood he was pleased by the news.

He gave her a hug and added, "*Félicitations, je vous souhaite tout le meilleur ensemble.*"

He was not exactly sure of the accuracy of his sentence but Annette's reaction and Marie's smiling face suggested that he wasn't too far off with his best wishes.

The training was broken up into specific days that finished mid-afternoon and covered training in specific areas on each day: shooting had been worked on, bombing, stealth/stalking moves, tactical withdrawals and hand to hand combat. The final day was stand down and the two new members of the Knaves rejoined them with their rather impressive rifles fitted with the German sights. On seeing these weapons, Daniel was envious and had to have a go down at the range; he did not disgrace himself but, in front of an interested section, came third in a shootout of three. Des and Johnny had been good to start with but had improved immeasurably over just a few days. They actually worked as a pair with each taking turns on the rifle while the other acted as the spotter with binoculars.

On the domestic front, there was also a familiar pattern with Daniel sticking to his word and getting back to Rue Mollien at a little after 3.45 p.m. each day, taking his afternoon glass of rosé wine and then, arm in arm with Marie, they attended the cinema to see a double bill of Charlie Chaplin, *Her Friend the Bandit* and *Mabel's Married Life* was a big crowd puller at the Excelsior, had a picnic on the dunes, took a bicycle ride along the promenade on two bicycles borrowed from the transport pool, but the most significant was the trip to Église Notre-Dame ("The Church of Our Lady") a Roman Catholic parish church located on Rue de la Paix. It was of splendid Tudor architecture, its origins dated from the 12th century, but chiefly from the 14th century.

Whilst sitting in the grounds after seeing the majesty of the interior, Marie had asked the faltering question "If you were to marry anybody of your choosing, where would you like it to be?"

Daniel had replied without hesitation not knowing if she had in a roundabout way actually proposed to him, "It would not matter where it was so long as it was to you, my love."

With that, Marie had thrown her arms around his neck kissed him and whispered, "I love you," and received the response she had hoped for, "and I love you with all my heart."

"I would like us to be married in Abbeville at St Vulfran Collegiate Church where all my family historically have been married."

It was obvious to Daniel that Marie had thought this through and although this pleased him beyond belief and said so he added, "However we really ought to wait for the end of the war, I just want this out of the way and everybody to survive it before making too many long-term plans."

This was the first time Daniel had ever sounded negative about the outcome of the war in front of Marie and the expression on her face told him that, although she knew it was bad, she really didn't know how bad and she certainly did not realise just what a lottery living and dying at the front was. He was determined that whilst ever he had breath to fight with he would not allow her to find out.

To put a happier note back to the occasion he said, "I think we should be married within a year of the war's end and that will give us time for you to come to England and meet my parents."

This more positive addition to the plans brought the smile back to Marie's face and she went on to say that she could go to England soon as Catherine was going back for a short spell.

This was the first Daniel had heard of this and somehow the thought of her being away in England seemed as though she was leaving him and struck at his heart a little. He knew it was stupid because his next leave away from the front would be weeks, maybe months, away.

Marie had read his feelings and reassured him, as she squeezed his hand, "I will only be a few weeks and Catherine and Henry are planning on going back as soon as your leave is over. We will stay with Catherine's family for a while before going up to Henry's and, with your permission, I would call on your family, I do so long to meet them."

"Well, I think there would be trouble if you didn't, my mother would never forgive me if I didn't insist on it. But I must warn you that our small house is nothing to compare to what you are used to."

"My darling Daniel, your parents will soon be my parents and their house was built on hard toil and love, it is no less a loving home than any castle or château, I will love it!"

He drew her into his embrace and vowed to write to them that night to tell them to expect the visit.

The final night's meal was a little sombre with all round the table trying unsuccessfully to put tomorrow out of their heads. The whole house was up for the farewell at 7.00 a.m., the more private farewells having been made in the privacy of their rooms. With tears all round they parted with promises to write whenever possible. It was several minutes before Daniel broke the silence as they travelled the well-worn route back to Merck.

"It shouldn't be too long before we get our next leave and the next one could be our proper leave not just time away to re-group and train, it'll be the big two-weeker!"

"That's if we make it that long!"

"Hey, stop that right now, we need to switch on and focus. The way we can make sure we do make it is ensuring we do our jobs and the section does theirs, the rest ... well, that's in the lap of the Gods of War. We can't feel sorry for ourselves, after all we have both got something or more precisely someone to fight for, remember that!"

Ray lifted his head, took a deep breath, looked Daniel in the eyes and nodded, "Yes you're right, I have so much more to live for than I did one week ago, I'll fight the very devil himself if I have to."

"That's the spirit Ray; we'll see this bastard war out!"

They did not have transport to take them back to the front so a long march was the order of the day. This did allow plenty of time for the usual banter, most of it directed at Sergeant Murray and his news about Annette and of course, Des and Johnny just because they were the new boys and that's what the new boys got. At first they marched on good roads with green fields with deep red and purple poppies gently dancing in the wind. In the wild meadows they saw blue and white cornflowers and there was a smell of camomile on the wind. The small village of Looberghe where they stopped on the first night and got their orders was in an area that was still almost untouched by the war with its pretty village square that they accessed over the Canal de la Colme. The population were welcoming and provided billets for all without hesitation. The following day Daniel followed his orders and marched the section to Bollezeele where they picked up their transport which took them to Poperinge which was a totally different scene altogether. They spent a night huddling in whatever cover they could find and received their new orders from Battalion HQ. The morning of 15 May 1915 saw the section strike out for their HQ at Bellewaerde, their route took them through Ypres itself.

Ypres had taken even more pummelling during the Battle of Frezenberg Ridge when the Germans had seen via aerial reconnaissance that the allied support lines were coming straight through the debris field that was Ypres. Their long range artillery hit the town hard with devastating effect. *The* Battle of Frezenberg Ridge started on the 8 May and carried on until the 13 May. The Germans moved field artillery forward and put three army corps opposite the 27th and 28th divisions on Frezenberg Ridge. The German attack began on 8 May, with a bombardment on the trenches on the forward slope of the ridge but the first and second assaults by German infantry were repelled by the survivors. The third German assault of the morning pushed the defenders back. The Germans were prevented from advancing further by counter-attacks and a night move by the 10th Brigade.

As they came out of Ypres, amazingly unscathed and headed for Bellewaerde, via "Hellfire Corner" the not-too-distant guns growled and got louder with every foot fall. They marched on across this Flanders morass where mud, dead and living became one and the same; the dead would not stay buried and kept reappearing as their bloated corpses filled with the gases of decay or overturned by explosions. You could not say that the poor sods in these surroundings were living, merely existing and the mud of Flanders engulfed or encapsulated everything. They followed the Menenstraat and turned off on to the Bellewaerdestraat picking up the first communications trench at the junction of the two roads. They walked close to the church whose crooked obelisk-like spire was hit at the very top by an exploding shell creating the effect of a giant dandelion that had gone to seed in a strong wind; the rest of the spire afterwards was left with a distinct list! Shells were busting every second all around; it was dizzying with the percussion abusing the eardrums upsetting the equilibrium. And then, sudden quiet; more to come? Nothing; a reprieve, a relief.

"Welcome to Bellewaerde," whispered Ray into Daniel's ears.

"Cheers, let's see if we can find Battalion HQ in this mire and then a little shelter before this all kicks off again."

After several wrong turns and a couple of about faces they finally found an old German bunker known as Fritz's Redoubt, which was being used as Battalion HQ. Lieutenant-Colonel Pickering was delighted to see Daniel and congratulated him and Ray on their promotions.

"We are having the very devil of a job with Fritz in this area. We know they are building for a bit of a do! But damn it if they don't almost every day send a bombing party of nearly thirty down over and hit us with what seems to be almost impunity. They seem to retire back towards the old communications trench. They also have two very handily placed machine guns that the chaps have christened, Mighty Kraut and Flailing Fritz. Whenever we have sent raids of our own they have put paid to them, we must have lost over fifty men by now. These raiders have managed to take three prisoners over the last week, when what we need more than anything is a few of our own to find out what this big bash is going to be about. Sorry to throw you straight back in the thick of it, but I need you to get up to speed with the lie of the land, plan how you can stop the raids and get these machine guns, every time our artillery set about them they just disappear underground and reappear when our bombardment is over."

"Well I am pleased you have missed us sir," replied Daniel smiling and asked if there was anywhere the section could set up their base so they could get some rest and start their planning the coming morning.

Lieutenant-Colonel Pickering's orderly took Ray to the dugout allocated for them in the support trench while

Pickering himself walked the front trench with Daniel showing him the ground as well as giving him a briefing of all that had gone on over the week they had been away. According to Pickering they had only just held on following the Frezenberg Ridge affair and if this was anything like that then they would be pushed to the very limit and that was why they needed intelligence on Fritz's intentions.

The weather had taken a change and the temperature had dropped and a sharp frost had been on the ground each of the last few days, which was a little unseasonal to say the least, but at least it was better under foot. Daniel had a word with a few of the front line veterans about their knowledge of the area, topographical understanding was key to planning any ambush, even if you are only stalking deer, but on this occasion the adversary would be a whole lot more deadly and were not likely to turn and run when confronted. He sent for Ray, Art and Des. Placing Ray in charge in his absence, he tasked Art to sketch the layout including the old communication trench with a special interest in a couple of old dugouts that the old hands had said still remained. Daniel explained that he and Des would use a listening sap to get out in towards the old trench and, as dusk was falling, traverse from shell hole to shell hole to gain the relative security of the trench which had, over the months since it was last in use, been severely damaged.

Ray didn't like the idea of his captain going out and risking his neck saying, "Danny, I know somebody needs to go out to have a look round but I'm your sergeant, it should be me, not you, going."

Daniel appreciated his wanting to protect his captain, however pointed out that it was he who had to come up with the plan, plus he and Des had their stalking and tracking experience and would be far better at moving around in no-man's land than somebody of Ray's size and lack of stealth!

"I don't want to put too fine a point on it Ray, but out there you would look like a grazing bull rather than going unseen!"

"Well that's a fine thing to say, I thought I had been losing weight," he responded with a resigned smile.

"Well yes you have," answered Daniel whilst patting him on his upper arm, "maybe I was a little harsh calling you a bull, you've trimmed down to a bull calf!"

"Charming."

"Ray, thanks anyway, just make sure you are here when we return after dark. I don't want any of these jumpy buggers, blowing my head off."

After discussing his immediate plans with Pickering and letting Des into his plans, the two slipped out up the sap with just a couple of pistols and Mills bombs between them, no packs, just their camouflage suits. It was 6.00 p.m. when they started their traverse across to the trench. Three shell holes linked the sap to the trench with only slight areas of ground where they exposed themselves. Just like when stalking, by moving slowly and smoothly, avoiding sudden movements at these times they did not bring their presence to Fritz's attention. It took nearly an hour to move the thirty yards required but they achieved it without incident. That is if you considered the continuous, random shelling and sporadic gunfire as without incident. The trench had lost the sharp edges of a newly built trench and all the parapet sandbags had been blown to hell, but by remaining on their hands and knees they were totally blind to both sides. There were clear signs of recent similar movement, hand, knee and toe prints, sliding marks of rough cloth in the mud told the story of how Fritz had been getting so close to the allied frontline. They clearly saw where they had left and returned to the trench, depending on the target they had been set. They got to a point where they were no more than twenty yards from the German front line trench and found the second of the two dugouts described by the troops, the first being not long after entering the trench. This second dugout was after the first jumping off point that Fritz had used. They continued and the trench seemed to follow a line back to the actual German trench, suggesting this might have been done deliberately by Fritz to give the raiding parties easy access into no-man's land. As they neared the enemy front line, Daniel could see one of the machine gun posts. Retracing their steps, they actually checked in greater detail into the dugouts, on the way out they had just ensured that they were empty before moving beyond them. They found boxes of German stick grenades that obviously the raiders equipped themselves with on the way out towards the allied lines. These were all in the dugout furthest from the German lines thus cutting down the distance they had to carry the rather cumbersome grenades. It was, by now, completely dark and the return journey to the safety and "comfort" of their battalion trench was only interrupted by non-specific, general machine gun and artillery fire that was the background noise of life at the front. On their approach, Daniel heard the bolt of a Lee Enfield rifle slide a bullet into its chamber. He was just about to give the password when he heard the reassuring voice of Ray,

"Empty that bleeding chamber soldier, or you will get this bayonet up your arse, that's my captain coming in!"

"Cheers Ray, me and Des coming in."

It was not the official way of standing down a sentry but Daniel new that if Ray had not been forceful in the matter a jumpy sentry would have shot first and asked questions later. This sentry had got the message loud and clear and on entering the trench he was still shaking at the prospect of Ray's bayonet tickling his nether regions. Art and Geordie were also there so it was a fairly formidable trio that had been on hand depending on where they had approached their line. They retired to discuss the plan adding as much extra information and detail to Art's maps and sketches as they could.

The Knaves ran through the plan time and again, each adding their thoughts and refining the plan accordingly until in the early hours they were set. The only thing that was not known was the exact location of Mighty Kraut. Flailing Fritz was the machine gun post at the end of the old communications trench, the Mighty Kraut was approximately fifty yards further down the trench line and would need to be dealt with silently if the assailants were to have a chance of returning safely.

The plans were passed by Lieutenant-Colonel Pickering with a, "Quite an ambitious plan Byrne but if anyone can pull it off it's you and your lads, good luck."

For the rest of the day they did their best to rest up and get plenty of food as the plan involved them being out for what possibly could be several days and, during that time, it would be iron rations and nothing else. Daniel was proud as he looked at his section all very carefully checking and re-checking their equipment. It wasn't necessary for him to carry out the normal daily equipment checks and parades. Unfortunately, Fritz had other ideas about them getting plenty of rest; their artillery bombardment that day was as constant as huge breakers hitting the coastline. The bombardment swept their front line like fire sweeping through a forest with all the ferocity of a hurricane. Fortunately it appeared to be focussed on the front line and not the secondary. In the periods of fitful sleep he got he was accompanied by lurid dreams of his long dead pals, it wasn't pleasant or restful. On waking, he only knew his hatred was burning with the intensity of the furnace and that was stoked every time he thought of how they had died. As evening came, the pals got together for a last run through and started out to the front line. The bombardment had finally decreased to just distant, sporadic shellfire, but on arriving at the front it was clear to see its earlier effect.

Death had been delivered across the entire front with total indiscriminate ease. It had struck down victims by the hundreds, entire groups dead, some dismembered and others decapitated, others simply dead in a multitude of other methods. However, just has many had been spared. How did that happen and which divine being made that decision, who got away with it and who this time was to cop the packet? Odin the god of war, maybe.

They waited until darkness had fallen and following Daniel (with Des bringing up the rear), the fully equipped Knaves followed the original route out and along the listening sap, across the shell holes and into the old communications trench. Daniel stopped and listened on numerous occasions, aware that the German raiders could have chosen that same night to launch another attack, likewise they carefully checked each dugout before moving beyond and towards Flailing Fritz. Both Lewis's set up just below the parapet at the second dugout to cover the rest, with Art, Ronnie and Des taking up position by Flailing Fritz. Daniel, Tommo and Johnny slithered out of the trench just under the eye line of the Germans and moved off on their bellies to find Mighty Kraut. It took nearly an hour to locate it. Tommo moved slowly under the barrel of the Maxim and slipped into the trench, whilst Daniel slipped directly into the trench placing him and Tommo on either side of the gun. Johnny got ready to pull the gun forward so it could not be retracted and used on his comrades if they were discovered. Just about then, and totally unplanned, the British artillery started up and Daniel saw the three Germans around Mighty Kraut visibly hunker down. The rest of the trench was deserted and, looking beyond the machine gun post, he could see Tommo was in place bayonet in hand. They caught each other's eye and nodded their readiness. With the speed of striking cobras they planted their weapons into the backs of the nearest two victims driving the blades upwards into the hearts. Their other hand firmly placed over their mouths pulling them back on to the blades. Daniel pulled his bayonet free and was preparing to move on to the third German when he saw he was just leaning, limply forward. Johnny had not only pulled the Maxim forward out of the way but had stabbed his victim straight through the eye with such force it had appeared through the back of his skull. The problem Johnny was now having was retrieving the blade of the bayonet which was stuck and in his moment of slight panic he could not pull it free. Daniel signalled for him to leave it and, placing the two dead Germans into the parapet so they were still standing as if watching out over no-man's land, he slid a Jack of Clubs down the blade of the bayonet that now protruded from the dead man's head. Up over the trench he and Tommo went. Johnny had quickly removed the Maxim's belt and plugged the barrel internally. He replaced the belt and then plugged the end of the barrel by pushing a spent cartridge case that had been widened for the task in the end of the barrel. Then slowly they made their way back to Art, Ronnie and Des. Art watched Daniel and the others get back around the first bend and towards the first dugout then signalled for his team to use their Mills bombs and dropped them into the sandbagged machine gun nest, housing Flailing Fritz. As the explosion ripped through the night air, they withdrew to meet up with the others at the dugout as planned.

The plan had always been to do this first which as Daniel had described, "It will be like poking a wild animal, you are always going to get a reaction, it's just a case of how long you wait."

Daniel guessed that the German reprisal for this act would be to rely on a tried and tested means of attack. Therefore, they would split into the two dugouts with a thin communication wire between them, if and when the raiding party came to wreak vengeance for the attack on Mighty

Kraut and Flailing Fritz they would catch them all in between the two dugouts.

It was twenty-four hours later that it became clear the predicted reaction was actually happening. In the meantime they had to endure artillery attack that swept up and down the trench. It was pleasing for Daniel to note that it was only rifle fire that raked across the top of the trench and not machine gun. He could only think that they had tried to bring Mighty Kraut into action and not cleared the blockages and therefore, as well as blowing its barrel, had probably killed another Kraut! After a few hours things settled down and, following the plan, both dugouts had a sentry posted at its entrance. Each sentry was attached to the other dugout by the wire so on each hour when sentries changed they signalled each other all was still okay and only random continual signalling would indicate action on the way! It was a long day with nowhere to go, and only iron rations to eat. To pass the time some played cards, others dozed, whilst Daniel wrote a letter to Marie, to whom he repeated his undying love and how he was willing the end of the war so they could be together, married and raise a family. He also wrote to his parents, who he told about their plans to marry and that Marie would be coming over to England shortly with Catherine and Henry. He mentioned that Marie had their address and would be writing with her dates when travel arrangements had been made. Daniel had started helping Ray with French lessons, Ray being determined to surprise Annette with this at their next meeting.

They had gone to the dugout nearest the allies' lines. Daniel's logic was that the officer leading the raiding party would be at the front and he wanted to take charge of the operation to take at least him prisoner. It was early evening when the communication wire started to twitch vigorously and then lay still, the whole dugout was thick with tension. All in that dugout had got several German stick grenades to welcome their guests whilst Ray had his Lewis primed and ready for action. They lay in the darkness of the dugouts and out in the semi-darkness of the trench they heard slight whispering getting a little louder. A head popped into the dugout and Daniel reached up and dragged the individual in towards the rest of the group who all hit him almost at the same time. He fell to the ground unconscious without anybody knowing which punch had done the job. Daniel came out first swiftly followed by Ray who opened up with his Lewis. Daniel had wrestled the first person he had come to down to the ground and landed a couple of right hand blows into his face. He dropped to the ground as fast as he could as he knew that both Lewis's would be paying homage to Odin the god of war and at the agreed slight upward angle the only safe place in the trench therefore was on the ground. The others threw grenades out and down the trench. It reminded Daniel of being a young lad and visiting his uncle at the castle farm and shooting rats in the barn. The infernal crescendo left an echoing silence and the floor littered with a grey mass of dead and injured whose moans and shrieks were those of the condemned. Daniel had his body flowing with pure adrenaline. He seemed somehow dislocated from the real world, what a buzz seemed to engulf all the Auckland Pals, at that point they were a truly murderous creation. Within a few minutes with the rush abating, Daniel took stock. As expected, neither side would know which group had ambushed who, but it was Fritz that had easy access into the trench so it was only a matter of time before they sent some more troops to check. As quickly as they could, without showing themselves, they moved the thirty-three dead up the trench and used them to create a barricade, taking their souvenirs and planting another calling card as they did. It was under the cover of total darkness that the second German party gingerly came along the trench. The Knaves, from behind the barricade of bodies, used the whole store of German stick grenades to drive their adversaries back. With recognition of the German defeat in this smallest of battles, their artillery started to pound the trench once again, but this time to add to the confusion and British artillery added to that chaos. Their withdrawal was more of a "run for it," than a tactical withdrawal. Daniel screamed at them to keep moving and, with their prisoners, got back to their lines with shrapnel spinning around their heads filling the air like a cloud of stiletto blades. There were cheers from the battalion who guarded the front line as the Knaves dropped in the trench. Daniel looked up as soon as he hit the bottom of the trench still holding his prisoner. Charlie was holding his shoulder and between his fingers leaked an ever expanding dark crimson mass. Ray was stood and shouting back into no-man's land.

The only words he could hear from Ray were, "Nnooo! Jack" as he tried to get back over the parapet. It was Geordie who managed to drag him back.

"It's no use Ray, he's a goner and if you go out there so will you be."

Ray's head dropped and it was Daniel's turn to move towards the parapet and Geordie grabbed him with his other hand, "No Captain keep down, there's too much iron work flying to go out at the moment. He's well dead so anybody else getting killed will really be a waste; give it a little time for things to cool he's only a few yards away, I'll get him."

After the highs of the ambush, they had paid the price with another Auckland Pal dead.

Daniel sat in the Battalion HQ in front of Pickering, who saw the hurt in Daniel's eyes.

"I know just at this moment in time this seems like no consolation, but if every attack ended in a kill ratio of thirty-three to one, then we would all be home for Christmas. From your report with the loss of only one man killed and another injured, your jaunt over there has been a startling success. The First Lieutenant or *Oberleutnant* you brought back was from the 11th Bavarian Division and they have just been brought up to support the 6th who have been here sometime, but more importantly some of your old friends from the 23rd Infantry Division, 1st Royal Saxon Corps are here and they generally support gas attacks!

"I intend adding to the report of Colonel Dupuis of our Canadian friends who is requesting a citation for your section and especially for you and Henry's part in the action at St Julien. I will be requesting a further citation as well as some form of recognition of your role here."

On 24 May, just four days after their costly adventure, the Germans released a gas attack across a near four and a half mile front. British troops were able to defend against initial German attacks but were eventually forced to retreat to the north and south. Failed British counter-attacks forced a British retreat in total of over half a mile northwards which was only a fraction of the distance that could have been, had the allies not brought reinforcements up due to the intelligence they had recently received compliments of the Knaves.

During the attack, the Knaves became part of the front line defence. The ground reverberated to a crescendo of hammer blows. Away in the distance, artillery of all sizes was thunderously belting out spouts of blue-brown smoke from which erupted tongues of white, green, red and purple flames as the German artillery went about their business with tedious efficiency. The Pals faced the menace of a grey wall of Bavarian Infantry that bravely charged the line. Behind the cloud of chlorine gas the storm troopers fell to the rattle of machine gun and rifle. Pre-warned, a gas alarm had been sounded and although still very new to the battle front the gas was not the unexpected terror of its first use. Everybody knew to stay out of the wind and therefore the gas cloud. They all had hastily cobbled homemade protection of goggles and urine soaked pads and scarves.

182

The German troopers were still very wary of the gas attacks and did not follow up too closely in case of a change in wind direction. This allowed allied troops to refill the trenches that had to be abandoned as the worst of the gas moved over them. It was the weight of the German attack that was so telling and the first notable use of the flamethrower or *flammenwerfer* came in this surprise attack. Across the front, immediately adjacent to Daniel's position, he saw four small groups of troopers around a spouting, spitting and fire breathing dragon.

"What in God's name is that?" screamed Pickering who was also in the defence of the front line.

Daniel instantly remembered that evening with his uncle on Battle Hill in Co. Durham and shouted to his section and particularly Des and Johnny to concentrate fire in the centre of the spouts of flame.

"Somebody in that group will be carrying a tank with fuel oil, hit that and they will all go up!"

Sure enough, one by one there was a small explosion followed by a ball of flame and each group disappeared. Daniel first saw Des then Johnny punch the air as they claimed their hits. As the last explosion died down the impetus of the attack died and Fritz started to retreat in disarray. Daniel surveyed the scene. Four small clusters of burnt bodies, so badly burnt in fact there was no clothing left and the crisped figures had twisted back to their embryonic foetal position as their tendons had contracted. Heavy fuel oil filled the air and mixed with the sickly, sweet smell of burning flesh.

This was only a momentary respite as a new wall of grey stood and charged across the fifty yards of no-man's land; what bravery, what stupid, foolhardy bravery, they fell in their hundreds. However, this time the waves kept coming and either side of their section the front line was falling back and fearing being trapped and surrounded,

Daniel gave the order to fall back to the support trench where fresh troops waited to take up the cause. They ran for all they were worth and leapt the support trench in a single bound, turning and dropping to the floor to add to the fire power. It was here that they held their ground and the German advance were brought to a halt. Fritz was now in the old British front trench and the exact coordinates of which the artillery already had, within minutes of the red signal flares arcing into the sky, a forest of lightning bolts struck, making the very ground that Fritz cowered in tremble and boil.

The British and their allies who had been hastily brought up thanks to the intelligence that had been gathered from the prisoners taken by the Knaves, established their new front line under this sustained artillery bombardment that went on for hours. This allowed a change round of the front line troops, so those who had faced the full force of the attack were relieved and sent to the rear. This included Daniel and his section who he was relieved to find unscathed by the onslaught. They moved back towards Hellfire Corner and came to a dressing station where they saw first-hand the effects of gas on the unprepared.

Hundreds of troops with bandaged eyes being led hand on shoulder, whilst others less fortunate would have taken lungs full of the chlorine gasped for air as they drowned in their own body fluids as the chlorine did its deadly work on the internal workings of the human body. A mighty chorus of pain and anguish sang out for all to hear. Even in the surroundings of such inhumanity that the Ypres Salient represented, Fritz had stooped to a new depth.

Geordie looked over the seething mass of pain and said to nobody in particular, "What depths have you sunk too Fritz? You must realise this can only lead to a backlash that will equal if not surpass this atrocity?" he shook his head in disbelief.

"You've got that right," spit Ray through gritted teeth.

Equally appalled at the sight, Daniel turned to the lads, "Take a long look at this and remember what you see. If you ever feel sorry for any of those grey clad bastards, remember this. If you wonder why we are here, remember this. If you wonder if we are in the right, remember this! Come on let's move off!" With that, he set off at a pace.

The Knaves Honoured

The battalion had been moved back to the town of Poperinge which required traversing Hellfire Corner and Ypres to regroup and take stock of their losses. It was over a ten mile march and they seemed to be harassed the entire way. Transport on the roads was in greater chaos than usual. Burnt out motor lorries and horse drawn carts alike littered the roadsides, the pitiful sight of dead pack horses, too numerous to count added to the carnage. Their huge carcasses disembowelled by flying shell fragments and shrapnel, these poor beasts of burden had gone to their deaths trusting their handlers, an innocent victim of man's inhumanity.

The battalion camp was on the southern edge of the town and consisted of rows of tents in fields. An old brewery had been taken over as the armies' bathhouse with the three large beer vats now containing soapy water to wash off all the filth, a slightly cleaner vat to do your final clean and then the final rinse. Having dropped their clothing at one end, they picked up new washed underclothes and then, if they were lucky, they would also get a clean uniform, but this depended on if they were early in the queue. Daniel had made sure of this, not just to ensure clean clothes. He had been summoned to Divisional HQ to report on their recent "stunt" and Lieutenant-Colonel

Pickering was to join him. Pickering had his orderly sort some polish for his boots and wipe down his tunic and cap that could not be exchanged due to the rank markings and the battalion insignia. Pickering was not very forthcoming about the meeting and rather pokerfaced and this concerned Daniel, surely he was not going to get hauled over the coals? After all it was Pickering who had said that killing thirty-three enemy and taking two prisoner compared favourably to one dead and one injured. He was hurting enough inside over Jack's death and Charlie's injury. To be put on a charge over it would really be a kicking, and he hadn't even managed to write to Jack's parents yet, or get news to Henry prior to his return to England. The staff car arriving for the pair further set him on edge. He didn't want to seem concerned by asking Pickering what it was all about, so he asked a few less direct questions, which Pickering played back to him expertly with a straight bat.

"So why are they not happy with your report, sir? Surely they don't need it duplicating by me?"

"Let's say they want it directly from the horse's mouth, Byrne," was his reply.

On arrival at the, not long built town hall, that was now Divisional HQ they reported to the sergeant on reception who pointed them in the direction of another reception room where an adjutant took note of their arrival and told them to be seated whilst he went to see if General Haig was ready to see them. The plot thickened!

Almost immediately they were ushered into a rather grand office which was the size of a small ballroom with just one desk offset from a log fire which really set off the wooden panelled room. As they marched forward, Daniel caught a brief sight of some other people in the rear of the room, but so nervous of being in these surrounding his gaze was straight ahead and he came to a smart attention alongside Pickering, who looked strangely relaxed for so formal a meeting.

Haig was sat at his desk and only looked up when both had come to a halt.

"Ah, Captain Byrne, you've come up in the world since the last time we met. You've also been making a bit of a name for yourself with this young rascal," he pointed to the group at the rear of the room.

He turned to see Henry, Catherine and Marie. His heart soared, this couldn't be a ticking off if these were present, but what was it all about? Henry moved forward alongside his friend and winked at him. At the same time Pickering moved away, Henry coming to attention. Haig approached and his adjutant followed with a silver tray in front of him.

"Well you two certainly have proved my theory correct. Intelligence is the key to winning this war, and for that reason it gives me great delight, nay, pride in presenting you both with the Distinguished Conduct Medal. The citation reads, this awarded for gallantry in the field and in the face of the enemy. Whose swift action helped avert the taking of St Julien 1915 and thus maintaining the line." He went on to state, "The Canadian Commander of the CEF (Canadian Expeditionary Force) has mentioned in Dispatches the whole section for those actions at St Julien. On top of this, I am pleased to repeat the award for your actions at Bellewaerde, where without the information learnt from your captives, we would have surely sustained a major reversal."

He shook their hands and asked Daniel if he had all he needed for the section to carry on their sterling work?

Rather hesitantly Daniel asked whether it would be possible for the section to be formally told by the general himself at tomorrow's morning parade, rather than hearing the news from himself.

"Excellent idea young man, and we will bring the cameras with us, we need all the good news stories we can get back in good old England. See to it Smythe, first thing in the morning at their camp, come to think of it, better not make it too early as they might want to do some celebrating in Pop [Poperinge] tonight, don't you think?" he winked at the two who very enthusiastically agreed.

"So young Byrne," he said in a more fatherly tone, "what do you think of my idea of getting Henry here to set up another section like yours?"

"Should work fine sir, providing you get the right members in the team."

"Oh I'll leave that to young Henry here, besides I hear he has become a bit of a lead magnet so you need shut of him and we need him at HQ," laughing at his own joke, (Henry had told him about the comments in St Julien), he turned and waved to the ladies who were still at the back of the room. "Please ladies come and congratulate your brave menfolk. This is the calibre of man that will push the Bosh all the way back to Germany and out of your beautiful land," he directed his comment mainly at Marie. "And you two, you are both two damn lucky fellows to have such delightful beauties at your side. If I was twenty years younger you would have been in trouble, I could turn a lady's head in my time you know?" With that he waved his dismissal and added to his adjutant and Lieutenant-Colonel Pickering, "Arrange the details for tomorrow".

They got out into the reception area of the former town hall and Marie threw her arms around Daniel's neck, hanging there whilst she gave him a long hard kiss.

"I don't think you have been telling me exactly what you have been up to, but somehow I knew my man would be up to something extraordinary."

With that she kissed him again and they all left for the staff car that had been made available to take them back to camp via the Hotel Palace that was situated on Ieperstraat in the centre of town. When they got to the hotel, Daniel saw Annette who ran down the hotel steps to kiss him and asked about Ray. It had been arranged that he was to go to the camp and tell all of them about a party that had been arranged by Henry that evening, but no mention would be made of the citations or Annette. However, Daniel was to insist on Ray coming back into town with him to help arrange the party and, of course, where Annette would be waiting to surprise him.

Daniel gave the group their orders, leaving Art to get them as smart as possible and to the Palace Hotel for 7.00 p.m. "in good order," meaning they weren't to be too drunk when they arrived, that would no doubt come later!

With that, they headed back to the hotel and to free up the staff car. Daniel led Ray into the bar where he ordered two glasses of red wine. Ray downed the wine in one and placed the glass on the bar and was about to order another round. Daniel had positioned himself so he was facing the door into the bar and Ray facing him. It was easy for Annette and the others to walk up behind him totally unseen and for Annette to put her hands over his eyes. She whispered something in French that Daniel didn't quite catch, but whatever it was gave the game away instantly to Ray, whose grin was like a small child's on Christmas morning. In one movement he spun round and lifted her off the ground in an enormous loving bear hug. With this signal the bartender brought out six ready poured glasses of champagne.

Ray looked accusingly at Daniel, whom pleaded his case, "I knew nothing about it myself until just a couple of hours ago, and it's his fault," pointing at Henry.

"We thought you were in England?" questioned Ray.

"No we haven't got there yet; this little affair cropped up and stalled our plans! I hope you are not too disappointed?"

"So what's happened then? This can't have been put on just on a whim, as much as it's lovely there's something happening, isn't there?"

They sat down and began to explain what had happened and what was going to happen the following day, asking Ray his thoughts on whether they should tell them all tonight or leave it as a surprise.

"I think you should tell them, some are going to get hammered to forget about Charlie and Jack, others might not enjoy the evening enough having had nothing but bad news recently. No, I think they should be told; there's no better way to start a party than a healthy helping of good news."

Daniel looked at Henry, who nodded and simply said, "Agreed!"

"Henry, you are the one to give the good news. You were in charge when most of this happened, it would be more appreciated by the lads coming from you."

This was a statement not a question from Daniel and Ray's nodding backed him up.

"It would be an honour," with that he raised his glass and toasted, "the Knaves and our lost comrades."

The two lads wholeheartedly repeated the toast but the girls were a little quieter as two of them knew their men would be returning to that arena shortly and the next toast could be including them.

At a little earlier than the allotted time, the lads arrived and made straight for the bar. Art had presented himself at the reception to request their arrival be passed on to Henry and Daniel. When the knock on the hotel room door came Daniel was nearly ready, having luxuriated in another hot bath which he had shared with Marie. The drying process had also taken considerably longer than would have been expected had he been on his own. The slow tender caressing of each other's bodies under thick, soft, warm towels had, unsurprisingly, led to a height of excitement resulting in a similar height of passion for the next hour. Daniel had managed to keep a little focus on the time and had been able, rather unwillingly to extricate himself from his very own version of heaven to get ready for the arrival of the lads. Within minutes he was down in the bar with his friends. Ray wasn't far behind with Henry arriving a few minutes later. Very fashionably, all the ladies arrived together but just a few minutes late, after the 7.00 p.m. agreed meeting time. But what an entrance, the three were dressed to impress and so they did. One by one, as the lads realised what the next was looking at, you almost heard their individual jaws hit the floor. Henry, Daniel and Ray very proudly moved across the floor to take their partners by the arm and escort them to the group where Henry and Daniel went about the introductions. Most of them did not know how to respond to the introduction. Should they bow, salute, shake or kiss the ladies' hands? Instead they followed the lead of the previous member which was to nervously grin and nod their greeting whilst going red with embarrassment.

They moved over to the tables which had been reserved for the group. The ladies were on the central table with their men and the others spread across the three other tables that had been positioned in a semi-circular pattern so all were equidistant from what was effectively the top table. Having ensured the group had fully charged glasses, Henry welcomed everybody and set out by thanking them for their commitment and support over the previous weeks and months.

"Gentlemen," plenty of jokers in the group looked around as though they thought he was talking to someone else. "It is not just the three of us here who realise just what professionalism and raw courage you have displayed over the last months, the fame of the Knaves has spread right to the very top of the military tree. Most of you met General

Haig on our night training exercise back when Battalion HQ was outside this delightful little town of Poperinge. He at that time told you how this little experiment was his idea and that he would be keeping a keen eye on our performance, well he has and he is mightily impressed with you. But it goes further than that. Not only is the general impressed, but the Canadian Expeditionary Force is and also very thankful for your assistance in St Julien. That is why the whole section has been mentioned in despatches by the British and Canadian Armies."

Suddenly there was cheering whistling and general bedlam. It was Ray rising to his feet that brought the unruly bunch under order.

"Our lieutenant-colonel and captain are far too modest to tell you their news so I will ensure their blushes by proudly mentioning that both have been awarded the Distinguished Conduct Medal to add to the pride of our small section!"

Again, more whistling and hooting of joy and disbelief.

Henry took over again and thanked Ray, somewhat sarcastically for embarrassing them. He had not intended sharing that news with the section and intended letting it filter out over the evening. Ray's comments had not really surprised him but he was touched by the sincere warmth they all had shown in the news.

"Any award any member of this section gains is a gain for everybody. No one person can achieve success without the whole team doing their jobs. So I think I can speak on behalf of Daniel and myself that although we have been presented with this honour, the honour is all of ours."

At that there was more rapturous applause and Henry looked towards Daniel to say something.

"I think everything that needed to be said has been said. I would like to endorse that any award is for all of the section regardless of who gets it and beyond that I would like to ask you all to stand and join me in a toast to ourselves and our fallen comrades, may they never be forgotten."

There was a more solemn and formal repeat of the toast as most of the group downed their drinks in one and then mass hysteria broke out as Henry announced a free bar. Daniel made sure he got to speak to everybody in turn over the evening and Marie was dutifully by his side. Her elegance and beauty won each man over in an instance; it was if she could cast a spell as she approached them. Her soft accented English had them eating out of her hand and she was a tremendous success, as was Annette, who had a little trouble with the lads' sense of humour when they asked if she knew what she had let herself in for; or "you could do an awful lot better than that you know." Ray had expected it and took it as it was meant; in good humour, in fact the more jealousy they showed, the wider he grinned.

It was a little after 11.00 p.m. when nearby explosions brought the evening to a close, the lads set off for the estaminet that they had passed on their way up to the hotel. With a final fatherly warning from Ray, not to be too tight for the morning parade, Art as usual was in charge of the group. They set off in great spirits, even though the loss of Jack and the possible fatal injury to Charlie was still raw.

Daniel and Marie had taken their leave of the group a little earlier, at the same time as Henry and Catherine. Daniel had impressed on Art the importance of being as pristine as possible for the morning's affairs. Both he and Henry had discussed the reason that Haig had been so keen to pick up on Daniel's suggestion (in fact by now he was quite sure it was his idea from the start). Making a big show of the citations would show him in a great light. Relations between Haig and French were to say the very least, strained. With such a lack of success the king was very disappointed in French's performance as Commander in Chief of the British Expeditionary Force (BEF) and Haig had been quick to make maximum mileage of this having direct access to the ear of the king. The snippets of intelligence the Knaves had been able to gather had on numerous occasions meant a greater reversal had been averted and Haig had optimised this to promote his part in the new means of waging war, which in his view needed to be more intelligence-led. The king was left in no uncertain terms that it was all Haig's doing that this crack, specialist unit had moved so quickly from concept to field operations on the front line, fed by undercover spies and aerial reconnaissance. It was actually not too far from the truth, he genuinely did believe this, but it was the speed at which his ideology had borne fruit that surprised even him. Henry was sure this situation could and should be used to their benefit. This did however mean, unfortunately, some might argue a continuation of specialist missions where the price of failure could be fatal.

As Daniel and Marie entered their room, the distant rumble of artillery bombardment gave a most unwelcome reminder that they were still within easy reach of an example of one of man's greatest follies.

Marie shuddered slightly in Daniel's arms, "When will it end Daniel? There doesn't seem to be anything happening to create a reason for peace talks, other than when everyone is dead! And who wins then?" she said in a very quiet, almost desperate voice.

"I'm afraid you're right, it seems to be a case of who blinks first, who starts feeling the political pressure back home. Unfortunately, for you and the Belgians it's happening in your homeland."

"I hate this!" she started to cry, "Every time you go away I die a little, longing for your safe return, but knowing you are very likely to be in grave danger."

"We are together now and that's what counts. Let's not forget if it was not for this war we would never have met and I for one am glad we did that! I could not have dreamed a year ago I would be in love with a beautiful French lady who amazingly enough appears to be in love with me?"

"Oh, I am and I thank the Lord every day for our meeting. I know it's very selfish but I want this war to end so I can have you to myself. Is that so wrong? I want the war to end just for my own reasons and nobody else's!"

Daniel drew her towards him, "It works for me!"

He kissed her deeply and passionately and they fell on to the bed in each other's arms. The ongoing distant bombardment was overpowered by a natural phenomenon, so much greater than the hatred of war that even its noise could just have been the crack of thunder during a rain storm on a wet spring evening. Nothing could unlock their love for each other and their joint heartbeats seemed to drown out all else. At least for the night, love would beat hatred.

Daniel awoke about 6.00 a.m. to the slightly unfamiliar sound of silence. No bombardment, no marching troops or artillery limbers moving along the street outside. Had he been transported to another time? He looked across at his sleeping Marie and thought of their night of passion and loving. Such passion, such wild passion it started with and then it grew gentler, a tender caressing. How often had they made love that night? He could not recollect, it mattered not, they had fallen asleep in each other's embrace and this is how he had awoken. Bliss!

He vainly tried to untangle himself without waking Marie up, but so tightly were their two bodies entwined that she woke immediately he moved. She opened her eyes, saw him looking down at her and smiled. She tilted her head back towards his and very gently kissed him, her hands cupped around the back of his head and pulled him closer, kissing harder. He responded in kind, his hands brushing over her nipples and across the flat of her stomach, between her legs.

It was nearly 6.45 a.m. when Daniel got out of bed to answer the knock on the door from room service. Breakfast and a new uniform were delivered with a note pinned on it from Henry:

A present from Haig. All the section are being issued with new uniforms for the citation presentation. Enjoy breakfast and see you downstairs at 7.30 a.m.

Henry and Daniel entered the camp at 8.30 a.m. to be met by Ray and Art, reporting all present and correct. New uniforms had been received at 6.00 a.m., these had been pressed prior to delivery, boots and weapons cleaned to within an inch of their lives. The section was having breakfast and if it was to the lieutenant-colonel's liking they would be ready for inspection at 9.00 a.m.? Daniel beamed with pride that both Ray and Art could be relied upon to ensure all was in order even after a night out. Ray had left at the same time as Henry and Daniel, but had been up and into camp to oversee and assist Art's preparations.

"That will be more than satisfactory, thank you Sergeant," was Henry's formal reply. It was more in jest than real formality then he turned to Art, "I take it that the lads managed to have a good time after you left last night, Corporal?"

"Yes sir! The boys did their best to reinforce the entente cordiale at the estaminet on Casselstraat called Van Bauwel and all back in camp before curfew."

"Excellent. Glad to see it's not just my captain and sergeant maintaining good relations with the locals!"

At that, he failed to maintain his pretence of formality and his straight face broke into a broad grin and began to laugh, with the others joining in.

At 9.00 a.m. the section had their inspection and it was up to the standards that Henry and Daniel had expected.

Henry took the opportunity in emphasising the importance of the section's relationship with their benefactor, General Haig, and that maintaining this positive support by such a man would ensure there long-term welfare, as the new uniforms and regular breaks from the front had demonstrated. He did point out the negative side to this arrangement and that was more of the same sorts of action they had seen up 'til then. He then gave all of them the opportunity to make any observations and ask questions and even if anybody had doubts at being in the section, giving them the chance to return to their battalion. He was pleased to hear that for all the dangers and losses of this close knit unit everything remained very positive. This was in no small measure to Daniel, Ray and Art and he knew it. Leadership was crucial to good morale.

Fifteen minutes prior to Haig's programmed arrival an official photographer and film crew arrived, along with members of the general press and set up to cover the great man's entrance and the events at the camp that morning. The camp kitchen had received the sort of food that only the chefs from the hotel could prepare so it became obvious to all concerned that the concept, formation and achievements of the Knaves was to be seen as a real stroke of genius on the part of Haig and the king and the rest of the country were to know about it!

The Haig cavalcade arrived with great fanfare. He was mounted on a white charger and accompanied by his Aide de Camp and a company of cavalry as his personal bodyguard. He was minute perfect with his timing, as his reputation would have you expect. The section was brought up to attention. He dismounted and was met by Henry and Daniel. The section were put into stand at ease, stand easy. The small group retired to the kitchen tent where refreshments were taken. After a few minutes they re-appeared, the section being brought up to attention once more. Henry and Daniel joined the group and Haig took his place facing the section, citation in hand. Haig briskly delivered his well-prepared speech which repeated, for the press's benefit his belief that whatever his troops on the front line could do, they did it so much more effectively and with much less cost if real time, accurate intelligence was available and that could only come from the ground due to the limitations of reconnaissance via the Royal Flying Corps aeroplanes and observation balloons. Again for the press, he emphasised it was his vision that had taken this section from concept to very successful operational activity and congratulated their success and wished them well repeating a similar message to both Henry and Daniel when they were presented with their Distinguished Conduct Medals. With that, Haig blatantly checked with the press that they had everything they needed before taking the salute and disappearing in a cloud of dust and hooves!

It had been a very calculated public relations exercise to gain Haig favours with the British public and of course the king. It did seem obvious to all on the parade ground, but at least the section got to eat and drink the refreshments that had been laid on and virtually untouched. It was Henry's job then to remind the section that regardless of the way they felt Haig had used them, they had received a section citation and with Haig wanting to make the most of "his" great idea, they would continue to be supported as long as they continued to succeed. In between hors d'oeuvres and a selection of main fish and meat dishes, washed down with copious measures of Sauvignon Blanc, the lads agreed that there was some advantages to Haig's support and even toasted his continued health, albeit tongue in cheek. Henry had already pre-warned Daniel but he also had to break the bad news that the section would be immediately sent back into the line, where a particular task awaited them.

Daniel had time to return to the hotel and say his goodbyes to Marie. On reaching the hotel he found her with

Catherine seated in one of the reception rooms taking tea. They were packed, but Catherine made some excuse about checking she had not left anything in her room and left them to take a stroll in the small garden. The distant thunder raps of artillery fire, as always, accompanied their walk. The love they had for each other made the parting all the more difficult and, tearfully, Marie held his hand as they walked.

"Please be careful, my love," she said choking back the sobs.

He squeezed her hand and rather poorly tried to joke, "Don't worry, old Fritz is not wily enough to catch Daniel Byrne."

Even before he had finished saying it he realised how lame and stupid his attempt was. There followed an awkward silence, until Marie broke it by explaining that Henry, Catherine and her were going to England the next week as Henry's recuperation leave was coming to an end and he was required to travel back to the War Office in London to talk over something that was so important that it was top secret and he could not discuss with them. It would however give the perfect opportunity for them all to go and visit Catherine's parents first, then up to County Durham to visit Henry's estate where, if she had Daniel's permission, she would like to visit on his parents. Henry had hinted on the trip back to Blighty being arranged soon during their journey into the camp that morning, but had obviously wanted to give Marie chance to deliver the details.

Daniel expressed his pleasure at this idea, commenting, "I think there would be all hell for me to pay if for some reason I said no! My mum would kill me! I wrote to them a few days ago warning them of your intended visit and if you can let me have your travel plans I will let them know when to expect you, I can do that tonight, I promise!"

Marie smiled and handed him a piece of paper with the timetable of the whole of the visit written down, "Just so you know where to send your letters to, I have kept everyone you have sent and read them a thousand times each, I don't want one going astray." She placed the note into his hand and folded it over.

She brought his closed hand up to her mouth and kissed it. They kissed long and hard, the sort of kiss only lovers parting could describe. Daniel had to pull himself away and so the sight of his Marie crying didn't set him away, he strode off out of the hotel and into the street without looking back. Ray was waiting outside with Henry, it was clear to see Ray had just had a similar experience with his goodbye to Annette. They looked at each other and nodded and looked away. Ray turned and joined the rest of the section who were in rank ready to march off back to the war and Daniel looked at Henry.

"Look after her, Henry and give my regards to my ma and pa as well as everybody else back home."

"Of course I will Danny. More to the point you look after yourself and the lads, they are counting on you. Here are your orders and a little birdy is talking about old Fritz has got a bit of a bee in his bonnet about the Knaves and is going to attempt to set up a trap to lure you into. It appears that we have managed to ruffle his feathers somewhat, unfortunately now you are the target that they are gunning for."

"Thanks Henry, don't worry about us, we will be even more careful if that is possible. Besides, they won't have anybody as sneaky as the sneakiest bastard in County Durham!"

"You've got a point there Danny!"

With that, Daniel turned and joined his lads, Art passed him his pack and they struck out for Langemark-Poelkapelle, north of Ypres. From the reception window,

Annette, Marie and Catherine comforted each other, tears flowing from all.

Langemark-Poelkapelle

Battalion HQ was based in a rather weary looking, old German bunker that had seen attention from both sides during the course of the war. Positioned at the end of one of the communication trenches leading up to the front line, the last mile approach was, to use Art's description, a little bit fruity!

On arrival, they were met by Lieutenant-Colonel Pickering who had recently been wounded by a piece of flying shrapnel shell casing. After receiving a dressing to his wounds at the nearby dressing station, where he had insisted on walking to, with the comment, "I don't need any bloody stretcher bearers, the damn injury is to my shoulder not my bloody legs!" he was back in his salubrious surroundings of battalion HQ within six hours. The bunker, named The Mayfair Club, was positioned alongside the Bikschotestraat to the east of Langemark-Poelkapelle. The front line at this point ran approximately west to east on the northern extremity of the town. The town had seen a lot of action over the previous few months and all but the hardy, or possibly foolhardy, residents had fled. The Knaves were shown their dugout that they had to set to extending to house the whole group. It hardly allowed the men to lie down without being pressed up against one another.

"Some contrast to the last couple of bloody nights!" observed Tommo.

"Well, you see now how that wonderful General Haig looks after his favourites!" came the broad, soft Irish brogue of Geordie.

"Yes, the sooner we get back into old Fritz and get more goodies for him, the sooner we will be back at Van Bauwel estaminet in good old Pop," added Art.

Whilst the lads settled in and extended their new home, Daniel and Ray reported to Pickering, who was full of praise and genuine congratulations.

Daniel presented his written orders and awaited further information. Apparently, over the past couple of nights, some of the work parties and normal patrols into no-man's land had been attacked by what appeared to be a deliberate ambush. This was not usual, when patrols ran into trouble in no-man's land, which they regularly did, it was down to accidently running into German patrols and during the ensuing fire fight both sides lost men and both sides had men escape or due to someone making too much noise a patrol would be discovered and shot to pieces by all manner of firepower from Fritz, including artillery. This was different. These patrols ran into something that seemed ready for them and gave them no chance. After a short but vicious, one-sided fire fight, it was over and there was no German artillery fire to add to the mayhem, almost as though they did not want to shell the area because they knew they had men there, which they wouldn't if their patrol was mobile and the encounter was accidental. No, this was deliberately set up and the most damning evidence was what had been left on two occasions and had been visible to all come the daylight of morning. There would be one of the unfortunate Tommies propped up in the kneeling position by his own rifle with a playing card pinned to his chest by his own bayonet. It was a joker. It was an obvious response and invitation to the Knaves to commence a deadly game of cat and mouse, one they could not turn down if the honour of the allies and the legend of the Knaves were to be maintained.

Over the next couple of days Art did his usual work sketching the terrain, catching with superb detail the topography that could be used by the section to get in to no-man's land undetected. As usual, he questioned the old hands in this section of the trench to get local knowledge. The more work and time he spent looking across this area, he started to see something that was rather interesting. He sent for Daniel and asked him to look out at the German wire. He could not see what Art was getting at until Art pointed to certain areas that he highlighted on his sketches, there was a clear path through the German wire. This was unheard of. Each night, just like the allies, the Germans repaired their wire for maximum defensive protection. So over the next two nights, come daylight, they checked and sure enough the gaps remained. Was this an invitation? That night Daniel and Tommo went out to see. Armed with nothing other than a couple of Mills bombs and a pistol apiece they worked their way out along a depression that had been another drainage ditch. They slithered through the mud almost like eels in shallow water. They had complete darkness provided by a cloudy night but this made finding the first gap all the trickier. Once located, the other two gaps took them all the way to within twenty yards of the German frontline which was clearly indicated by timber boards. Just before the last line of wire, Daniel's face came up against and thin wire stretched across the gap which was attached to small cans hanging on the wire, this was obviously the alarm for the waiting ambush. He very carefully lifted the cans away from the wire so they had nothing to rattle against before untying one end of the thin wire and placing it to one side. It was clear to see that footprints on these boards and the adjacent mud belonged to British boots and they only travelled in one direction. They paused for nearly ten minutes in the third gap and during this time it was clear that two saps had been dug out from the German front line and at the terminus of each sap was a small dugout. It must have been covered until the team in either dugout heard the approach of a patrol as nothing could be seen but the slight murmur of voices and the slightest leak of tobacco smoke came from either side of the invited course. With practiced hand signals, Daniel and Tommo came to an agreement on position and numbers then slithered their eel-like way back, replacing the German alarm system, to the relative safety of their lines. Ray had not moved from his covering position with Geordie on the other Lewis a few yards away. The whole section was stood too awaiting their safe return or the fire fight that would be needed to cover their urgent withdrawal. As they slithered into the trench covered in mud with only the whites of their eye showing, Ray could not help himself.

"Well if it isn't a couple of bloody mud monsters," he laughed out loud at his own joke, and the others joined in but they all knew it was laughter of relief rather than the poorest of poor jokes.

Plans were put in place for their stunt for the following night. As usual the preparation was painstaking in its detail. Everybody had a role and just in case the worst happened everybody had a secondary task which covered someone else not being able to do theirs. They poured over Art's sketches and the existing maps. They knew distances by time taken to slither in mud from trench to allied wire, allied wire to German wire and between each row of German wire. They even knew which star constellation was to be found over the German and British lines so if they got separated they would not lose their bearings. The format was to be the same as usual, with the Lewis's setting up to cover their withdrawal. If things went wrong a red Very light would bring down heavy artillery on to the German front line to keep their heads down and the Lewis's to give heavy ground level cover to discourage even the most spirited Hun. They went over the plan again and again, everybody memorising their roles. They checked their weapons, and they ensured they had a full stock of Mills bombs. They ate and rested up readying themselves for the challenge that had been thrown out by their adversaries. Daniel had already written, as promised, to his parents so he composed another letter to Marie. No mention of where or what he was up to, just his hopes and plans for their future together. He told her how Ray's French lessons were coming on and that Annette would be surprised at his progress, as he was. When he had finished he tried to sleep a little. He would report to Lieutenant-Colonel Pickering at 8.00 p.m. for a final briefing, but the overall plan had already been discussed in detail. Basically, Pickering was more than happy to leave the planning of such a specialist operation to someone who had been there and done it before, which as Daniel thought, was credit to the man; many a commanding officer would insist on having the majority of the say in such plans regardless of their ignorance.

He was woken by Ray at 8.00 p.m. He must have been much more tired than he had suspected, and he had been sound asleep for a full two hours. His heartbeat was steady and strong, he felt the buzz of anticipation and excitement course through his veins. He was full of energy and eager for the off, but there was that cold professionalism about his movements now as everything was channelled into ensuring the mission and his lads came to a positive conclusion. He never understood why but he had complete faith that it would be the case. The positive aura he gave off was infectious and the whole section picked up on it and that same clinical approach. Daniel looked around and saw a group of warriors preparing for battle. His pride in his lads swelled almost to bursting point, he would die for these lads and he knew they would do the same for him. If he had to die then, other than in old age, this was the way he wanted to go, surrounded by his own kind, his brothers at arms.

He went to see Pickering who had little to say but wish him luck and assure him that the trench would be stood-to and alert during their time out in no-man's land. Everyone was aware that the clash of two specialist teams was about to take place and they prayed that the Knaves would come out on top. He offered Daniel a slug of whiskey which, as usual, Daniel thanked him for but declined. He did not want anything to blunt his senses for the night ahead. Pickering nodded his head in understanding and offered his hand, Daniel took it then, rather more formally, saluted, turned and left to re-join his men. They were going over their camouflage suits one last time and he joined in that ritual. At 10.00 p.m. they went over the plan one last time. For no reason, or so they hoped, Fritz started a bombardment of the front line along their front, so they hunkered down and waited it out. It was always a total lottery. At any moment a shell could land directly between them and that would be it, no more Knaves, no more Marie, no more future. Again he was totally convinced that was not his destiny and, although he hunkered down with the rest of them, when any of them lifted their head to look around they saw Daniel with his head held high, steely determination. The bombardment made the slithering through the allied wire quite easy. It gave good cover and Fritz would not be expecting anything to happen through this, so it only took about an hour to make their way to the first row of German wire, where the two Lewis's were deployed off to the right and left with the support of a rifle grenadier to add more fire power and to carry extra magazines for the Lewis's. Between the second and the third row of wire the riflemen set up leaving just four to move forward. This was the critical stage, if they had not been heard, then their foe would not be waiting and just like the night before Daniel heard quite voices and smelt tobacco smoke. Daniel was disappointed in his enemies' lack of stealth; out on the County Durham moors he and his uncle had spent hours and hours silently stalking deer to mark their tracks so when the paying customers came out they could easily locate their prey. It was just inconceivable that in a life and death struggle that they were in, they could not refrain from smoking or talking.

Daniel was sure that he could smell both pipe and cigar smoke and, after several minutes of lying still, he also had a good idea that each dugout was home to three Germans. They moved off again removing the alarm cans and the thin wire. They moved around the outside of the dugouts that, as before, were covered with hessian sacking to make it look like a continuation of the surrounding terrain, an ingenious trap, thought Daniel, unfortunately spoilt by the quality of the men setting that trap. When he had got to a position alongside the right-hand side dugout he started to inhale the foulest smell imaginable, decay. He had smelt animal carcasses decaying up close before and on the battlefield he had smelt human decay but this was so intense it took his breath away. He moved his hand forward and it sank into the mud as before but then touched a dome-like object a couple of inches below the surface. The dome tilted backwards and, as it did so, the ground under his head started to rise; the stench became even move vile. Daniel realised he had pressed down on to the head of a corpse and, by doing so, the torso had risen. The entire front of the torso had been ripped open by something and his face was almost into the corpse's abdominal cavity. Daniel choked back the bile that entered his throat, he had to remain silent. He signalled behind that he was moving further right, pointing to the reason. He did not want anybody else to be taken by surprise and possibly give them away. They continued round until both teams, Daniel, Tommo, Johnny and Art, Ronnie, Des slid down into the saps that led back into the dugouts. By entering from the direction of the

German trench, Daniel hoped it would buy the few extra seconds it would take to despatch their quarry. Daniel looked across and could just make out Art in position and awaiting Daniel's signal. When he gave it, Daniel and Tommo entered their chosen dugout with Johnny standing by with a pistol, whilst Art and Ronnie entered their dugout with Des standing by. Both Daniel and Art made sure of the position of the first victim from outside and plunged their bayonets deep into the unsuspecting individual then the pair of attackers pulled back the hessian and went about their bloody butchery. Such was the speed and the ferocity of their assault not a shot was fired and only the faintest cry was allowed to escape. As agreed, they fell upon their victims quickly and pulled the hessian back over the top of them, so if anybody from the German trench had heard anything they would not see anything too out of the ordinary. They lay on their prey for several minutes all the time expecting all hell to break loose, but nothing. Slowly they crawled out of the dugouts taking with them the forage caps of the dead. In each forage cap they placed a Jack of Clubs and hung them on the top of the wire for both sides to see come daylight. Just as carefully as they had moved out, they slithered back regrouping as they went until all the section were in line heading for the allied lines. Lieutenant-Colonel Pickering, good to his word, had the entire line stood to and Daniel found out later that he himself had not moved from the sentry post for the entire time they had been out. They returned with a tunic from one soldier to show which unit was being used against them and a couple of souvenirs such as the Iron Cross, Second Class which Art had managed to locate on one of his victims and the dagger with a German eagle inlayed into its handle that Tommo had acquired. Daniel reported the success of the mission and advised that lookouts should check the wire at first light for confirmation, but he did warn that they should probably expect old Fritz to be pretty pissed off by the night's events and to show his displeasure with a bit of a backlash!

Pickering was delighted but was having difficulty concentrating on the report and had to ask Daniel, "What is that God Almighty smell that you've managed to gain while you were out there Byrne?"

When Daniel had finished telling him about the close encounter along with the dead corpse, he added, "Well in that case I guess you will be ready for that slug of that whiskey now then? And I suggest after that you might want to get a bit of a wash!"

Whilst Pickering wrote up the report to send to Divisional HQ back in Poperinge, Daniel returned to the section's dugout which, every time they had entered, they had enlarged slightly, it was now quite a little home from home. Several skeletons were contained in the walls and very artistically their hands had been freed to hold candles, whilst any timber they could find was used to prop up the roof. The lads being predominantly miners found this work almost therapeutic in a nostalgic type of way. The opening had been reduced in width by sandbags to keep out the drafts with weighted hessian sacking acting as a door. Kenny and Anders had been down to the kitchen where, with the success of their mission already having spread like wildfire, the cooks had managed to rustle up some hot food and tea for them, treating the lads as heroes. Everyone was hard at work cleaning as best they could their mud-clogged weapons and their clothing whilst eating the bully stew and petrol-flavoured tea (it as usual had been transported in old fuel cans). They had just about got body and soul back in a state of feeling almost human again and their equipment serviceable when their attention was raised by shouts coming from the front line. Their dugout was actually off one of the communication trenches but it did not take long for them to travel the one hundred yards or so to get to the front line. It had been the German sentries who had first spotted their colleagues' forage caps on the wire; their shouts of consternation were added to by the further shouts of derision by the British. Insults were being traded across no-man's land when the lads arrived and this started as being reasonably light hearted, bearing in mind it represented to Fritz six dead comrades. These insults gradually became more threatening and obscene, followed by the trading of rifle shot, progressing into machine gun fire and finally both sides turned to a full-scale artillery bombardment. The British made certain that the two ambush dugouts were destroyed using the forage caps to home in on. Fritz would not be trying that stunt again, at least not at that location. The lads retired as quickly as they could with shells falling all around. They could no longer hear the solemn rattle of those monstrous machine guns, spitting their deadly venom. As disconcerting as that was, it was drowned out completely by the flood of high explosives which arced into the sky falling like waves crashing on to a shingle beach washing across the British lines. Daniel looked back towards the German lines. The red, yellow and brown ghostly flashes of explosions through the smoke from previous hits were visible wherever he looked. Up ahead there was a tremendous eruption at the junction of the communications trench and the support trench a large forward base for the artillery observers had just taken a direct hit. A rain storm of debris of building materials and other more bizarre objects came back down to earth. A bed head, drawers, chairs and even a mirror landed and if the explosion hadn't shattered them in the first place then the heavy landing did. The only thing to land in one piece was amazingly a chamber pot!

It landed at Des's feet, "Well, how the hell did that survive when everything else is kindling?" Des instinctively picked it up and carried it with him.

"Well they don't seem to have taken that very well do they?" giggled Ray as the lads ducked into their dugout.

"Old Fritz is well known for not having a sense of humour, you know," replied Geordie as the last of the group found the safety of the dugout.

Daniel looked round to check that everyone had made it. He had to take a second look as his eyes scanned Des and saw the chamber pot, "Des, what are you carrying a bleeding chamber pot for?" his voice couldn't hide his amused amazement.

"Well it just fell at my feet; it looked very pretty so I just couldn't leave it behind."

Ray couldn't help himself, "That'll keep us out of the shit, then!"

There was a groan at his feeble joke and then the whole group started to giggle in a nervous energy sort of way.

They excavated another pair of hands from the most recent corpse they had uncovered and used them to hold the chamber pot. These hands belonged to a long since dead Frenchman if his uniform was anything to go by. This went to prove how long the sides had been facing each other across this actual section of line; the French had not been here since the very early stages of the war.

This rickety, ramshackle dugout did not exactly embody Daniel's notion of a bombproof abode, but it was all they had. They now could do nothing other than sit out the deadly game of high explosive tennis that both sides threw at each other for no other reason than they could. These shells were being fired from the relative safety of the rear and, as usual, it was the PBI that paid the ultimate price. After a few hours there was a marked decrease in the British bombardment but the Germans kept up their intensity, almost trying to make up for the obvious defeat in the war of stealth that had just been played out. The enemy onslaught continued for three more hours keeping everybody's nerves hanging on tenterhooks. At any time from any gun a shell could strike their dugout. Of the hundreds of shells that landed it would only take one direct hit to wipe out the Knaves just as it was doing up and down the line. It was a sick feeling that you were not in control of your own destiny and in actual fact in the lap of the war gods. But Odin was looking after the Knaves, as Daniel knew he would, he always protected his warriors. The most horrendous game of chance imaginable. Daniel had received orders from Pickering that, at the cessation of the bombardment, his section was to fall in to the front line and to expect a German attack. When it did stop and he led his lads out and up towards the front line, they could see only devastation all around, entire sections of trench collapsed in on itself. Here, to move forward you had to expose yourself above the protection of where the original trench had been and Daniel felt the bullets fly past him as though attacked by hundreds of deranged hornets. By the time they got into the front line trench, it was too packed to allow them any room on the fire steps, but he did drag a few men off to allow Ray and Geordie to position their Lewis's. There had been a fatal delay between the end of the German bombardment and the assault. Like cattle being driven to slaughter, the grey-clad hordes stormed across no-man's land with screams of rage and bravado, challenging the British Tommy to stand and fight – they did. It was ridiculously brave but totally foolhardy. They were mown down in their droves, in a matter of minutes the German attack was in ruins and their troops staggered slowly to a halt, turned and, what had been a fine looking sight of row upon row of Bavarian disciplined infantry, was now a fleeing mass of panic and all the way back to their trench the British continued to snipe at them.

Daniel surveyed the scene after the last German was either back in their trench or was lying face down in the sea of mud that extended between the two lines. He felt nothing but satisfaction in a job well done. His sensitivity to death in this grotesque environment had diminished to nil. It was easily quantified in Daniel's eyes: kill or be killed and, as far as he was concerned, he had far too much to live for. His job was to look after the living; there was no time or place for the dead. The desolate and lifeless scene that stretched out before him would have given him nightmares a year ago and back then he would have expected this to haunt the very devil himself. But not now. This was the nature of the beast and he had to deal with it, for himself and the others.

Following the end of the bombardment, the assault had taken no more than an hour but it had been a harrowing twenty-four hour period. A very weary section made their way down the communication trench that had already been temporarily repaired by the working parties. It was early evening and the quartermaster had sent up ammunition to restock and hot food and tea was brought forward. With replenished ammunition and full-ish bellies they fell asleep through almost total exhaustion. Only one man stayed awake on sentry duty for the group in case they were needed. Daniel took the first spell and then on through the night on an hourly rota they took their turn overseeing the safety of their pals.

Over the next month, the section had very little in the way of specialist tasks so they became part of the battalion once again and the daily chores and monotony of front line infantry was their lives. There was an element of risk from the sporadic shelling or sniper fire if you lifted your head too high, but with no attacks from Fritz and no planned attacks on the allied side for the most part it was tedious:

Daily trench and rifle inspection, which meant cleaning their rifles, cleaning themselves and trying to get rid (an impossible task) of lice and rats.

Stand too, half an hour before and after dawn and dusk, which was the most likely attack times.

Breakfast was a mess tin on wood chips to boil water for tea, a slice of bacon with bread placed into the fat or breaking hard biscuits up into the fat.

Other meals were served up by the working parties that would bring the occasional hot stew but, more often, just bully beef with bread or hard biscuits and the speciality of the house, petrol-flavoured tea!

Latrine duty which was a punishment, but some troops liked it as it took them back from the front. None of the Knaves received such a punishment, it would have not only let them down but the section would have been let down and nobody could allow that to happen.

The only action was the odd patrol into no-man's land and once they stayed out until the next night. They manned a listening post, but that could only hold three men, so Art, Ronnie and Johnny spent the night in a shallow dug trench that led out into no-man's land. During the night, any action would be caught by Very lights fired from flare guns used by both sides for illuminating the darkness and enabling all manner of weaponry to range in on the unfortunate soldiers caught in the open.

On a daily basis Fritz would shell with an array of artillery – high velocity shells, shrapnel shells and the worst were the heavy trench mortars (*minenwerfers* or whizz bangs!).

Relief crews would arrive after about a week allowing R&R into the rear, this could be up to a mile behind the front lines. Here, billets could be anything from a chateau to bivvies. Unfortunately for the lads, it was, on their two occasions the latter. Here, they tried to get baths and had a chance to meet the locals plus using the military brothels. Unfortunately, the small hamlet near to Langemark-Poelkapelle where they got their R&R was called Kapsalon Cathy. Daniel viewed what had previously been a peaceable, quaint hamlet that had been reduced to nothing more than a miserable pile of rubble. All of the buildings had been damaged, and most devastated. What had been previously homes to normal people was now the playground of soldiers as they rifled through the personal belongings looking for anything that could be salvaged.

They were back in their homely dugout when orders arrived which was to transport them back to Poperinge and a briefing with Lieutenant-Colonel Henry Neville. Daniel's heart skipped a beat. He would get news of Marie and how the visit with his parents had gone. Hopefully Henry would be carrying the latest letters from Marie and his parents as the mail had stopped flowing for the last few weeks for some reason. They left under the cover of darkness and were well out of range of the guns before daylight. Without any pre-arranged transport it was a case of hitching lifts wherever they could. The seven miles or so were covered very easily with the good weather. As they marched, Daniel was amazed, how absurd it was that, in amongst all this desolation, there appeared many corners of Flanders which had been missed by the violence and hooliganism of the war. But he knew this was probably just a temporary oversight and the gods of war would rectify this in due course.

Amien

The Windfall

As they marched into Poperinge, Daniel could hardly contain his excitement. He knew he had to get the troops billeted before going to the Divisional HQ where he was to meet Henry, but as the camp got closer he got edgier. It got to the point where, as soon as they arrived, Ray turned to him.

"Give me your kit and get yourself off and see Henry. You're like a kid at the fairground!"

It took no persuasion. "Thanks Ray, I'll be back as soon as I have news." And with that, he was off towards HQ.

Daniel reached Divisional HQ a little after 6.00 p.m. and he half suspected Henry might have already left for the evening. To his pleasant surprise this was not the case. As they greeted each other, Henry explained he was about to leave when word had reached him from the camp that the section had just arrived so he had delayed leaving for the Palace Hotel.

"How did it go?" Daniel blurted out.

"Oh fine, the injury is all but healed and I am officially back on full operational duties."

"I don't mean that!" cried Daniel.

With that Henry started to smile, "Not for a single minute did I think you did. Forgive my teasing Danny, but I couldn't help it ... Relax, everything went fine, your father and uncle are both smitten with her. You'd have serious competition there if either was twenty years younger, and well your mother, she's just found herself the daughter she never had and probably a best friend. They were inseparable from the moment they met. Marie says that when they are alone together your mother wants only to speak French so she can polish her language skills up, but Marie says she does not need it and realises why your French is so good. Anyway, I have letters from both of them back at the hotel. If we make our way there now I will let you have them and a big bundle for the rest of the lads. The U-boats have been up to mischief in the Channel and have managed to sink a couple of ships over the last couple of weeks and both were carrying mail as well as troops."

"Where is she now? Has she come back to France with you? Why is she not here, or is she?"

"Steady on Danny! One question at a time, you're asking questions faster than I can listen! No, she is not back in France. She is coming in a couple of weeks' time with Catherine ... and your mother! That's how good friends they have become she is coming back with your mother to show her Château de Noyelles, Abbeville and the Somme Bay area."

"Is that safe, what's the action like down there?"

"Nothing really happened since the early part of the war when we gave Amien up rather easily, then took it back just as easy. The trenches run to the north-east of Amien at the moment and Abbeville is untouched, with the château further still to the west; it is clear of any risk really.

"Anyway by a stroke of coincidence this will bring us to the mission I have for you and the lads. It will have you operating down there for a while so you should get the opportunity to meet up. I suppose you'd like that?"

It didn't take long to get to the hotel in the staff car that Henry had at his disposal. En route it was decided that Ray should be in on the briefing so, as the pair retreated into the bar, the car was sent on to the camp to bring Sergeant Murray to the hotel for the mission details over evening meal. With the formalities of the meal out of the way and having found a corner of the lounge in which to talk confidentially, Henry started with a brief history lesson about Amien and followed with the mission brief.

"There has been a textile tradition of Amiens for hundreds of years and recently it became even more famous for its velours. The textile guild and the merchants had amassed over one hundred thousand pounds in gold bars which, at the outbreak of war, the merchants removed from the bank and stored in the vaults of Amiens' 18th-century City Hall where they kept its presence secret from both the French and British armies, not trusting them to leave it alone. With the war ongoing the price of gold has rocketed by two hundred per cent of its pre-war price.

"At the start of the war, in August 1914, Amiens had been the advance base for the British Expeditionary Force. It was captured by the German Army on 31 August 1914, but recaptured by the French on 28 September. The proximity of Amiens to the Western Front and its importance as a rail hub made it a vital British logistic centre, so we intend holding it at all costs.

"Unfortunately, during the short German occupation one of the noble merchants who decided that good old Kaiser Willy was going to win the war turned informer and the Germans got their hand on the lot. When the French took it back the Germans retreated with the gold and several grand masters that hung in the city hall, they were last seen leaving the city on the troop paymaster's wagon down the Rue Voyelle through the area of Camon on to the

Rue de Lamotte-Brebiere wetlands following the River Somme towards Peronne. The speed of the French attack meant that they captured many of the retreating German forces. The paymaster wagon did not reach Peronne, and neither did it get captured. The only conclusion we can draw is that it was camouflaged and hidden to be retrieved at a later date. It has been brought to my attention by my contacts in Peronne that the Germans have realised they will not be able to retake this land, anytime soon so they are about to send in a team to recover it."

Henry started to lay out a couple of maps;

"Amiens lies on the basin of the Somme River more or less where its tributaries, the Selle and Avre, flow into it. The old town is situated in a swampy area at the bottom of the valley. Amiens is also known for the *hortillonnages*, gardens on small islands in the marshland between the River Somme and River Avre, surrounded by a grid network of man-made canals, known locally as *rieux*. They are also known as the 'floating gardens of Amiens'. Because of the canals, the *hortillonnages* are sometimes called 'Little Venice of the North'. This wetland area follows the River Somme all the way to Peronne and presents thousands of hiding places for our shipment. The Frenchies can only say that they overtook the last of the retreating forces at Bray-sur-Somme. I think it's safe to say if it were behind or on the German lines they would have had it away by now. No, it must be behind our lines.

"So gentlemen, somewhere between Camon and Bray-sur-Somme there is a shipment of over three hundred thousand pounds of gold at today's rate, several priceless grand masters and an undisclosed amount of German marks waiting for your boys to retrieve before this German unit does. There is one more twist to this; the leader of the German unit is one Oberleutnant Rex von Grapon, who if my sources are correct, was the mastermind in setting up the trap they set to catch you at Langemark-Poelkapelle. If I may say so, your result there was a work of art, another famous mission for the Knaves, Haig is in seventh heaven when he retells that story!"

Henry handed over the maps of the area and one very useful surveyor's map of the valley which showed elevations. Two areas of high ground appeared along the entire twenty miles of the valley bottom from Camon to Bray-sur-Somme one of which was a wooded area above a small hamlet of Etinehem. Daniel immediately thought that this would be a good place to watch and wait for the German team to make their move, explaining to both Henry and Ray that the only way they could find such a well-hidden shipment was to wait for the Germans to take them to it. They all agreed with that basic principle but a lot more planning was needed and an immediate start the following day was also required as they did not know exactly when the Germans would be setting out.

"Annette's cousin, Pierre, is a fisherman in the Somme Bay and plies his trade up the Somme River all the way up to Peronne. Actually, he crosses the front line with his trade, he could possibly help with guiding and transport," suggested Ray.

Both Henry and Daniel knew the importance of local knowledge and were quick to encourage Ray to send a despatch to Annette requesting her to ask her cousin to meet with them in Amien. Henry called his aide who was still working at HQ to arrange a despatch rider to deliver Ray's request to Annette immediately. Knowing they would have an early start the next morning, Daniel and Ray left Henry by about 9.00 p.m. Henry, returning to HQ to check the despatch rider was ready, carried Ray's letter to hand over in person.

Ray left to get in the car with Daniel close behind, when Henry stopped him and pulled him to one side, "Danny, you understand that we are officially only after regaining our French friends' gold and there is no proof that any German pay chests are with it, and even if there is nobody knows how much. Haig would be very excited by the return of the guild's gold and nothing more, if you understand my meaning," he winked at Daniel.

Travelling down to Amien was by train from Poperinge to Calais and then transferring on to another train directly down to Amien. The first train was the usual cramped cattle wagons where there was not enough room even to sit. The train creaked and groaned along a very sorry looking track that had been patched together more times than the average pair of socks on the front line! With it being the main means of new troops getting to the front from the allied ports of Calais and Boulogne, the Germans had constantly given it some close attention. There were several times when the train and carriages lurched violently to one side or the other as they ran over areas of embankment that had been undercut by artillery bombardment. As fast as the engineers repaired it, Fritz did his level best to destroy it. The observation positions of the Germans picked up on a train leaving Poperinge and the predictable bombardment commenced. With all the practice the Germans had had at hitting the line they only managed to hit the track directly behind the train as it limped its way out of the station and on into open country. No sooner had the bombardment stopped when the rattle of machine guns started as an aeroplane bearing the dreaded cross of the Imperial German Air Service bore down on them. They had all heard that the German planes had now got forward-facing machine guns which could be operated by the pilot, but this was the first time they had seen proof of it. It swept into the flank of the train spitting its flashes of fire, raking the carriages at the rear. Its first pass was relatively easy as it had caught the occupants of the train unawares. The pilot was in for a nasty shock on his second attack as every available gun, including two Lewis guns belonging to Ray and Geordie, let rip. From being a deadly menace it became a death trap in seconds, so much lead was put up into the air in the bi-plane's direction it could not fail to run into some. Its wings folded, the engine smoked and then a small explosion (possibly an on-board bomb destined for the train) saw the machine crash almost pathetically into the field adjacent to the track. With the demise of the bi-plane, the journey became much less fraught and they arrived in Calais within a couple of hours with just a couple of stops to check the track's integrity rather than risking a derailment. With the lads de-trained from this journey, Daniel and Ray left them on the platform while they found where they had to be to get the next train to Amien. They only had two hours to wait so stayed close by to the station and used the estaminet just outside the Gare Calais Frethun to replenish their stock of food and wine. This set them up in good spirits for the longer but much more pleasant journey down to Amien. They were still in carriages that had been used for livestock but at least they had one to themselves and they had old bails of straw to sit on. The train pulled into Gare d' Amiens a little after 6.00 p.m. and, as ordered, they marched through the town to the north of the railway station to pick up the Rue de Verdun which led directly on to the Rue Voyelle and into the Camon area. They were already on the trail of the German retreat back in 1914, but only Daniel and Ray new the significance of this route. They came across a small factory unit on the side of the River Somme next to the Rue Marius Petit. It was closed down but still in good structural order, the house next door was number 45 and, as his instructions directed, he knocked on the door and was most warmly met by an elderly man who, impressed as he was with Daniel's French, insisted in speaking his much poorer English. Monsieur Olivier was one of the textile merchants who had lost his gold to the Germans and represented the entire guild in his capacity *de president*. He showed the lads to the offices attached to the factory where they found washing facilities and a small kitchen and, with the factory still having lots of unsold bolts of cloth, enough material for adequate soft and clean bedding for the night. Monsieur Olivier left the lads to get set up and assured Daniel that food, coffee and wine would arrive shortly. The largest office which Daniel suspected would have been Monsieur Olivier's was set up so he could go through the briefing with the lads and finalise the plan that he had with their input. It basically had five stages to it.

Moving up to the front line and meeting the commanding officer in the area to get any intelligence off him, he had been made aware of a possible incursion by a group of German troops, but not what their purpose was. Plus they would scout the valley on the way.

Setting up the two observation posts on the two pieces of higher ground he had identified off the maps that Henry had given him. He suspected that if they had been given enough time it would be the post at the wooded area above a small hamlet of Etinehem. That would be the first place that they would pick up their guests, but just in case by the time they got there the Germans had proceeded beyond Etinehem, another one would be set up at Sailly-Laurette. Between the two, they could keep an eye of the whole of the Somme Valley from the front line to the outskirts of Camon

They would pick up the German unit and follow them, by moving over the higher ground the two groups would be able to keep in contact without being seen. Daniel had no fear that the Germans would travel up on the high ground, they would be too visible up there when they were operating behind enemy lines.

It would be a simple case of waiting for the Germans to locate and get the load ready for the journey back when they would spring their ambush.

Boats could be used to get the treasure back down stream to Amien and using different boats would lessen the risk of losing all if the water was running high.

They had just finished the briefing when Monsieur Olivier brought Pierre Gabon into the office. It was a slightly strange meeting, introducing themselves to Annette's kin, who they had never set eyes on before, especially when they would have to let this stranger into a few big secrets. Sensing the situation, Pierre made his introduction in a way that proved he had been sent by Annette.

He immediately walked up to Ray, "I see why Cousin Annette has been so taken by you, you are so like her husband it is quite amazing," he turned to Daniel and said, "and you must be the English captain who has stolen Mademoiselle Marie's heart?"

They all shook hands and Daniel translated for Ray, who although his French was improving, struggled with the speed and accent of Pierre. Unabashed, Ray ripped into a brief welcome in his best stuttering French. It was far from perfect but surprised and impressed Daniel, and Pierre appreciated that he had made the effort. Daniel explained to Pierre that Ray was just learning French and wanted to surprise Annette at their next meeting, this again seemed to win favour with the likeable French fisherman. There was nothing for it but to let Pierre into the whole story. If they expected him to guide them he had to know what he was letting himself in for.

Pierre listened to the story and the basic plan. Then let them into a little secret of his own. "I carry intelligence messages out of Peronne to the French Army HQ in Amien; my hatred for the Germans is huge. My family have been decimated by this war and myself, I have lost my left leg just below the knee or I would be still fighting the filthy Hun," he said whilst tapping it with his knuckles, there was a resounding wooden reply to the percussion. "You may need more observation points, there are many twists and turns to the Somme and the valley is deep?" he suggested. "I have arrived here with a full catch and in the morning I will sell to the market traders in Amien before starting out for Peronne. I could go ahead and scout for you if that would be of help?"

Monsieur Olivier was good to his word and when the plans had been discussed they ate and drank before turning in for a good night's sleep. Daniel was excited, this was something very different and the whole plan was down to him. The buzz of anticipated action was not sufficient to stop him from sleeping and it was a well-rested Daniel Byrne and the rest of the Knaves that woke at 5.00 a.m., breakfasted and moved along the road that ran parallel to the river until they reached the village of Lamotte-Brebiere where they dropped down to the side of the Somme. This was their rendezvous point with Pierre where Ray, in borrowed civilian clothing, joined Pierre in the boat which moved off up river and the others started to follow it east towards Peronne and the oncoming Germans.

There were three boats in total, the front being a small skiff with a square sail and the two others, Daniel would describe them as small rowing boats, were tied in line behind. These were the boats that actually carried the fish, the skiff had a small cabin which acted as Pierre's home during his three-day trip to catch his fish, sell at Abbeville, Amien and Peronne and buy cheese and wine in Perrone to sell back in Amien and Abbeville. It became clear to Daniel they had a perfect cover story.

Pierre's advice proved correct, the terrain would not actually allow just two observation points to cover the whole of the valley. It just proved a point to Daniel who made a mental note that what looked like a plan on paper rarely survived the first view on the ground, which in fact was Haig's own reason for setting their section up in the first place.

As they moved forward along the river, it was a different world to that of the Ypres Salient. There were no background rumblings of distant artillery, the sun was shining and everything seemed peaceful. You could see *anguillères* (eel traps) and the shining scales of carp, enjoying the calm of the surrounding waters. Pierre had stopped a couple of times to talk to the anglers next to the eel traps to ask if anybody had seen German soldiers, explaining that if they did they should get to the bridges at, Corbie, Sailly-Laurette, Sailly-le-Sec or Chipilly where they would find British troops to report to. He told Ray in slow, studied French that all these people hated the Germans and would not fail to inform them of any sightings and that nothing travelled along the valley without them noticing. With Pierre's guidance Daniel had placed two lads on each of the bridges and Pierre had arranged a bicycle to be made available to allow quick contact between each via the roads which everybody agreed the Germans would not dare to use, at least on the way down to locate the treasure.

They reached Etinehem by mid-afternoon where Daniel left the rest of the lads under the watchful eye of Art. They camped in the woods just west of the village and, with the permission of the local priest, used the church tower to watch the river all the way back to the point at which the French had overrun the retreating German forces back in 1914, Bray-sur-Somme.

Daniel, wearing one of Pierre's fishing smocks to hide his tunic, Ray and Pierre set off up the river towards the front line which was just a few miles west of Peronne following a straggling line from Arras in the north to Roye in the south. On reaching the allied front line, Daniel and Ray went to report to Colonel Davies, who commanded in this region. At that particular time the war seemed to have forgotten the Picardy region in comparison to other areas where industrial slaughter was a daily expectation. Pierre had carried on about his normal business and proceeded up river to Peronne, for his fish needed to be sold and this would give him the opportunity to speak to his contacts.

"So the famous Knaves are amongst us!" was Davies' reaction whilst shaking Daniel's hand enthusiastically.

At first, Daniel thought he was being sarcastic but it was evident by the way he vigorously pumped Daniel's hand his enthusiasm was very sincere. Daniel was quite taken aback that the Knaves should be known even in this part of the line. He accepted Davies' invitation to coffee in the rather plush surroundings of Le Château l'Oseraie, in the village of Hem-Monacu.

Davies explained, "There is a very good understanding between the two front lines at this moment in time, in so much as if we leave them alone then Fritz leaves us alone! I know this won't always be the case but for the moment I can't see the reason for stirring things up and spoiling this tranquil setting any sooner than necessary."

Daniel could tell that Davies wanted to be in on the game but was too straight-laced to ask. He also realised that he needed to know just in case things didn't go to plan and the Germans managed to get the treasure back to Hem-Monacu and tried to cross the line. Davies was ecstatic at being part of such a stunt and working alongside the Knaves, he could not wait to share his piece of intelligence with Daniel.

"My boys picked up on a strange floating object moving down stream by our floodlights during the night. It was about midnight and it appeared to be a couple of large logs side by side but what was suspicious was they were almost perfectly parallel to each other and there seemed to be objects between them. Head-shaped objects! So at first light I sent two teams, one on each bank down river to see if anything could be seen. They had just got back when you arrived and it appeared that the two logs were tethered together and they had come ashore and been carried up on to the bank just a mile beyond here, on the northern bank," Davies unashamedly beamed with pride at his news.

Just then there was an urgent sounding knock on the door and a sergeant entered, saluted and apologised before explaining that Sergeant Murray and a Frenchman needed to speak urgently.

"Bring them in man, bring them in," he waved almost beside himself with growing excitement.

Ray came in with Pierre behind him. He saluted and Colonel Davies had him and Pierre sit and insisted on not being so formal in these intimate circumstances. Ray explained that Pierre had learnt that the Germans had crossed the line under the cover of darkness last night so there was no time to lose. With corroborating information it was clear that the Germans were downstream of their current position. Daniel was not too concerned with this; he knew that if he were in Oberleutnant Rex von Grapon's position, to remain unseen until at least they recovered their treasure they would only travel during darkness. Even then they would stay at the river's edge, so the way Daniel reckoned it, as he explained to his waiting audience.

"If they passed through the front at midnight and travelled a mile downstream before coming ashore, it will have taken them probably an hour or so before they would be ready to move off. They would need to hold up undercover by 5.00 a.m. to ensure they are not spotted by any fishermen out on the river, so at best they have had four hours travelling, through hard going, probably only making a couple of miles per hour," he opened up his map and looked hard at it, then tapped on a point on the map over a village called Cappy. "With the best progress they could have made I would say this is the furthest they could have travelled, what do you think Ray?"

Ray was not too good at strategy and was happy to go along with Daniel's logic, but knew his friend needed backing up in front of the colonel so agreed, "Can't see how they would get any further than that without taking risks and they won't want to do that until they are forced to when they pick up their loot!"

"So," concluded Daniel, "if we set off back down river at about 9.00 p.m. by the time we are in that area they should have started to move once again and, with luck, we might actually locate them."

Daniel checked with Pierre that he had concluded his business and would be happy to set off at the planned time, and when Pierre had agreed they had more coffee and Colonel Davies insisted on them dining with him.

Pierre had suggested that if Daniel was willing to go in one of the other boats and they did locate the Germans, and he thought it was very possible due to there being a clear sky and a near full moon that night, he could continue down river to meet up with the others whilst he and Ray kept an eye on the German progress. This seemed like an excellent idea so was quickly adopted into the ever-developing plan. Daniel sat in the small boat that was being towed by the skiff. He had managed to get a civilian cap to wear with Pierre's smock from the gatehouse at Le Château l'Oseraie. They pushed off and, without the sail on the skiff being up, due to travelling with the flow of the river, they moved in almost total silence. The current flowed steadily and Pierre had estimated that they would arrive in the Cappy area at about 10.00 p.m. They had been keeping a sharp lookout from the minute they had pushed off but from the big sweeping bend just east of Cappy where the river separated from the mass of ponds that filled the valley. They paid even closer attention to the reeds on the northern bank. Just as the river started to converge with the ponds on the eastern edge of Cappy, Pierre raised his hand and steered the skiff to the southern shore behind a small crop of trees, pointing across at some tall reeds a little way ahead on the opposite bank. Daniel could just see movement, an unnatural swirling of the reeds that suggested several people travelling undercover. Daniel was impressed; firstly by Pierre's eyesight, although it shouldn't have been too surprising as the man's safety relied upon this for safe navigation of the river on a near daily basis. Secondly, the Germans, they had not shied away from taking the hardest possible route in a bid to remain unseen. Unfortunately for them, they had been spotted and their slow progress would now allow Daniel to move ahead of them and prepare their welcoming committee. Prior to setting off, Pierre had given Daniel a quick course in steering a boat with the flow of the current by paddle only. By using it like a rudder over the rear, it ensured a quick and silent passage ahead of the Germans and down to Etinehem whilst only running aground once. That had not proved too much of an issue, Daniel had just allowed the small boat a little too close to the shore where it caught a sandbank just below the surface. He had simply got out and re-launched it and was at Etinehem within two hours. Daniel knew that at the rate of progress that von Grapon and his men were making, it probably would not be until the following night that they would arrive at Bray–sur-Somme at which point they needed to have continual observation on von "Crapun" (as the lads had taken to calling him!).

The bicycles proved their worth and by the following morning all the group were together. Daniel sent two riders up the road towards Cappy to locate the skiff with Ray and Pierre in and between them they were to convey progress reports on the Germans. Using the boat, he sent Ronnie and Des across to the southern bank to cover that side just in case von Grapon decided to cross over.

It seemed to be an age and Daniel had been having doubts about his plan when finally Johnny arrived back on his bicycle to inform Daniel that, "Von Crapun has gone to ground just to the east of Bray-sur-Somme near to a 'D'-shaped section of water away from the actual river close to a road. Ray has gone on to the shore to keep an eye on them and says that they appeared to be having a good look around the area before first light when they went to ground again. It was almost as if they were looking for something."

It made sense thought Daniel, if the retreating Germans had to hide their treasure quickly it would need to be close to a road. They would be unlikely to have sufficient time to move it across marshy terrain by hand and still escape the pursuing French.

Ray had shown Johnny exactly where they were on his map which Johnny now showed Daniel on his. It was clear that if the Knaves moved quickly they could be in position by dusk and wait to see what von Grapon had planned. They moved off on to the road into Bray-sur-Somme and out, on to the Cappy road. Just outside Bray-sur-Somme they took a small turn off which dropped down and forked either side of the 'D'-shaped pond. They stopped at the fork in the road and the group was split into two.

Ray had joined them and had made it clear that he was convinced that this was where Fritz's loot was, "They could have made much more progress down river if they had wanted, but instead they have gone on to the island in the middle of the 'D', this must be the place."

"Okay Ray, if you take your Lewis and your lads along the left fork and I will take Geordie with his Lewis and the others to the right, set up so we are shooting over towards that bush," he said pointing at it, "we need to take care not to shoot each other whilst taking out von Grapon!"

"How are you going to give the signal?"

"Well we may as well leave it until they have recovered all the loot, no use in doing the dirty work ourselves. Besides, once they have done some hard labour they will be tired and have less fight left, hopefully. I will use the whistle and then just let rip with everything we have got. We haven't got enough men here to take prisoners and transport the treasure back."

When Daniel was in position he could see that the Germans were actually still up and about very stealthily, however they were working at constructing a couple of carts. When the treasure had been hidden they had obviously dismantled these carts to allow then to be hidden more easily. The wheels and sides had been disassembled and hidden in the reeds just under the water level. As the carts took shape, two men started pulling on submerged ropes and in total fifteen small chests appeared from out of the water with one further one which seemed to be longer that all the others coming up with a lot less effort. Daniel was not quite sure what von Grapon's plan would be to try to find horses to pull the carts, but he was concerned that some of his men or collaborators could be meeting them. It was for this reason that Daniel decided to commence the attack. He was just about to give the signal when another German came through the reeds and shallow water on the end of the island where the bush was that they were using to align their attack. He had Pierre at gunpoint. Daniel choked back the air in his lungs that had filled to blast the whistle. Unfortunately, Pierre would not know that the Knaves were in position to commence the attack or what the ambush plan was. He was now directly in the line of fire. It was impossible to hear what was being said as they whispered but several slaps across Pierre's face were delivered by the person who appeared to be in charge. This was presumably Oberleutnant Rex von Grapon. The final slap was sufficient to knock Pierre off his feet and he landed down the sloping bank towards the water. Knowing that this little turn of events would have Ray ready and chomping at the bit, he blew his whistle hard. All hell broke loose. All shots were aimed towards the bushes as arranged but managed to cut the Germans down at torso height. Men and reeds were scythed down together, only the men hit the ground quicker and harder. When the firing had stopped, the reeds still floated down to earth having been torn apart and propelled skywards. It was eerily quiet after the devastatingly noisy and violent preceding seconds. As both groups from either side of the pond stood up to survey the scene, they cautiously made their way on to the island by two small land bridges. It was a scene of tangled mayhem, already the pools of blood spilt from the tattered German bodies soaked into the dry dirt island. The dust of the disintegrated reeds, the cordite of the bullets and the thick sickly smell of bloody death was overpowering to both the eyes and the nose. Very slowly across the island a body moved, it was Pierre. He had been fortunate enough to have remained down the bank below the level of the guns. As he got to his feet, with lightning speed a second body moved in behind Pierre, pistol in hand and thrust into Pierre's back. Oberleutnant Rex von Grapon was alive!

As the flying chaff and dust settled, there was a silence. Just for a second, then suddenly with a thrashing of reeds, a screaming of threatened violence and a blazing pistol in hand another German appeared, presumably, thought Daniel, this was another sentry. Shooting from the hip, Geordie let him have a two-second burst of his Lewis. The air-cooled gun featured a 47 cartridge circular magazine which Geordie and Ray replaced immediately on ending any fire fight to ensure the gun's preparedness; with a firing rate of 500–600 rounds per minute it meant that half the magazine was emptied into the German and, at that range, Geordie didn't miss. As Daniel looked on, he firstly thought of the mistake he had made by not deploying sentries himself, the next was relief as nobody seemed to have been hurt and finally it was one of mild humour as he has just witnessed this German cut in half by the twenty plus British 303s-calibre bullets. Poor old Fritz's legs had almost comically carried on running not realising that his owner had been knocked backwards, dead, it was only after two further paces that the legs fell in solidarity with its severed torso. Again silence.

Still standing facing him was von Grapon, pistol pressed into Pierre's back. Von Grapon did not even flinch at the demise of his (hopefully) final comrade.

Daniel stood out in front of his lads, "Ray post sentries to cover the perimeter," he never took his eyes off von Grapon whilst giving the order.

"Captain Daniel Byrne, I presume, Oberleutnant Rex von Grapon, at your service," he very slightly bowed his head in salute and there was the faintest sound of his heels clicking together although Daniel could not see as the pair of them were still partially down the bank.

"I am aware of whom you are and what you are doing here, but it does look like your efforts have been in vain. We have been following you since you crossed the front line in between those logs. You appear to have nowhere to go and half the allied army is aware of your whereabouts. I suggest you place that gun on the ground very carefully or you will end up in the same state as your comrades!"

"So it appears that the British have finally started to gather credible intelligence? Captain Byrne I schooled in England and was educated at Oxford," he spoke in perfect English, considerably better than Daniel's, "I am more aware of the British sense of fair play than you are. I don't think you will endanger this French fisherman, as pathetic as he is. In fact he could be part of your infamous Knaves, albeit just for the purpose of this little enterprise. I am just going to back down here into the reeds and through the shallows where my friend here will continue to serve as a shield but also will take me back up the Somme and across the lines. If you try in any way to stop me, then he has landed his final catch!"

With that he started reversing down into the water through the reeds with Pierre protecting his front. Daniel knew that now was not the time to take action. With poor visibility through the reeds and Pierre not being as fleet of foot as he would be if he had two good legs, there was too much of a risk. After all, Pierre was almost family to Ray even though they hardly knew each other and he had courageously helped their cause. No, von Grapon was right; he couldn't do anything to endanger Pierre. Besides, when they had ensured the skiff was heading up river they could use the bicycles to get to the bridges that crossed the Somme and its wetlands at Cappy. There they would meet up with von Grapon and Pierre would have more of a chance of escaping if they could catch them by surprise.

"Stay where you are boys," ordered Daniel, "we don't want an innocent civilian getting hurt!" He turned to the disappearing German, "Von Grapon we will meet again and next time you will not have anybody to hide behind, that's a promise!"

"Captain Byrne, I look forward to it and when the time comes I will be the one holding the cards, if you excuse the joke on your choice of calling cards, and you, you will be dead!"

Ray stiffened and started to move after the voice in the reeds, but Daniel stopped him. "Let him go Ray, we can get him later."

Daniel's head was spinning with the number of thoughts he was trying to process at the same time, but this was what he thrived on and in seconds he barked out his orders.

"Geordie, follow at a distance to the water's edge, don't let him see you, but just check they are moving up river. Ray, Des and Johnny get the bicycles together, we can get up to the bridges at Cappy faster than they can, they are moving against the flow. Art get the rest to bring the other two boats over here and start loading the loot into them if there is not enough room in the boats then wait for us to come back down river and we will need to separate the haul into what we take by river and road. Keep a watch to ensure they don't double back and head down river if they do you will have to stop them at all costs and, unfortunately, Pierre will have to take his chances. If they do double back, signal with a short blast of Geordie's Lewis, is that understood?"

"Right, Danny."

"Okay. We'll see you in a little while with that pompous Kraut, dead and floating!"

The bicycles were ready and they were off. It was no more than a mile and a half to get to the first of the four bridges that crossed the mass of water that made up the Somme at this point, but from these points they could see anything that was approaching from whichever of the four narrow strips of water that actually passed under the bridges from the numerous interconnecting ponds and the main river.

The wait was agonising. No signal from Art. They must be coming, just be patient. Doubts! Have faith. Have they beaten us to the bridges? Are we waiting here and they are sailing merrily towards the front lines?

There was a sail, yes it was a boat. More importantly it was Pierre's skiff staying close to the southern bank. Not surprisingly thought Daniel, he should expect us to pursue him and not just give up so easily. At the tiller was Pierre, but Daniel could not see von Grapon.

"The bastard is probably hiding in the cabin with his gun trained on Pierre," growled Ray who, like the others, had come over to the southernmost bridge to join Daniel when he signalled to them that it was that bridge that the skiff was heading for.

"I could pepper that cabin and in seconds there would be nothing left alive under that roof," suggested Ray rather enthusiastically.

Just then the bow of the skiff hit a tree root that reached out into the river. The boat stopped with a thud and Pierre fell sideways down into the bottom of the boat.

"I think Fritz the fox has fled the coop!"

Daniel could not hide his bitter disappointment and frustration. When they got down to the skiff it was difficult to tell if Pierre was alive or not. Ray got to him first and lifted him up into a seated upright position. Daniel posted Des and Johnny as sentries not wanting to get caught out again.

"He's breathing but has got one hell of a crack on his skull. We need to get him to a doctor as soon as possible."

Johnny had left Des and Daniel to guard the reeds and woodland that covered the bank and beyond. Daniel knew it would be impossible to track down von Grapon and now their priorities had changed. They needed to get Pierre to a doctor and save his life rather than hunt down and take the German!

With bicycle stowed and still covering the south bank, they dropped the sail and Daniel used the same technique that Pierre had taught him just a few days before to take the boat back to the others at Bray-sur-Somme, approaching with caution making sure that Art knew it was them approaching in the boat.

Sentries were already deployed and with a "Well done, Art," Daniel got the lads to put Pierre into one of the completed carts and Geordie and Ray set off pulling it up the hill to the village.

Daniel turned once again to Art and said, "Keep everybody on guard, that vicious Kraut could return although I doubt it, I'm going to the village with Pierre to get someone to send for a doctor."

"Shouldn't take too long to get there now you've got your oxen harnessed up," chuckled Art nodding in the direction of Ray and Geordie.

The nervous tension of the last few hours was finally broken and the whole group started chuckling in unison.

Ray could not help himself, he had to return humorous insult for humorous insult, "We might be the size and have the strength of oxen, but at least we don't stink like one!"

Art smiled in quiet victory; by getting Ray to bite he had won the battle of wits and humour!

In turn, Daniel smiled to himself as they moved off up the hill. Even after the stress and pressure of the last few days, the lads still had something that was irreplaceable and could not be trained into troops. It was much more than the usual military camaraderie, this was being part of family and that's what made the Knaves function so well and stand out from the rest.

By the time they got to the village there was quite a commotion. The villagers had heard the gunfire earlier but had been too scared to investigate. Nevertheless, soon after their arrival and the locals' recognition that they were not German, an elderly retired doctor had looked over Pierre who had started coming round on the cart ride. He had checked his eyes out by moving his finger from side to side and staring closely into each of his eyes and ears. The old mad pronounced him fit and well and to have the skull of an ox!

"There's a theme forming here," laughed Geordie when Daniel translated the old man's diagnosis.

It was a very poorly looking Pierre that joined the four Knaves on the walk back to the boats. Art had sent Des up to inform Daniel that they had shared the chests out across the three boats and with the lads evenly shared out, the boats were still very stable in the water. With the river so benign, Pierre had agreed that there should not be any issue in using the boats for the return journey to Amien. So Daniel had therefore given the cart to the villagers and told them where to find the others. There was a gruesome price that they had to pay however; they had agreed to bury the dead German troops that littered the reeds around the 'D'-shaped pond.

Daniel was pleased to see that Art had maintained the guards throughout the three-hour time lapse they had been away getting Pierre's head checked and bandaged. The chests were shared out across the vessels but the more common shaped chests were in the skiff along with the oddly long chest. This was the first time Daniel had had the time to look closely at them. The ten similar sized and shaped chests all carried the Amien Textile Guild crest that had been very evident at Monsieur Olivier's factory. The long slim chest was painted with a pitch-like substance and Daniel presumed this would be the old masters. It was the other five chests in the other two boats that intrigued him and one by one he forced them open to investigate. Four were of equal size and shape but one was much larger. All had the Imperial German Eagle burnt into the chest's timber. Four were full of silver German coins and the excited group's whistles soon turned to silence when the larger chest was opened. It was full of fine gold jewellery. It looked like a scene from the Robert Louis Stevenson book, *Treasure Island*: gold coins, sovereigns, old Spanish-looking coins in a bag that was labelled "Urca de Lima", small golden ingots with crests on them that Daniel did not recognise. The most stunning of the chest's contents was the array of bracelets, necklaces and tiaras studded with countless coloured stones.

All Daniel could think about at that moment in time was Henry's words back in Poperinge where they had got the mission brief, "We are officially only after regaining our French friends' gold," and "Haig would be very excited by the return of the guild's gold and nothing more".

Without further delay, Daniel arranged two of the pay chests to be placed in the skiff, whilst the other two and the gold jewellery chest were loaded into the middle boat with Ray and Geordie in it. Daniel was with Des, Johnny and

Pierre in the skiff with the rest in the empty boat bringing up the rear. All tied together, with Pierre taking the tiller of the skiff, they made steady progress down river whilst Daniel discussed a suitable landing place just before the wharf at Amien. Pierre had just the place and within three hours of steady cruising they arrived in a little pond whose entrance was almost obscured by reeds and was so densely surrounded by reeds that you could not see any civilisation, although the noises of Amien were clear to all.

The group listened in disbelief as Daniel explained what was about to happen. Ray, Geordie and Pierre were to wait in the second boat that had the jewellery and two pay chests until the rest of the group took the skiff and empty boat down on to the wharf at Amien where they would bring Monsieur Olivier to meet them and let him open the chests that contained the guild's bullion, old masters and some of the paymaster's marks. They would explain that, due to his head injury, Pierre had been detained until he was fit to travel and under the cover of darkness they would move down river to Abbeville where the other chests would be unloaded and transported to Château de Noyelles. Pierre would return to Amien with Ray and Geordie once everything was safely stored. Their treasure would be divided up between all the group who had taken part including Henry whose idea it had been from the start. If during the remainder of the war anybody was killed the group was to swear an oath right there and then to ensure the family of the deceased got their share. The disbelief turned to unbelievable excitement, but Daniel quelled it before it got out of hand. Within thirty minutes they had moored on Amien wharf close to the bridge of the Rue Voyelle not half a mile from Monsieur Olivier's house. By 10.00 p.m. all the chests were situated back at the factory with an armed guard around it until the authorities could come and take the treasure off the Knaves.

Monsieur Olivier could not contain his excitement. He had gathered all the guild members in his house and they awaited the arrival of the mayor and other town hall officials as well as a few French troops who were garrisoned in the city. It was an impressive sight when the chests were opened. Each chest was full of neatly stacked gold bars all stamped with the guild crest. No wonder each chest had weighed so much. Not so impressive as far as the lads were concerned was the rather drab looking paintings that apparently were priceless and belonged to the town hall; in the morning, carts were arranged and the recovered treasure returned to the vaults within the town hall. On seeing it safely installed in the town hall vaults, Daniel reported to the British HQ where unsurprisingly he found Henry waiting. Henry had been there since the previous day having heard an update from Colonel Davies at Château l'Oseraie.

"Well you've done it again Danny, Haig will be over the moon, another successful mission by his team, he'll have some mileage out of this!" he boomed across the HQ hall so everybody could hear.

He was slapping Daniel on the back but was clearly trying to steer him away out into the gardens of the old mansion that had been commandeered by the British as their HQ.

Once out of earshot he cut straight to the chase, but much more quietly asked "So what did we get? I've already heard that you brought back the bullion, paintings and some of the German paymaster's money, so we must have got a little something for ourselves?"

As they walked, Daniel explained how the whole mission had unfolded including the escape of von Grapon. He was enjoying the fact that he could sense that it was Henry's turn to become impatient for the real news, but when he had built the tension up enough to see Henry ready to burst he told him of the share they had and that it should be somewhere near Château de Noyelles by now.

"Danny, don't you just love it when a plan comes together? You are going to be English and French heroes after this and wealthy to boot! What a result! Oh and just to add to the good tidings, Marie and your mother are here as well."

"What! Why didn't you say so?"

"Well if you are going to play that game with me I'm sure going to have my turn," he replied, punching Daniel playfully on his arm, "where are the lads now?"

"They were making their way back to Monsieur Olivier's factory where we have our billets, awaiting further orders."

"Well the guild members had been talking about putting on a bit of a do if you brought the goods back, which obviously you have so we need to find out when and you all are to be given the freedom of the city for preserving its wealth, albeit when they say the city's wealth they really mean their wealth! Anyway you are due more furlough and that starts immediately after the public recognition, which if I don't miss a guess, Haig will want to be in on for more photographic opportunities." He leaned even closer to Daniel and whispered, "Rumour has it that he is about to take over from French as commander in chief, this will be another nail in French's coffin."

"How can I get to Marie at Château de Noyelles? Besides we all need to get over there so we can sort out what we are going to do with the loot?"

Daniel went on to explain about the oath they had taken and how they would get the share of any fallen to the remaining family.

"Very noble but I would prefer if we don't need to invoke that oath."

"Let's be realistic about this Henry, anyone of us could buy a packet at any time. If this war goes on much longer we are unfortunately bound to lose more, even all of us!"

"Good God man, what's put you in such an optimistic mood? Is it not enough for you for one day: Hero in two countries, wealthy, about to meet up with the love of your life, not to mention you mother!"

The thought of meeting Marie again brought a smile to his face and then he felt a little guilty at not including his mother in that thought, but just momentarily, "So how are we going to get over to the Château?"

After a short pause Henry answered, "If you go back to the factory and pick up you equipment, I will come over in the staff car and pick you and Ray up. I will arrange for transport for the rest and by evening we will all be at the château. I will arrange a despatch rider to inform us of when the celebration back here is to take place, or more importantly when Haig is likely to be turning up, we'll need to be back to meet him. When we return, the ladies can join us in the celebrations. I don't think your mother realises what a hero you are."

Feeling rather pleased with the plan Henry had concocted, Daniel set off for the factory in Camon. With a spring in his step it only took thirty minutes, and he gathered all the Knaves together to explain the plans for the next few hours. He was surprised to see Ray and Art back already. They had left Pierre in Abbeville where he had arranged transport for the loot to the château and a lift back to Amien for the pair.

Henry arrived and was greeted as he should be, like a long lost friend, inside the factory there was no need for military formalities, the normal micky-taking prevailed with comments of, "look who's here, it's that pen pusher" and "here's the lead magnet" and the last one they heard before they headed in the direction of Abbeville and

Château de Noyelles was, "hope he drives better than he kicks a football!"

The roads were empty and in fairly good condition, even with Henry driving like a demon, which in normal conditions would have had Daniel and Ray sick but neither noticed as both could not wait to see their ladies. On entering the grounds and passing the farm they stopped to check whether Ray and Annette was there or at the château. She was at the farm and so was Pierre, who, after a good night's sleep was looking a lot better than the last time they had seen him. Ray had stayed with Annette and had faced the introductions to her parents, they promising that they would walk up to the château shortly. Henry and Daniel proceeded and it was with a lump in his throat that he saw the grand house appear through the wooded pastureland. Due to them arriving unannounced they had entered the house and were half way across the great hallway when Margot saw them. With a beaming smile, she put her finger to her mouth to caution them to remain silent. She called to Marie, Catherine and Daniel's mother to come into the hall to assist her. Marie entered first and squealed with delight at seeing her beloved Daniel before her, she almost flew across the hallway into his arms and they did two full spins before kissing each other. Catherine had come in second and smiling she walked over to Henry and planted a kiss on his cheek; Henry had been there for evening meal and stayed the night before, so this was no big reunion for the two. Finally, Daniel's mother had followed the two younger girls and stood back smiling at the reunions going on before her. Having put Marie down, Daniel looked at her and quickly covered the few yards between them sweeping her off her feet. Until that point he had not realised how much he had missed her, Marie joined them and the three hugged for all they were worth.

"I can't believe my luck," he rejoiced, "holding the two most precious ladies in my world; life can't get better than this!"

So many conversations happened at once that it was bedlam for a few moments until Margot took charge of the situation by ordering them all into the reception room overlooking the front gardens where she produced the same decanter and this time five glasses as she had done on Daniel's first meeting with her. He explained to Margot that Ray was at the farm with Annette and would be walking over soon. It was the first time that Daniel had seen Margot look flustered, when she was about to meet somebody who most probably, if Annette got her way, was to become her son-in-law. Next, all the women of the house got flustered when they were told that the whole section was about to descend on them. It was something that neither Henry, Daniel nor Ray had considered being any problem at all.

Daniel's mother shook her head, smiling at Margot, "*Hommes!*"

"*Oui seuls hommes,*" agreed Margot also shaking her head and smiling.

There was then a frenetic hour of running about sorting out the spare bedrooms so everybody had somewhere to sleep. During this time, Annette and Ray arrived and Margot was even more flustered to a point where she was in tears, thankfully they were tears of joy. She did not totally disappear when Ray gave her a bear hug when she had put her arms around him, but she nearly did. It was decided that everybody would dine at the château, due to the expected numbers. Ray would go back to the farm and pick up Annette's father and Pierre, but to ensure enough beds, Ray and Annette would sleep back at the farm. All the ladies set about producing a large vat of coq au vin which was supplemented by adding a couple of partridges and a pheasant that Annette's father had shot earlier in the day. The menfolk started fetching up several bottles of local red wine from the cellar whilst Ray and Pierre was sent back again to the farm to bring the old man's home made Calvados. They had just started their first round of toasts when there was the unmistakable sound of tyres on gravel, followed by the even less unmistakable voice of Art.

"Bleeding 'ell! It's bigger than all West Auckland put together!"

Art was somewhat taken aback when he was scolded by Mrs Byrne (as he knew her), "And we'll have less of that kind of language, if you don't mind, Arthur Moore!"

"Bloody 'ell, Mrs Byrne, what are you doing here?"

"Arthur, language!" she repeated and started to laugh as she hugged each of the lads in turn.

Each one, she had taught at some stage of their early lives.

The night was one of true joy to all and full of celebration and raucous banter. Only at the start of the meal did it get serious when Daniel gave a toast to "fallen comrades". There were tears in the eyes of almost everybody around the table. All had been touched by death to some extent or other by this damn war.

It was well past midnight when Marie and Daniel made their way to bed. His mother had already made her excuses and Pierre had driven Margot and her husband, Tomas, back to the farm leaving Ray and Annette to walk back in the cool of the summer night. Daniel dropped on to the bed sitting facing the distant wall. He had taken his boots off when Marie appeared before him, naked. Until that point, he had started to feel tired, the trials of the previous days catching up with him. She slowly undressed him, starting with his shirt and moving down to his trousers, very slowly undoing his fly buttons, her hands brushing his rapidly growing excitement. When he was also totally naked, she pushed him down on to the bed on his back and straddled him kissing him as she lowered herself down. He was enveloped by heaven and the table light silhouetted her Venus-like shape in his view. As she rode him up and down he reached up to hold those perfect firm breasts. God, how he had missed this!

The morning arrived all too early as far as Daniel was concerned. He got up to find his mother the only other person downstairs. He was a little embarrassed as he knew that she knew he and Marie had been together during that night and no doubt she knew what they had been doing.

Just as she had always done, she read the situation and put him at ease, "I don't know how you did it Daniel, but you have certainly got an angel there. I hope you have a life full of joy together." With that she gave him a little peck on the forehead, although she had to tilt his head down and stand on her tiptoes! "There's a man arrived on one of those motorbikes in army uniform and says he had a letter for Henry. He is in the kitchen having breakfast. He must have been up early to get here all the way from Amien at this time."

Daniel entered the kitchen and the private stood to attention, "Stand easy, private. You have a despatch for Lieutenant-Colonel Neville?"

"Yes sir, I am to give it to him in person!"

"Okay, so what does it say, I dare say you were there when the message was taken down?"

The private looked a little disconcerted. Confused by what this captain had said and his uncomfortable shuffle conveyed that to Daniel.

"Relax, it will be about General Haig's visit to Amien, we are waiting for it, it's just the timing we need to know. Do I need to raise the men immediately or not?"

The private handed the sealed message over, "The general will be arriving in Amien on the 4.00 p.m. train and there is something going to happen at 6.00 p.m.".

"Good, you can report back to say we will all be there by 2.00 p.m. Once you've finished your breakfast you can set off. Carry on."

Henry was coming down the staircase just as Daniel came out of the kitchen.

"Message from HQ, Haig arrives at 4.00 p.m. I suggest we need to be there no later than 2.00 p.m., I will chase the lads up."

"Good, we need to sort out the windfall and ensure it is safe before we leave. Then we have to be shipshape for Haig."

"That shouldn't be a problem; I will send for Ray and get the lads together. When we get to Amien we all still have that new uniform we got at Poperinge."

Daniel was off knocking on doors and within ten minutes all the lads were down and waiting for an update. Des was sent down to the farm to bring Ray up, but just as he got out of the door he saw in the distance the staff car arriving with Ray, Annette and Pierre.

Down in the cellar they all crowded round the open chests. The chest with the gold and jewellery spoke for itself but, on closer examination, the two chests with the silver coins were not German, but old French silver coins from the court of Louis XVI which had obviously been raided by the Germans during the early advances across France in 1914. Marie read and translated the script on the coins: "Louis XVI, By the Grace of God, King of France and Navarre," on the front and "Blessed Be the Name of the Lord, 1785," on the reverse. The true value of this was hard to say but it was clear to Henry and he explained to all the goggle-eyed observers that it was many more times' the value of just a chest of current, German coins.

The group agreed that, due to the need for secrecy, all present would get an equal share and the earlier oath reinforced with the new members of the group pledging their support. Henry would be the one who had contacts and the opportunity to get the horde valued and then he would be able to get a rough idea as to how much it would be worth to each individual. There was a need to keep it safe and let any possible repercussions settle, it might be that the authorities were aware of this missing treasure and they might have to return some or all to the bottom of the pond at Bray-sur-Somme! Marie revealed that the château had a hidden room where it could be stored. It was agreed that that would be the safest place for it to remain until they were sure nobody knew of its existence.

When the lads had left to start preparing for the journey back to Amien, Marie showed Daniel and Henry a secret room behind large wooden wine rack shelfing which appeared to be fastened to the wall at the far end of the cellar. In fact it was hinged at one end and had hidden castors at the other. A latch just under the second shelf from the bottom released the rack which opened into the room revealing the vault. The three chests were stowed safely and the three joined in the preparations for a return to Amien.

The journey back to Amien was uneventful although slightly crowded in the staff car where Henry, Catherine, Marie, Daniel and his mother crowded in. Ray and Annette were in the front of the Associated Equipment Company (AEC) transport lorry which had been used to get to the château. There was a little tension between the group as they all held their own thoughts of the rights and wrongs of keeping this windfall. Henry reconciled it for everybody. It was clear that everything they had was stolen by the Germans from across the country and therefore returning it to its rightful owner would be impossible. Anything that was traceable and more had been returned to its owners. It didn't sit well with Daniel's mother but she was happy to remain quiet and the others just accepted Henry's reasoning. On reaching Amien, the ladies were dropped off at the 19th century Hôtel Marotte close to the centre of Amiens.

With Daniel joining the lads in the lorry, they returned to the factory and were reunited with Monsieur Olivier who was over the moon to see them again and brought food and wine to refresh them after their journey. He got his maid to operate a press that was in the factory so all their spare uniform was as good as new. He produced some polish so the boots got a quick bulling and off they set in the lorry back to HQ where they managed to find time to give their weapons a further clean prior to the expected arrival time of Haig.

Henry was at the railway station to meet Haig with his staff car and took him directly to the same hotel where the ladies were stopping. After thirty minutes to freshen up, he was at HQ to meet Daniel and the Knaves again.

They had fallen in, to form a small guard of honour for his arrival and as Haig arrived he realised it was "his" Knaves who had formed his guard and beamed with pleasure, taking the salute from Daniel then offering his hand to shake.

"My goodness Byrne," he pumped Daniel's arm emphatically like a water pump, "are there no end to your talents? Not only a hero but a treasure seeker!"

Daniel heard himself saying, "Thank you sir, just doing our duty," whilst thinking under his breath, "thank you sir just helping ourselves," that thought made Daniel genuinely smile.

There followed two hours of photography at the town hall, the vault and at the wharf where there was a recreation of the landing of the chests. Then it was back to the town hall for the celebrations where the speeches went on forever (or so it appeared). There were lots of very passionate speeches in French which Daniel started to follow but then gave up until they were asked to come forward in line and were given a scroll apiece, apparently giving them the freedom of the city of Amien. That allowed them, amongst other things, to drive their cattle through the centre and along the Promenade de la Hotoie, grazing and watering them in the park. Pierre, however, was slightly more fortunate; whilst he also got the freedom of the city he was given a reward of one thousand francs, due to him being a civilian and having received an injury. Bearing in mind the windfall back at the château, everyone found this quite amusing! At last it was over and the provision of food and wine was abundant and of the quality you would expect for such a gastronomically demanding community. (That was the dignitaries of Amien, not the Auckland Pals, they were just happy to be fed, watered and to be rich!). Whether they stayed alive long enough to enjoy it, only time would tell!

The celebrations went long into the night with the good folk of Amien really making the lads feel special. Later still, they set out to discover the delights of the night time economy of Amien with one of the mayor's assistants as a guide. It seems that everywhere they went their reputation preceded them and nothing was too much trouble and no price asked!

Haig had retired much earlier having spent most of the evening playing the gentleman in front of Daniel's mother, Florence. He was retelling stories of John Byrne, her brother-in-law during the Boar War.

"Heart of a lion that man and his nephew proves time and again he is from the same mould. Henry says your husband is quite a formidable character also. What a family, I congratulate you Mrs Byrne."

Florence Byrne was proud of the fact that her menfolk were held in high esteem by such a man, but couldn't help thinking that it meant her only son was time and again standing in the way of harm.

Daniel saw his mother come across the room to say goodnight so walked her up to her room. As they walked she was a little pensive before she started to speak, "I know that you are very good at what you are doing, and I don't expect you to tell me everything you and the lads get up to, but in your letters you never hinted at the obvious dangers you are in constantly. I have listened to Uncle John's stories and seen the look on your face when you were listening. You don't have to prove anything within our family; me and your dad love you and are very proud of what you have done now. You don't need to do anything else in our eyes and I have talked to Marie about this and she feels the same."

Tears were welling up in her eyes when Daniel replied. "I have kept a lot of the detail away from you, so you would not worry. You must understand the excitement I feel when I am on these missions is incredible and if I wasn't doing this I would be still there, only I would be cowering in some trench somewhere wondering if the next shell over had my name on it, or waiting to bravely go over the top into the jaws of the massed ranks of German machine guns. I am good at what I do and am surrounded by people I trust implicitly. I am safer doing this than anywhere else on the western front," he squeezed her hand, "try not to worry." They were outside her room and this time he kissed her forehead. "See you in the morning, I love you Mum and tell Dad the same when you are back in England, I will be careful."

Daniel returned downstairs to join Marie who was talking to Catherine and Annette. Henry had just ordered one last round of drinks, Armagnac all round, Ray returned from seeing the last of the lads off down the street.

When everybody had a drink in their hands Henry raised his in salute, "Well, here's to many more days like the last few, profitable and surrounded by friends, cheers!"

They all drank and agreed. Daniel's eyes caught Marie's and it spelt out one message and Daniel knew she could see the same in his. Finishing their drinks, they made their excuses and headed upstairs. He did not know how she had managed it but a hot bath was run with mountains of soap suds protruding above the top. Without a word she led him to the bath and undressed him. She guided him into the hot soapy water then began to strip each of her garments, one by one in a slow arousing way that had Daniel transfixed and excited in a way that was only too plain to see. Marie climbed into the bath and the water poured over the sides, but this was no time for concern about trivialities. The water was either nearly cold or on the floor before they climbed out of the bath, dried each other and fell into bed. With the section's group furlough just starting, they had managed to have a long lay in the following morning. When they both came downstairs everybody seemed to have gone about their own business leaving them to have a leisurely breakfast.

Most of the lads were going to spend their downtime in and around Amien. They had intended to stop on the camp close to the western edge of the city but to Monsieur Olivier this was unthinkable. He had arranged for beds to be brought to the factory where they had been staying. There were sufficient individual offices for two to share and utilise as bedrooms with cupboards doubling up as wardrobes, the washrooms were cleaned up and gave an excellent ablution area. The factory's small canteen gave an adequate eating area with all meals being brought in, compliments of the Textile Guild of Amien. Daniel had negotiated and overseen this transformation that only took that first day, but in all fairness to Monsieur Olivier he didn't need any cajoling. What was a few hundred francs when these lads had returned millions?

Geordie had headed off back to Poperinge where a certain nurse by the name of Jane Holiway had arranged some time off from the dressing station just outside Ypres to, "reacquaint themselves with each other," was Geordie's phraseology. Unlike before, instead of the, "dirty lucky bastard," phrase Ray had used, with his great turn of fortune and circumstances, this was a much more encouraging, "Go on Geordie my lad, good luck and enjoy!"

Henry, Catherine, Marie, Daniel and his mother headed back to Château de Noyelles in the staff car which made for an even bigger crush than the journey over to Amien after they called into Abbeville to stock up at the market. This was after a quick shopping spree in Amien. Ray, Annette and Pierre had taken the more sedate means of transfer, via the ever reliable River Somme. Having done sterling work, Pierre's boats needed returning to the coast to allow him to return to his life of fisherman and part spy.

Henry had been handed sealed orders just prior to setting off. On reaching the château he disclosed that he had been recalled to the Intelligence Section at the War Department in Westminster and had to be there by the end of the week. This meant he and Catherine would need to leave in a couple of days. Florence Byrne suggested that it would be the best time for her to return to England seeing as she would have company for most of her journey back to County Durham. This was disappointing to Daniel but he did realise that she had been away from her home, her husband, his father, for several weeks although he had only had a few days with her.

On their final night together, everybody had a great meal at the château. Florence had insisted on cooking for her new French friends, Margot, Tomas, Pierre and his wife Claudette as well as Annette, Ray, Henry, Catherine, Marie and her son. A starter of light vegetable soup was followed by roast beef and Yorkshire pudding, finished off with an apple and blackberry crumble. Tomas insisted on supplying the wine and the calvados, commenting that, "it was no wonder that Henry, Daniel and Ray were such big men if everybody in County Durham ate so well".

The following morning was on one hand a day of sadness when the group parted but in a very selfish way exciting for Daniel and Marie, who for the first time would be able to spend an extended period of time together living as if they were man and wife. Henry, Daniel and Ray had taken out one share of the treasure so that Florence could take it back and Henry could use some of it to get it valued and possibly find buyers for some on the items which were very obviously collector's pieces and worth far more than their market value as precious metals and gems. Pierre was in no rush for his share and was happy to let Henry dispose of it and give him the money. With his reward from the Textile Guild he was financially comfortable for a while.

It was a tearful goodbye. Daniel squeezed Marie's hand tightly as they watch the staff car head down the driveway toward the farm, on to the D940 and on up to Calais. They turned towards the château once they could no longer see the car. As they got to the front entrance, Daniel stopped, looked at Marie and bent slightly, lifting her off her feet and carried her across the threshold. She laughed, put her hands around his neck and pulled herself tight.

Daniel kissed her and said, "I'll explain this old English tradition later, but right now I have an idea how we should spend the rest of the day!"

Each day was bliss for the young couple. They spent their days engrossed in each other's company, with walks and horse rides in the grounds where Marie showed Daniel the extent of the estate. He saw the tenancies that the château had responsibility for, one of which was totally empty since the father and son had lost their lives in the early stages of the war. Similar to the New British Army of Lord Kitchener, whole groups of local people had joined the French army together to protect their lands and it was in these groups they fell, now entire communities had lost their menfolk.

They took rides along the Somme estuary and took lunch in the many quaint villages such as Saint-Valery-sur-Somme or they would picnic if the weather permitted. On the second day, they visited Abbeville and Marie's mother. Daniel had wondered how she would welcome this stranger who had so swiftly taken her daughter's heart and seemed to have moved in to her home. On arrival it was plain to see that the old lady was hardly conscious and barely alive. Marie's tears fell and dropped off her high cheek bones like the morning dew dropping of the tips of leaves.

"This is how she has been for the last few weeks. She took a turn whilst I was in England. Your mother spent several hours with her when she was here and talked to her constantly about us. It appeared to work for a while as she started to respond, but the effort was too great for her and she relapsed to what you see before you. Sister Geraldine says it's only a matter of time."

Daniel held the old lady's hand from one side of the bed whilst Marie did the same from the other. Daniel and Marie held hands across the bad so all three stayed hand in hand for many minutes.

The evenings were spent dining at either the farm with Margot, Jean, Annette and Ray or in their nearby village of Noyelles-sur-Mer which was just a pleasant walk away and where Daniel was treated as a honoured guest being a member of the country's allies fighting a common foe and the partner of Marie who seemed to be personal friends with everybody.

The nights were spent in what Daniel could only think of as pure unbelievable ecstasy. Without the time constraints of previous times, there was so much tenderness and exploration in each other that neither wanted it to end. But end it must and both knew it.

Two days before he was due to return back to Amien they received a telegram from Henry. It assured him that his mother had got home safely and that all was well. Also, that, having seen his contact in London, she and Daniel's father now had 25,000 reasons to be happy, and that his contact was very interested in doing more business! This was obviously the value they had secured for one share of the treasure and that the other shares could be sold in the same manner.

This was more than Daniel could have hoped for. Not only did it mean that his parents, friends and comrades were set for life, but he and Marie had a £50,000 nest egg to start their lives together. Ray and Pierre were quite happy to let Marie and Henry arrange that their shares were similarly disposed of and Daniel vowed to ask the others if they wanted theirs to be sorted out by Marie and Henry.

With all that good news and happiness, it was a bitter pill to swallow when they faced their final day and night together. They spent it alone in each other's company. It was almost as if they didn't want to share each other with anybody else because it would dilute their precious memories of such a special time.

Inevitably the morning arrived when Daniel had to leave. They walked down to the farm where Ray was waiting and Pierre took them back up river to Amien to re-join the war. They left heaven for a rendezvous with hell, but their individual hopes for the future were so full of positivity that neither intended not returning. Kaiser Willy and company would not stop them getting back to their destiny with happiness.

As arranged, the Knaves all reunited at the camp outside army HQ in Amien. Immediately, Daniel checked his men where all okay and, after a full kit inspection, they had a private meeting at the shooting ranges where they were sure not to be disturbed. Jaws aplenty hit the floor when they heard the news from Henry and without any delay it was unanimously agreed that all shares were to be "cashed in" and, if it could be arranged, forwarded to the families back in Co. Durham. Daniel brought up the matter of their fallen comrades and their families.

It was Art who suggested, "With that amount of money, I certainly wouldn't mind putting £1,000 into a kitty to share between the families of Davy, Lazzer and Jack. We don't have to tell them how we came by it or we could even make sure they don't know where or who it came from."

Daniel was pleased to hear all the others agree without any persuasion from him. Once again it went to show just what a close knit team this group of young lads were. They reached out to the families beyond the immediate members, never forgetting even beyond death.

With this sorted and telegrams sent to Henry and Marie they went back to what they all did so well, soldiering. They had two further days retraining and awaiting orders.

Henry sent another telegram confirming that he could arrange all the details of the "business arrangements" but also that they were to proceed to a place called Nouex–les-Mines just south-west of Lille where the front line ran through the area of Loos. Nouex–les-Mines was on a railway line and was the army HQ in that area. This was where they would meet up with their commanding officer, the newly promoted Colonel Neville. They entrained the usual cattle trucks, that this time was furnished with benches and a few tables and settled down to their trip. The wagon door was open and Daniel looked out across the French countryside as it flicked past, reminiscing over the past months. It was only September 1915, he had only been in the army a matter of months and so much had happened in such a short space of time. How the fate of war favoured some and not others. He looked skywards thinking of his north-east roots. The Viking warrior kingdom of Northumberland had covered everywhere between the Scottish Boarders to York. He was not a religious man, but he did believe in fate favouring the brave and his ancient forbears had believed the same. He thought of Odin, god of war and father of all the Viking gods.

Historical Note

There is no record of any of Lord Kitchener's Pals Battalion being called the, "Auckland Pals". Neither was there ever a regiment called the "Durham Fusiliers" in World War I and the stories in this book are purely part of the imagination of the author. The stories do revolve around true battles of the period and the outcome of those battles has not been altered from popular history.

It is true that some of the worse duties on the front line (and there was plenty) was to go on missions into no-man's land, whether that be to set the defensive barbwire protection of the front line, prisoner grabs, general patrols designed to keep the enemy on their toes or to layout in listening posts. Teams that succeeded in these missions understandably got chosen time and again, many times, usually until their luck ran out! The author has not found any evidence that specialist teams were trained at this point in time to act as what is now known as "Special Ops".

Douglas Haig is a contentious character of this time being known by his men by several names, amongst them: Master of the Field, being one of the most favourable, whilst The Butcher of the Somme or Butcher Haig suggesting another view. When he died he was given an elaborate funeral and it was reported that "Great crowds lined the streets many of which were his ex-soldiers who openly wept". It is not the intention of the author to give credit for the invention of "Special Ops" or Specialist Intelligence gathering to Haig but it made a useful connection that allowed this fictitious band of brothers to roam around the Western Front with impunity. Hopefully this book does not enter the debate of national hero or villain.

There are brave soldiers who fell in the Great War whose names are quite correctly revered on the role of honour that can be found on the village green in West Auckland. This book it is hoped, only adds to their memory and is in no way designed to detract from those young men who so many years ago gave the ultimate sacrifice for king and country.

The first section of this book is purely the author's understanding of events leading up to World War I. Being no historian, please forgive any inaccuracies. It is the intention to paint the picture of the global mess that sucked the common man on both sides of the war into something that they had no chance of comprehending, or influencing.

When politicians fail, soldiers die!